sing me to sleep

sing me to sleep

ANGELA MORRISON

razOr
bill

An Imprint of Penguin Group (USA) Inc.

Sing Me to Sleep

RAZORBILL

Published by the Penguin Group
Penguin Young Readers Group
345 Hudson Street, New York, New York 10014, U.S.A.
Penguin Group (USA) Inc., 375 Hudson Street, New York, New York 10014, U.S.A.
Penguin Group (Canada), 90 Eglinton Avenue East, Suite 700,
Toronto, Ontario, Canada M4P 2Y3 (a division of Pearson Penguin Canada Inc.)
Penguin Books Ltd, 80 Strand, London WC2R 0RL, England
Penguin Ireland, 25 St Stephen's Green, Dublin 2, Ireland
(a division of Penguin Books Ltd)
Penguin Group (Australia), 250 Camberwell Road, Camberwell, Victoria 3124, Australia
(a division of Pearson Australia Group Pty Ltd)
Penguin Books India Pvt Ltd, 11 Community Centre,
Panchsheel Park, New Delhi – 110 017, India
Penguin Group (NZ), 67 Apollo Drive, Rosedale, North Shore 0632, New Zealand
(a division of Pearson New Zealand Ltd.)

Penguin Books (South Africa) (Pty) Ltd, 24 Sturdee Avenue,
Rosebank, Johannesburg 2196, South Africa

Penguin Books Ltd, Registered Offices: 80 Strand, London WC2R 0RL, England

10 9 8 7 6 5 4 3 2 1

Library of Congress Cataloging-in-Publication Data

Morrison, Angela.
Sing me to sleep / by Angela Morrison.
p. cm.
Summary: An unattractive seventeen-year-old who has a beautiful singing voice undergoes a
physical transformation before performing in a singing competition with her choir in Switzerland,
where she meets a boy with troubling secrets, and they fall in love.
ISBN: 978-1-59514-275-7
[1. Secrets—Fiction. 2. Singing—Fiction 3. Beauty, Personal—Fiction. 4. Love—Fiction.
5. Sick—Fiction.] I. Title
PZ7.M82924 Si 2010
[Fic] 22

Printed in the United States of America

For Matt,
who left us too soon.

Please Return To
your Seasons Institute

prologue

Damn, she's ugly.

My bio-dad's first words when he saw me. It's my only image of him. A shadowy figure bending over Mom wearing a hospital gown, holding a flannel-wrapped bundle in her arms.

Damn, she's ugly, Tara. What did you do?

Like she ate or drank something strange that made me come out red and pimply with a purple blotch on my forehead. No hair. Cone head from the delivery. My baby face screwed up and screaming at him.

Mom didn't hate him enough to actually tell me that story. She doesn't talk about him—not to me. He played in a rock band. Not a big one. That's all I know. I've seen the picture, though. It's in our family album with the rest of my baby pictures. The only one that survived with him in it. But Mom did hate him enough to tell that story over and over to his sister, her best friend since high school, every time his name resurfaced between them.

It's my first clear memory. Stacking Cool Whip bowls and margarine containers on the kitchen floor, listening to Mom talk on the phone, tuning into the quiet intensity of her voice.

"*Damn, she's ugly.* Our beautiful baby. That's all he had to say."

I was her beautiful baby. She called me that all the time.

Beautiful? Now I knew the truth. I was ugly. *Damn ugly.* No wonder Dad took off. Never looked back. Not at his ugly daughter making a fairy-tale tower from white and yellow plastic bowls, singing the first song she ever wrote, quietly to herself.

Da-amn ugly, da-amn ugly.

At least I can sing. Got that from my mom's side. I may not look like a songbird—more like a song stork—but if you close your eyes, it's beautiful.

chapter 1

THE OFFERING

Crap. There's a naked freshman chained to my locker.

No. Not naked. Briefs. Not a good look, kid. Spindly white legs, wimpy chest, shaking arms. Black socks. Maybe his mom didn't do the laundry all spring break, and that's all he's got today.

A bike chain encased in lime-green plastic goes through my locker's handle down the poor kid's underwear and out a leg, loops up, locked tight. He could escape if he wanted to streak.

Sniggering behind me. I don't turn. That's what they want. The sound multiplies. Amplifies. Magnifies into an audience.

I didn't see it coming while I slumped into the hall traffic, sinking lower into my baggy sweatshirt and loose Levi's, my eyes tracing the regular lines in the floor tiles, as I hid behind my long brown frizzed-out mane, face rigid just in case.

My progress was strangely quiet. No guys darting in front of me telling me to "get my effing ugly face" out of their way. No one shouting, "Take cover. The Beast is loose." No dying animal moans echoing off the lockers as I walked by. Only silence. Deadly silence. I thought I'd escaped this morning. I should have known. The hunters are on the attack.

But I'm not the only one they attacked this time. I focus on the trembling kid. "Did they hurt you?" I accidentally brush his arm.

He jerks back, stares at the spot I touched like it will burst into flames or harden to stone and turn to dust. Can't blame him. I'm Beth the Beast. Too tall to ever stand straight. Bony body. Face full of zits. Bug eyes magnified by industrial-strength glasses. The braces have been off for three years, but no one sees my straight, white teeth. Just fangs, long yellow ones. Dripping blood.

"They said" —the kid shudders and swallows hard— "to tell you I'm the offering."

They. We both know who *they* are. Colby Peart, Travis Steele, Kurt Marks. The Horsemen. Aren't there supposed to be four? And I think that's biblical. Ironic. Nothing biblical about Colby and his senior ultra-jock following who hold Port High School in their grasp. Apocalyptic? That works. But the end of their reign approaches. Seniors graduate. Unless by some sick shake of fate's dice they fail, next year this place will be liberated. The Horsemen will ride off into the sunset. I hope warriors hiding behind the hills get them and tear them to pieces.

The kid's talking again. The press behind me seethes in close enough to hear. "They said the Bea—you—require a sacrifice." He shudders again and looks down at the floor. "Every full moon."

The crowd behind us roars. Laughter is supposed to be healthy, uplifting. Not in Port, Michigan.

"It's okay." I restrain myself from patting his shoulder. "We'll get Mr. Finnley to bring his bolt cutters."

The kid won't shut up. His head comes back up, and he grimaces at me. "They said you'd drag me into your lair—"

More laughter.

Heat pours into my face, and I mumble, "I don't eat freshmen for breakfast."

"Eat me?" Confusion knits the kid's brows together. "That's not what they said you'd do."

Riot levels break out behind us. It sounds like half the school has crammed into the hall.

I don't turn and look. "I'm not going to hurt you."

"Can you knock me out first?"

The laughter, mocking and harsh, bounces back and forth across the hall, off the metal locker stacks.

This kid must have swallowed every word of the Beast legend. I'm a giant. I'm hideous. But a crazed female rapist preying on skinny freshmen?

I hold up my hands and back off. "They got you, okay." My eyes sting. They got me, too. "You're safe." I turn and try to push through the wall of unyielding bodies to find the custodian. My eyes are blurry. Crap.

Don't lose it. Don't lose it. Don't lose it. "Excuse me. Please." The surging wall of cackling bodies solidifies.

Then I see Mr. Finnley's head. Scott's there, too—leading him through the crowd. I swallow hard.

"Sorry, Beth." Scott bites his lip. "I wanted to get this cleaned up before you got here—but the kid wouldn't leave his whities."

"That's enough, people. Don't you have classes to go to?" Mr. Finnley glares, and the masses scuttle off back to the cracks and drains they came from. The Finnster shakes his head and gets busy cutting the chain. "I'll have to report this."

That's all I need. Another session in the office. Questions I can't answer. "Who did this?" Silence. "Who do you think did this?" Who do *you* think did this? We all know. Colby and his clones are behind everything nasty that goes on here. Nobody names them. We have another assembly about bullying. Nothing changes.

I glance down at the binder I'm carrying for first period. I scribbled out the words, but I know what they say:

> *Your words—*
> *Why do they define me?*
> *Why do I believe you?*
> *Your face,*
> *Your lips, and your fingers—*
> *Don't spill them on me.*
> *I'm bones, blood, and flesh*
> *Not clay to be pounded,*
> *And scorched in the fire*
> *That seethes in the hate you feel.*
> *I bleed when you wound me*
> *Just like the pretty girls do.*

It needs some kind of hopeful chorus. Can't seem to squeak anything like that into the equation. No music, either. Just those thin lines that make me sound so angry. I guess I am—angry. But I don't want everyone knowing that. I do a lot of erasing, burning, shredding, hiding, hurting. I run back to *Da-am ugly* and stay there.

The end of the year can't come fast enough. If I tiptoe next year, I'll be able to breathe—like when they left junior high.

Scott reads my mind. "Only three months, eight days, thirteen hours, and twenty-nine minutes until they graduate."

"Why do you help me?" Scott and I were best friends in preschool, and then he was in my class again in third grade. He was skinny and had to go to the nurse's office for hyper drugs at lunch. I was already taller than everyone else and wore thick, round glasses that made me look like an overgrown bush baby. My hair was short back then. Cut it now? No way. Where would I hide?

Scott doesn't have to hide. Doesn't have to help me and doom himself to eternal loserhood. He's cute since his face cleared up. I don't think he sees it. He's still way short, Quiz Bowl captain, core nerd. Still my friend.

He grins, nonchalant, self-sacrificing, Clark Kent to the core. "I don't take gym anymore. They can't steal my clothes and throw them in the toilet."

"But they could hurt you."

"You're worried?" He pats my shoulder. "That's nice, Beth. See you in choir."

Choir. School choir. Not my real choir down in Ann Arbor. Not the choir I begged Mom to let me audition for when I was thirteen. Not the competitive *all-girls* choir where I sit unobtrusively in the back and anchor the altos. Not the one I have to drive a hundred miles to, through Detroit's rush-hour traffic down I-94 every Tuesday and Thursday to rehearsals in a freezing cold church. Not Bliss Youth Singers of Ann Arbor. The choir I live for. The choir that takes me away from who I am to what I long to be. Beautiful? I guess. Isn't that what everyone wants? They all probably want love, too. I live with so much hate that I'm not even sure what love is. Neither is on my horizon.

Scott's just talking about our struggling school choir. Kind of a joke. Marching Band is almighty here. But choir passes the time. Easy A. Music is music. Singing is singing. A respite from the madness. No jock senior boys allowed. Out of this school of nearly two thousand kids, there are only eight guys in the whole group, so I sit by Scott and sing tenor. I've got a decent low voice and perfect pitch so sight-reading parts come naturally. I can sing high, too. I can sing as high as anybody if I want. I help out the sopranos and altos when we run parts. They go to pieces when I go back to tenor.

Scott can't sing, but he tries. I asked him once why he takes choir. Any guy who signs up is instantly labeled "gay" by Colby and his jocks—and the rest of the school.

Scott turned kind of pink. "So I can hear you sing."

That was probably the nicest thing any guy had ever said to me. Not that Scott was serious.

I played along. "Be careful." I punched his arm. "You'll ruin your reputation."

He got serious then. "I'm not gay, Beth."

"Of course, you're not."

He was going to say something else, but he just shook his head and walked off.

I dare you to say I'm not ugly.

So, back to this morning. Scott's halfway down the hall, but I catch up easy. Long beast legs cover ground quickly. "Thanks, Scott. I mean it. School would be hell without you."

He puts out his arm like he's a prom princess escort. "My pleasure, ma'am."

A shuddery, weak laugh comes out of me. I rest my arm on top of his and let him lead me down the hall, grateful for the support.

He smiles up at me. No braces for him now, either. Teeth recently whitened. A bit dazzling. "I wonder what people think when we walk down the hall together."

I laugh, stronger this time. "Beauty and the Beast. Dr. Namar did a great job on your face." We go to the same dermatologist. So far the miracle of clear skin hasn't happened for me. Dr. Namar keeps trying. He says the scarring will be minimal. But I have eyes.

Scott stops and turns to me. He's got a dreamy look on his face. "Beauty and the Beast? So if we dance in the moonlight—"

"You better bring a stool."

"One of the wheelie ones from the library?"

"Perfect. Mind if I lead?" Then I feel dumb. This giant girl dwarfing sweet, little Scott. I let go of his arm and move forward, head down, withdrawing into myself again. My shoulders round to their usual downward curve.

Scott hustles to catch up. "What I want to know is," he grabs me by the elbow and makes me stop walking, "if I kiss you when the music stops," he stands on his toes and whispers in my ear, "will you be my Princess Charming?"

I snort. "Dream on. No magic's going to help this." I pull back, deeper into my beastly cave.

Scott smiles. "I wouldn't mind an experiment."

I don't like it when he gets like this. "You don't want to waste your virgin lips on me. You could dazzle a half–decent looking freshman into making out easy." I head for my class. "Look in the mirror."

He scurries along beside me, scowling. "I wish you'd get over the looks thing."

I scowl right back at him. "Look at me, Scott." I part my hair with both hands and pull it away from my face long enough to give him a frightening glimpse. "How could I *ever* get over the looks thing? I am the Beast."

"If you believe that, they win."

"Wake up. Look around." I wrap my arms across my chest, trying to control the delayed reaction that shudders through me. "They won a long time ago."

chapter 2

UGLY IN ALTO

Scott isn't in choir. I look for him after school. No luck. I have Bliss practice down in Ann Arbor, so I can't dawdle. I need to talk to him, though. I know he's trying to be sweet, but him saying stuff about kissing and dancing hurts worse than "The Beast" spray-painted in bright green across the trunk of my faded-orange Ford.

I want to be kissed as much as the next seventeen-year-old girl. The ugly genie gave me plenty of hormones. But why even go there? When I'm forty, some blind bald guy can fall in love with me. My sight is bad to awful so we'd have that in common to build a relationship on. I'm too hideous for a guy who can see to even touch. I read somewhere that women peak sexually at thirty-eight—so that should work well for me. We can get married and have ugly blind kids. I don't even care if he's fat.

And I like kids. It's sad Mom didn't marry again and have more. Sometimes I wonder if she still loves my father—after all this time, all the pain. The only thing she got out of the whole deal was me. Not much of a prize. A baby sister to look after would have been cool. I work summers at the library—tons of toddlers and frazzled moms. I tried to help with the crafts a couple times, but the tykes got scared. Blind kids would be good.

I could find a blind high school to volunteer at and make a play for love now. Or maybe I'll just go home, slam a sandwich, and hit the road so I'm not late for practice.

I drive myself these days. Mom always hated the drive—had to leave work early every Tuesday. The whole thing was doable when Bliss practiced once a week, but last fall, Terri, our director, decided she wanted to try to get us into the Choral Olympics this year and bumped up the practices to twice a week. Mom decided my driving skills were excellent and bought me an old Ford so I could drive myself. At least the orange isn't off-the-lot bright. Looks like a dying pumpkin. Perfect to join my ugly stepsister gig. I named her Jeannette, nice and lovely so her feelings don't get hurt. Misery does love company. Look at Scott and me.

Slushy sleet chases me all the way through Detroit. I'm way late. I hate March weather. Spring around here is dark, cold, and nasty. Gray rotting snowbanks that hang on as long as they can. Sleet and ice instead of pure-white winter snow.

Traffic is a mess tonight, and poor old Jeannette is gutless. Everybody cuts us off. I don't ever dare try that. This is Detroit. I may be ugly, but I still want to live to sing another song.

I finally shake free of metro traffic and zoom into sleepy Ann Arbor, upscale university town, dozing on the banks of a quiet creek. The stone church we sing in is as old as the town. I slip into the sanctuary halfway through their warm-up.

No problem. I'm already hot. I played our practice playlist the whole drive down. Sang through the drills. All the songs. I downloaded all the parts, not just my alto. I love the soprano solo in this gospel piece we used for our Choral Olympics audition—"Take Me Home." I cranked Jeannette's dying CD player until the speakers were popping and sang the solo. I was a total star in the car.

I love it when we get to sing gospel stuff. None of us in Bliss are purist enough to prefer the classical religious pieces. We all beg Terri for more Broadway. That's the best stuff to sing. Most of the girls get pumped over the stupid pop pieces Terri throws in to keep the audiences happy. I admit I have my favorite contemporary divas packed in my iPod—who doesn't? But when I'm performing, I want more than that. I want the music to have heart and soul, desolation and joy—some meaning, for gosh sake. It's so hard to find anything that means anything.

Terri's kind of delusional with the whole Choral Olympics thing. There's no way we're going to get an invitation. We nailed the classical test-piece when we recorded it for our audition recording, but "Take Me Home" is challenging. Even the alto is incredible to sing—all that great stuff about *the sweet, sweet River Jordan.* There's this huge climax with everyone singing something else in kind of a round. Celebration and heartbreak all at the same time. Awesome. But Meadow, our soprano soloist, choked. She's had lessons her whole life, makes the most of her breathy, pop voice. But "Take Me Home" needs power. And emotion. Terri kept trying to get Meadow to go there, take after take, until we were all angry and exhausted. Meadow was in tears and then she just disappeared. Terri had to splice something together to send to the committee.

The Choral Olympics are in Lausanne, Switzerland, this July. Terri keeps putting pictures of the Alps and lakes and castles and Swiss houses overflowing with red geraniums and flags up on the Web site. It's going to be such a downer when we get the news. We should hear back any day now. We also applied to this festival out near Vancouver, Canada. Got into that easy. Better than nothing.

But not Switzerland.

I grab a spot at the end of the row of standing altos and fall into the rhythm of oohing and aahing, rolling higher and higher. Good. I missed the zings.

"That's great, girls. Keep singing. Ah-ah-ah-ah-ahhhh." The piano hits the chord for the next note up. "Everyone turn to the right. Shoulder rub the girl in front of you."

I pivot and start massaging Sarah, the girl beside me. She has for-real, not dyed, blonde hair that hangs down her back. Silky straight. Never a hint of a wave. Hair I'd kill for. No one is behind me.

Terri steps up and rubs my neck and shoulders. "I'm glad you made it. I was getting worried about you."

"Kind of nasty out."

"You be careful, Beth."

"In a few more weeks, it'll be just rain."

"And you can drive through anything."

"Almost." Mom wouldn't let me come a couple of times last month. Bad storms. Tonight is nothing.

"It may ice up later." I know I can stay at her place. She offers it all the time. I've never been brave enough to take her up on it. "Eees, girls. And I don't want to hear any witches." The choir keeps moving up the scale.

"I've got new tires. The interstate should be fine."

Terri squeezes my shoulders one last time and bellows, "Now everybody—left." She runs around the room to massage the girl on the other end of the line.

We sing through a couple of numbers. The first is one of those old pop song fillers. Boring. There's this one girls' choir in Europe that sings crazy rock songs. Sounds dumb, but they are a huge hit. I'd like to try one of those pieces.

The second song is our third competition piece. It features the altos, and we're all over it—carry the whole performance.

"Excellent." Terri beams over at my section. "That was gorgeous, altos. Good work." She puts her hand up to her forehead. "Sopranos. You're not getting the harmony right."

"I don't know why we have to sing harmony." Meet Meadow. Beautiful. Dainty. Skin so perfect you want to touch it to see if it's frosted on. Big dark eyes, long black lashes, perfectly plucked brows, pink lips—always glossy. Long, perfectly layered, and highlighted blonde hair. Never even a hint of black roots. A bustline her mom paid for. Size-one designer jeans. Heels all the time. Diva attitude. "First sopranos are supposed to sing the melody."

Terri is way too patient with her. "The altos carry the melody through that section. It's only eight bars. Let's go over it again." Meadow's parents are loaded. They keep Bliss afloat. Terri has to be patient.

"I'm sick of this song." Meadow flips through the sheet music in her open binder.

Terri bites her lower lip. "Would you like to practice 'Take Me Home'?"

An approving murmur runs through the girls. We all get off on that song, and we haven't sung it since our disaster recording session. It gets the blood flowing. We stomp and clap. Some of us get rhythm instruments and drums. One girl even gets to shout, "Hallelujah." It's as wild as a competitive all-girls choir gets.

Meadow shakes her head, retreats as fast as she can. "That's okay. We should get this right first."

I have to agree with Meadow. Singing "Take Me Home" now would be torture. We won't get into the Choral Olympics, and Meadow can't sing the song. It's weird Terri brought it up.

Terri pushes her hair off her high forehead. What I would give for her cheekbones. "If that's what you want. When we perform this at the Choral Olympics, your part must be perfect." She smiles to encourage Meadow. "The altos are doing a fantastic job. The sopranos need to catch up."

"Okay, girls." Terri enlarges her smile to include the remaining sopranos. "Let's run that part."

It's an easy descant. I can sing it in my sleep. They finally get it. Fall apart when we put it together. Sopranos can be so annoying. We sing that part twenty times. Just those eight boring bars. Now *they* can do it in their sleep.

"Excellent work." Terri gets the sopranos high-fiving each other.

I can't figure out why Terri keeps Meadow as soloist. Who cares if Meadow's mom promised a check for new costumes if we make it to the Choral Olympics? Our old ponchos are still serviceable. Mine's kind of short, but I stand in the back—way in the back. I glance around at the other girls. I guess Meadow is the best we have.

"Take a minute, girls." Terri glances at Meadow. "We're going to practice 'Take Me Home' next." She sounds kind of defeated. She knows how bad Meadow sings this song. She knows the Choral Olympics is a fantasy, but she can't let the girls see. I see. I'm wearing mega-thick glasses. I see everything.

I grab my water bottle, drain it halfway, stretch, and sink on the hardwood pew behind me. We practice standing in the church pews. There are eighty of us, so we don't fit in their choir seats on the stand. The sanctuary is full of warm old wood. Great acoustics. Perfect for "Take Me Home." Especially when we all get rocking—until Meadow gets lost, and we have to go back to the top.

Terri squats in front of Meadow, giving her a pep talk. Then she's on her feet again. "Leah, pass out the instruments." Leah's the choir president. Nice girl. Her straight long hair is dark brown, almost black. Matches her eyelashes and ballerina face.

Buzzing confusion. The jingle of the triangle. Someone hits her drum. Sarah shoves the croaking shaker that I play into my hand.

Terri glares us into silence, raises her hands, and cues the pianist.

The notes climb through the air, engulfing us all in the mournful sound. Eighty pairs of eyes glue to Terri's every move.

Now it's Meadow's solo opening. Terri dips her hand to bring her in and—

Nothing.

Meadow runs across the front of the room and out the side door.

"Leah, go after her."

Terri folds her arms, studies the music, tapping her foot.

I stand frozen with the rest of the choir. No one even rattles a shaker.

Leah returns with her doll-like face in a frazzle. "She's throwing up."

Groans and confusion. Everyone is disappointed. Terri seems really upset.

My hand creeps into the air. I'm not quite sure what it's doing up there. I've never raised my hand in choir before.

"Beth?"

I swallow hard and look around at my altos for strength. I can do this. I can. "I know the solo." My mumble is lost in the shuffle of the girls around me.

"Quiet, girls. What was that?"

Now everyone is listening, staring, questioning. I force myself to stand up straight, pull my shoulders back for courage, and take a deep breath. "I can sing it if you want. Meadow's part. So we can practice."

"You're an alto."

"I know the solo."

"You can hit those notes?"

I shrug my shoulders. "Sure." A smile breaks free from the churning pit of cowardice in my stomach.

Terri looks at me for a beat, smiles back. "Okay, then. Thank you, Beth."

Sarah takes my instrument. Her eyes are big—scared for me.

I close mine. Breathe deep. In and out. I'm in the car. Alone. That's not our pianist delicately caressing the opening from the black and whites. It's just the practice CD. I've done this a hundred times.

It's my cue, and I'm there, singing—

> *I take me down to the river,*
> *The sweet, sweet river Jordan,*
> *Stare across the muddy water*
> *And long for the other side.*

My voice flows pure and strong through the andante opening solo verse. I get a chorus all to myself, slow and mournful—lots of great runs.

> *Take me home, sweet, sweet Jesus.*
> *And wrap me in your bosom,*
> *Where my master cannot find me.*
> *Lord, I long for the other side.*

Then the choir comes in singing, *Take me home, take me home, take me home.* My voice soars high above them.

Verse two. No solo in this section. I open my eyes and sing with the altos.

> *I lay me down by the river,*
> *The sweet, sweet river Jordan,*
> *My fingers touch the muddy water.*
> *There's rich grass on the other side.*

The tempo ramps up on the chorus. Things start to get wild. We're all singing full power, top of our voices, shaking the windowpanes.

Oh, the glory of that bright day
When I cross the river Jordan.
The angels playing banjo
And the good Lord on the fiddle.

Terri's smiling all over herself—having the time of her life. She's jumping up and down, getting everybody into it. Oh, crap, it's me again. High and fluid over the harmonic jumble of the rest of the choir.

There's me pappy and me mammy—
Singing like they've never sung before—

I keep my eyes open this time. The choir sings back to me. I let loose, throw in another run at the end of the line.

The dark boy who said he loved me
And fills my dreams at night.

The place is rocking, building to the climax. All of us, full-throated, sing, *Take me home, take me home, take me home,* like *we* never have before. Electric sound magic. Music flying everywhere. The key changes, and we're into the bridge.

But my babe, Lord, my sweet child, who wears my master's eyes,
Wraps his sweet, sweet fingers so tight around my heart—

Each section wanders down its own tangled pathway until we wind back together into a perfect sustained chord: *HE AIN'T READY FOR JORDAN!*

We're one with that tragic girl so far away in time and place. A bunch of white girls finding their souls.

Terri hushes us into reverence for the next line. *A mother breathes because she must.*

Like my mom who kept going when my dad bolted. For me. She kept breathing, kept working—too wounded to ever love again. And I stare at her with his eyes, his height, his face, his zits. Every day, I'm there to remind her. The Beast incarnate.

The girls around me chant, *Pulls me back, pulls me back, pulls me back.*

My voice finds its way out of the harmony. Alone. One small slave girl looking for salvation.

> *I bid farewell to the river,*
> *The sweet, sweet river Jordan,*
> *Turn my back on the muddy water,*
> *Close my eyes to that other side.*

I don't know how I keep singing the final chorus. I'm so full of her agony. My voice breaks when I sing, *Where my master cannot find me.* I get control, and the choir joins me in a harmonious, heart-throbbing, *Lord, I long for the other side.*

I'm weeping on that last note. So is Terri. So are Sarah and the girl in front of me. All the girls are wiping their eyes. The final piano chord dies away. Terri drops her hands.

Pandemonium.

Everybody crowds around me. Hugging me. Pulling on my arms. Patting my back. They're all cheering. For me. Massively unprecedented emotion surges heat into my face.

Terri plows through the choir and hurls her tiny self at my giant frame. "Why didn't you tell me you can sing like that?"

I sniff and wipe my eyes. "I'm an alto."

That's when I see her. Meadow. Standing in the doorway. Her face matches the pale-green walls behind her in the hall. "What's going on?"

chapter 3

TAKE TWO

What Terri says next bounces in my brain but doesn't get through to me.

She clears her throat and says it again, "Meadow, I'm giving Beth the solo in 'Take Me Home.'"

Me? The soloist? For real? My legs go jelly. I sink onto the pew behind me.

"But it's mine." Meadow clutches the wood doorframe. "You can't give it to that—"

Hideous beast. She doesn't need to say it. Everyone knows what she means.

"You can't dash out to the bathroom when we're onstage in Lausanne."

"It's not like I do it on purpose."

"We need a soloist for this piece, hon. You've tried and tried. I know that. Beth can do it. You heard her, didn't you?"

Meadow stamps her foot. "Give it up, Terri. We're not going to be on the stage in Lausanne."

Her cold words blanket the room, silence the glow of the music we welded in the midst of the night. We all remember the pathetic recording we submitted.

I can't believe Terri is finally getting real with Meadow. I'm sick of all the babying, but Meadow is right. It's way too late. It doesn't matter now. I guess we'll need this piece in Vancouver. Singing is singing. I'll be the soloist there. Maybe that trip won't be up to Meadow's standards, and she'll skip the whole thing.

Meadow glares at me. "I say we dump that stupid piece. I hate it."

"Unfortunately, Meadow, I think we'll still need it." Terri stands up on a pew so all the girls can hear her. "You're not going to believe this, ladies."

"Quiet, everybody." Leah hops on the bench and waves her hands around. "Listen. Shush."

"I heard from the Choral Olympics yesterday."

Dead silence.

Please let it be *yes*. Please let it be *yes*. Please let it be *yes*.

"The MP3 file I sent them with our audition performance was corrupted. They need a new copy. I was going to resend the recording we made back in January, but I got busy today. Put it off."

Somebody squeals. And then another girl. It's getting noisy. Terri has to yell to be heard. "How about we get together on Saturday and record this again—with Beth."

"Hold on." It's Meadow. She looks even worse than before. "Who is going to tell my mother?"

I float home. Float into the house. Float up to Mom's room, totally amped that I can give her this. A fragment of "Take Me Home" runs through my head when I knock on her door. *A mother breathes because she must.* That's my mom. For sure. She breathes for me.

I tell her, and she flips out. "You're going to be the soloist?"

"Yeah. Me. And Terri's pretty sure that with me singing, we'll get in. You should have heard me tonight." I drop onto her bed and curl up on my side next to her, still trying to believe it's true.

"Too bad Grandma Lizzie is gone." Mom smoothes her hand over my head. "She would have loved to see this." Grandma Lizzie is where I got my voice. She was in a big band, sang for the troops in World War II. She died just after I was born.

"Maybe she did. Maybe she was there tonight. Holding my hand."

Mom gets all teary and hugs me.

I get settled for the night in my own bed but can't sleep. Stand up and stare at myself in the mirror. The girl that looks back isn't a soloist. She's the one you hide behind the floral arrangement. That would work. I can sing from anywhere. I don't want this face to wreck what they hear. I'm still that damn ugly daughter, still defined, still believe them.

I'm floating at school next day, too, but I'm so sleepy. I keep nodding off. Finally wake up by choir. Scott sits down next to me. I'm too happy to go back to where we left off yesterday. He'll never have to cheer me up again. He can be sweet and stupid if he wants. I'm so high—nothing will hurt. At least nothing Scott can dream up. Colby could probably get through, but he's done his worst for a while. He'll have to lie low after his naked-freshmen stunt. Only a couple of guys directed crude remarks in my direction as I crept through the hall this morning. Life's good. Really good.

"What's up with you?" Scott is still grumpy. He does need to go find a cute, short girlfriend. He's starting to fill out. He has a neck now. He never used to have a guy neck. And he's letting his baby-blond hair grow out. Crew cuts no more. He's almost got locks. It goes good with the neck.

"Are you lifting weights?"

"I go to the gym with my dad."

"That must be nice."

"He needs encouragement. You want to come with us—Saturday?"

"I'm recording on Saturday."

"You sign with Motown when I wasn't looking?"

"Hardly. But—" I can't help breaking into a foolish, sappy, I-can't-believe-my-good-fortune smile. "I'm the new soloist for Bliss."

"The fancy chick choir? About time."

"This is huge. Is that all you can say?"

"Congratulations. When you sign with Motown, let me know."

I want to grab him by his sexy new guy neck and throttle him, but class starts and he needs it to sing.

Saturday I'm up early. Out the door. I'm so pumped and alive. Wonder if love feels like this. Who needs it when you can have this rush, this excitement? Maybe that's why divas churn through men. What guy could match this high?

The roads are clear for once. No traffic, no slush, no construction. The sun even makes a brief appearance. I sail down the freeway, singing *my* solo with the practice CD cranked, coaxing Jeanette up to seventy. She shakes and vibrates, but I don't let up until the speed limit drops back to fifty-five.

I get to choir early enough to help Terri set up the recording equipment. Rental stuff. Huge microphones. A double-reel tape recorder this time to back up the digital. We get lost in the wires and don't notice Meadow and her parents when they arrive.

Her dad elegantly clears his throat. "Can I help?" He slips off his brown leather driving gloves, takes a bundle of mike cords from me, and adeptly straightens the mess. He wears a camel-colored wool coat, perfectly tailored. Really handsome. Not just the coat.

Terri's cheeks go pink when she talks to him. "After what happened to our last file, I don't quite trust digital anymore." She nods at the extra equipment.

He turns to hook the mikes into the recording system. "Yes. Meadow told me you're re-recording this morning."

"That's right. The Choral Olympics couldn't get the file we sent with our application to work. So we've got a rare chance—the girls are so much better now than they were in January."

Meadow glares in my direction. "But this is cheating. You should send the same recording."

"It's kind of messed up." I wonder what she did to it. "I called the committee and explained we need to rerecord. They said fine." She throws a look at me.

I turn away, biting the insides of my cheeks to keep my face in check.

Meadow's father turns knobs on the soundboard, pretending to be preoccupied. "Meadow says you're giving Beth her solo." He looks meaningfully at Terri.

She sort of wilts. The man knows how to use his powers. He sells cars. Thousands of them. Terri swallows and starts shuffling through her music. "Meadow was too ill to sing it Thursday."

"Ill?" Meadow's dad glances at her mom.

She wraps the fur collar on her coat tighter around her neck. "Meadow was not ill. You bullied her into performing when she wasn't ready." She's got full-length real furs in her closet at home. She wears them to our concerts.

Terri continues. I can tell she memorized this speech. "Beth filled in. The girls feel we should record both soloists, play it back and vote on which recording to send."

Way to go, Terri. So sly. How can they object to that?

Meadow's mom stares me down. "Beth can go first. Dear," she addresses her husband, "you better stay."

I can tell that no way does Meadow's high-powered dad want to spend his Saturday at a tedious recording session, especially if Meadow's singing, but he prepares to obey. "I can man this stuff for you." He flashes a smile made for movies at Terri. "Old hobby."

I can imagine the sound system they've got at their place and smile to myself. I bet Meadow is way into karaoke.

By 8:30 a.m. the pews are packed. Warm-up and neck rubs. Everybody's loose and spirited. It feels like a party. Recording sessions are usually stressed, but not this one. Whispers run around the room. No one seems to be able to hold her instrument still. Terri rolls with it. Normally she'd be uptight, glare down any girl who made a single unwanted noise.

All the girls are eager to see what Meadow's mom will do when she hears me sing. Sarah thinks she'll walk out and take her checkbook with her. The girl in front of me says, "No way. She's so delusional. She'll think Meadow is better."

Terri calls us to attention. Silence. She cues Meadow's dad to start recording. I should be nervous, but there's a fierce desire in me that doesn't leave room for butterflies. I stand tall so I can pull a huge breath in with my diaphragm and close my eyes. The piano intro starts. By the time the pianist hits my cue, I'm that lonely slave girl again pleading with her Lord to take her to a better place. The choir joins me. The music swells and twists. I'm lost in it. No mikes. No digital recorder picking up every hint and color of my voice. No Meadow sitting in the choir seats with her mom, who watches with a stunned look on her face. I'm transported—lost in the words and the tragedy and quiet heroism they spell. I am this music. The celebration mounts, comes to its climax, and then it's just me, my voice throbbing with emotion, sanctifying the song as I sing:

> *Turn my back on the muddy water,*
> *Close my eyes to that other side . . .*
> *Lord, I long for the other side.*

My face is wet again. I don't know when the tears came.

Then silence. No one breathes. All eyes are glued on Terri's upraised hands. She nods to Meadow's dad. He pushes buttons, and it's over. Perfect take.

First time.

That never happens.

Our eyes pivot to Meadow and her mom. They're whispering. We're still silent. Meadow's mom stands up. Hang on. Here comes the cyclone. The woman shakes her perfectly styled head sadly and helps Meadow to her feet.

"I told you they'd split," Sarah whispers. "Kiss those new outfits good-bye."

I nudge with my elbow to shut her up.

Meadow's mom guides her to the podium where the minister delivers his sermons. We're all looking up at her. Meadow's face is set, her mouth a firm line. "I really want to go to Switzerland." She licks her lip gloss off. She points at me. "We'll get in with that." Meadow glances back at her mom. "Mom says it's okay. I don't have to do the solo."

Stunned silence.

She can't be giving in. Not so easy. I guess I was counting on her leaving in a huff when she lost the vote. But she wants to stay and let me sing? I don't get it.

"What?" Meadow looks around the room. "You think it's easy to have to sing the solos all the time? You think I want that kind of pressure?" She shrugs her shoulders. "Let her do it for a change."

Pandemonium, take three.

Good thing we're not taping again with Meadow because no one has a voice left after all that screaming. Terri passes around a big bag of honey-flavored throat lozenges, and we sit down and listen to the playback.

I've never heard myself like that before. Gives me chills. That rich, beautiful sound dancing above the choir is me? Doesn't seem real. We're sending this off to an international selection committee. Me.

We're sending *me* off. I get lost in the fantasy. I'm singing on a stage with lights shining all around.

> *Can this be me?*
> *A microphone in my hand.*
> *Lightbulbs flashing,*
> *People screaming when I take command.*
> *Can this be me?*
> *Taking the stage for gold dreams.*
> *A true princess*
> *Winning glory like the tales say*
> *I can—*
> *Is it me?*

After the playback, I avoid Meadow. She's dealing with rejection better than I ever thought she could. Maybe she's telling the truth. If I had her voice, I wouldn't want to sing the solos either. She's got ears like the rest of us. She's allowed to want to go to Switzerland no matter what it takes—like the rest of us.

Her mom is another story. She hovers in the back, rapid-fire whispering to her husband while he winds up the mike cords.

"Okay, girls." Terri ignores the angry woman at the back of the room. "If we're going to get our act ready for the world stage, we've got a lot of work to do. See you Tuesday."

I hang out so I can thank Terri, but Meadow's mom descends on her. "If you're actually going through with this, we need to talk gowns. They must have something elegant. My daughter will not appear on an international stage in one of those old capes."

I get myself clean out of her way. Guess our capes are doomed. The handpainted flowers on the front are kind of hokey, but they're pretty. And we get to wear comfy black pants and a cotton choir T-shirt under them.

Meadow's mom continues in a loud voice, "They'll need an entire travel wardrobe."

Terri's eyebrows shoot up. "We better keep it basic. Most of the girls don't have a budget for a new wardrobe."

"Don't let that worry you. I have suppliers." She's getting excited. "A few classic pieces. Mix and match."

"Comfortable." Terri's not going to win this one.

"Well-made clothes are always comfortable." Meadow's mom launches into a list of exactly what we must have.

"Thank you so much," Terri finally says. "I'll leave it all up to you." Good going, Terri. We won the war—let her have this battle.

"I insist on it. At least they'll all look good." She catches sight of me. "Well, most of them."

I can't thank Terri properly with this woman in the way. Terri sees me. She knows. I give it up, heft my music bag onto my shoulder, and turn to go.

There's Meadow. Right in my face.

I mumble a weak, "Hey."

She frowns. "I'm not going to bite you."

I hold out my arm. "Take a chunk if it will make you feel better."

"What? And blow my diet?"

"Thanks for—"

"That solo has been driving me crazy. I can never get it right. Terri's always crabbing at me to stay after and go over it and over it and over it. I've got better things to do with my time."

"Better than singing?"

"You would say that." She laughs and flips her fake blonde hair back. "There's lots out there better than singing."

I'm guessing Meadow rates love over singing. Maybe she's not a fair judge. It's obviously way easier for her to get guys than sing a solo. Her mega-hot boyfriend picks her up sometimes in his mega-hot red sports car. Maybe he gives her the exact same high I get when the music pours through me, engulfs the choir, and transports us to a different plane.

Sarah laughs from behind us. "Have you seen who's on the program? The Amabile guys are one of the host choirs."

The Amabile guys are a tenor and bass choir just across the border in Ontario, but light years away from us in the youth choir universe. The entire Amabile organization is like that. Their girls' choir kind of invented the whole movement. Hatfield composes for them. I have all their CDs. They set the standard. The girls are legends.

But the guys?

Rock stars.

I have their CDs, too. I can't believe we might get to meet them. Every girls' choir in the world is crazy in love with them. It's not that they are amazingly hot. A few are. Most are just gangly teen boys. Cute and sweet. Kind of like Scott. But when they sing—that's hot. Amazingly.

Meadow turns on Sarah. "Really? Are you sure?"

Sarah sighs. "Funny, we have to go all the way to Switzerland to meet them."

Leah is in the pew behind us, sorting the rhythm instruments. She leans into the conversation. "Have you seen the latest pictures on their Web site's gallery? The ones of their Christmas concert? I die for a guy in a tux."

"Who can sing." We all say it at the same time. Even me, Beth the Beast who never got a guy in her life, gets this.

Sarah kind of writhes. "Ooh, why does that make them so hot?"

Meadow narrows her contact-blue eyes at me. "So Miss Soloist, what are we going to do here?"

I look around for help. "Ummm." Leah and Sarah stare, too. "Practice hard, like Terri said."

"No, silly. Listen, I don't know how you came up with that stunning voice completely out of the blue but," Meadow shrugs and wrinkles up her whole face, not just her nose, "the rest of you is a disaster."

I look down at the hole worn through the knee of my Levi's, rub my hand over it. "I'm sure your mom will come up with some great looking clothes for us."

"Don't worry about the wardrobe. We've got that handled. Easy fix. At least you're not obese, too. You've got a bust under there somewhere right? But—"

I drop my head and stare at her shiny black pumps. "I was thinking I could stand behind something. Flowers. Curtains."

Sarah and Leah laugh.

I smile up at Meadow. "I'll sing from backstage, and you can lip-synch."

Leah says, "We'd so get kicked out for that."

"No gold medal," Sarah adds.

Leah snaps the lid closed on the instrument case. "No press conference."

Sarah winks. "No finale singing with the Amabile guys."

Meadow's eyebrows tease up. "We wouldn't want to jeopardize that." She scrutinizes my face. "Drop your bag. Try to stand straight." She walks around me. "Statuesque. Nice cheekbones. The jaw is a little heavy." She grabs a chunk of my hair. "At least there's lots of this to work with." She pulls off my glasses. I can't see much, but I can tell Meadow is in her element now—way more than when she's singing. "We can do a lot with your eyes. Have you ever tried contacts?"

"Whoa. Hold on. You think you can Glinda me? It won't work. I'm magic proof."

"Oh, honey." Meadow rubs her hands together. "Glinda's got nothing on me."

chapter 4

REMAKE

"What happened to your hair?" Scott flicks it with his finger and makes a section puff up as he sits down beside me in the caf.

"Being soloist has a price." I feel naked. It's still frizzy. No way am I going to add hours to my morning routine straightening my hair with that nasty tool of torture they gave me. It's just school. But my hair is way layered and a good foot shorter. It looked fantastic at the salon. Today I'm the Beast on shock therapy.

"They made you cut your hair?" Scott shoves a forkful of spaghetti in his mouth. "I liked your hair."

Only Scott could like my hideous hair.

As soon as our official invite to the fourteenth annual Choral Olympics arrived, Meadow got started on me. She called it a makeover slumber party and invited Sarah and Leah and the rest of the prettiest girls in the choir—and me. No bones about who was getting made over.

I put down my sandwich. "They ambushed me."

"A bunch of skinny wimp choir girls ambushed *you*?"

"Meadow sat me down in her glitzy bathroom." She's got a Hollywood-type vanity mirror. "And did my face—troweled it on." All the girls gasped and said I looked beautiful. I put my glasses back on so I could see what they were talking about. Kind of ruined the effect. Then I had to tell them all about getting contacts when I was twelve, how excited I was, what a disaster it ended up being. I remember telling my mom that my fiery red hypersensitive eyes didn't hurt at all. She flushed them down the toilet.

"Jeez, Bethie, that's rough. Explains the new breakout." He goes back to his spaghetti.

"So nice of you to notice." Last month's fading crop of hormone-induced zits are being crowded out by a fresh load of fine red bumps all over my face. Not just my usual zit zone.

He swallows. "Stupid brats. Who do they think they are?"

"Beautiful. They don't understand ugly." I tear my sandwich in two.

"You're not ugly, Beth." He opens his milk.

"I just wanted to go home and scrub." I take a bite and chew. "They made me sleep over."

Scott puts his milk carton back down. "They waited until you fell asleep and then whacked your hair off?"

"Does it look *that* bad?"

"It's all uneven."

"Layers. Supposed to be stylish. Meadow got us up early, and we went to a salon."

"Crap, Beth." He picks up my hand. "You're wearing nail polish."

"I know. I can't get it off. You should see my toes." They waxed my bushy eyebrows to a thin line. I'm not telling where else they waxed. They tried to glue fake eyelashes on me, but after the waxing, I got a bit hysterical, put my foot down.

"You should get your money back from that haircut." He guzzles down his carton of milk and eyes my apple.

"Meadow's mom paid." I roll my apple over to him. "She's the mastermind behind the madness. She got her stylist to fit me in." He washed, conditioned, hot oiled, relaxed, and dumped an entire bottle of detangler on my hair—like I'm a bag lady who never brushed it. Then he ironed it flat, cut long layers, and a "fringe" that I can't keep out of my eyes. "Meadow's mom wanted him to dye it, but they ran out of time."

"What color?" Scott takes a big bite of my apple.

"Maybe blonde." I shove the bangs out of my eyes, but they fall right back into them. "I stormed out of there in the middle of the debate. I don't want to be blonde. Can you imagine me blonde?"

"No." He reaches over and slides my bangs out of my eyes for me. "Your hair color is nice."

"Mousy brown? Kiss it good-bye. How do you think I'll look with highlights?"

He puts the apple down, gets serious. "Just like the rest of them."

"That's the idea."

"But it isn't you." He stares hard right into my hyper-magnified eye-balls. "I thought they wanted *you*."

"They want a star. Meadow's mom says my nose is okay. We don't have time to change that, anyway."

Meadow gave me a bag of bra inserts. Since her surgery, she doesn't need them anymore. Gross. I'm not using her cast-off inserts. Next Saturday we're all getting measured for our new performance ward-robe. Then Meadow's mom, Meadow and I—I begged Leah and Sarah to come along to keep it sane—are going shopping for the perfect push-up bra, designer jeans, and scoop-neck tops that show off my "striking clavicle."

Scott puts his hand on my arm. "Will I recognize you when they're done?"

"Just look for the tall girl with highlights bumping into things."

"No plans to cut your legs off?" He glances down at my jeans.

"Shhh. She's got spies everywhere. We don't want to give her ideas." My cell buzzes. I jump.

"Poor Bethie. I've never seen you like this. Are you sure it's worth it?"

"To sing on the world stage? What do you think?" I pull my cell out of my Levi's pocket and glance at the screen.

"Is it her?"

I nod. "Her mom's cosmetic team can see me Thursday morning. Want to come? Hold my hand?"

He takes the cell from me and studies the screen. "What's this about lasers?"

"Erases the scars."

"You trust these guys?"

"Meadow's mom could pass for her sister. They must be pretty good."

"You really want me to come?" His hand slips down my arm to squeeze mine. The sweet side of him oozes out. I like it today. I need some honey.

"No. That would make it worse." I pull my hand out of his and take back my cell. "They aren't doing anything drastic. Just the laser treatments on the scars. Something new for the zits. No collagen shots for my lips or anything like that."

"Your lips are really beautiful." He stares at my mouth, kind of hungry. "They are so expressive when you sing." He traces my lips with the tip of his finger. His voice gets husky. "Don't let them touch your lips."

I'm stunned speechless.

Scott really needs to get a girlfriend. I should tell him that. He's a heart melter. Mine is doing strange things. I should encourage him to find somebody, but I don't want to mess up this moment. I'm sure he doesn't realize what he's doing to me. How effective that wispy wave of blond hair over his left eye is.

I should tell him. He needs to know. He'll never figure it out on his own, but I'm going to need him over the next few weeks. Something real to hang on to while Meadow's crazy mother hacks away at the rest of me. If Scott gets involved with a perky short girl, what happens to me? Disgusting. Selfish. I know. He deserves to be happy. Get a little lip action for once in his life. If he pulled this move on any other girl, she'd be making out with him by now.

But I need him.

He cares about me. One of the few people who does. He wants to help me—wants to be my friend. Is that using him? Unfair? Don't I deserve something? Somebody to be my best friend. To know me inside and out and still like me. Everybody else has someone who loves them. All I'm asking for is this nice boy to keep being my friend.

Until I'm ready to fly.

Sounds like a pop song, huh? *Lift me up until I fly. On your shoulders I'll touch the sky.*

A creepy pop song.

I need to tell Scott he's a babe. I need to tell Scott not to worry about me. He can have a girlfriend and a girl who is his friend. I need to tell him.

I don't.

I lean over, kiss the top of his head, and clear his tray for him. Least I can do.

A day later I'm lurking in the shadows, trying to get from the front door of the school to my locker. I tamed my new hair cut with an elastic this morning. We have to wear our hair up when we perform, so the stylist left the layers long enough for updos and ponytails.

"Hey, Beast." Colby steps in front of me. "What happened to your mane?"

I don't answer, keep my eyes down. I study the new Nikes he's wearing. They zip. No laces. Hideous, but on Colby they're cool. Everyone will want a pair.

"It's not fair, Beastie." He pounds a finger into my shoulder. "You shouldn't make us look at that face. Here." He shoves something cold and rubbery at me.

I don't grasp onto it. The thing falls to the floor. A green witch mask with hairy warts and cracked lips lies at my feet.

"Put it on."

I've got to get away. I start to step around the empty mask and Colby's shoes.

He blocks me, grabs my arm. "That's no way to treat my present."

I struggle to wrench my arm out of his grip. He squeezes hard. I look up at him. He's laughing, loving this. His eyes go past me, signaling. Travis and Kurt appear—grab my arms with their clammy hands and pull them back, hold me pinned, smashed against them. I can feel the heat from their bodies, smell their sweat.

I try to shrink into myself away from them, but I can't hide. They have me.

Colby nudges the mask with his toe. "Make her pick it up."

Travis and Kurt force me to bend down—hold me there until I open my clenched fist and curl my fingers around the mask. The vinyl is slick and cool—elicits an urge to scream and run. They force me to my feet.

Colby, who is the only guy in school taller than me, takes the mask from my hand and forces it over my head, knocking my glasses and pinning them crooked underneath it. "Wear it until your hair grows back."

I can't breathe in there. Can't see. My glasses are jamming into my face. I'm dying to rip the mask off, but my arms are still pinned.

Colby bends over and whispers, "Perfect," in my ear. He's got hot, sensual breath that invades my head and sends bolts of unwanted desire like interior lightening strikes into my gut. That creeps me out worse than the mask.

His body is touching me.

I go nuts, fight to get free. Can't scream. Why can't I scream?

They laugh at that. "Don't worry, Beast. You're too ugly to want to mess with." Colby backs off, and the guys behind let me go.

I run toward the girls' restroom—crash into a wall of people watching. Laughter. A hand grabs my butt. I rip the mask off, grab my glasses, and let it fall. Head down, arms wrapped around myself as if that will keep me from falling apart, I scuttle down the hall.

My face is wet. Crap. I'm not supposed to let them do that. I crash through the restroom door—startle some smokers. I lock myself in a stall. Colby's truth beats inside me.

> *This is me, don't you know?*
> *Touch the sky?*
> *Who am I kidding?*
> *Clip my wings, weight me down.*
> *I thought my time had come.*
> *But the dream turns to dust.*
> *As I bow to do your bidding,*
> *Now I see the truth—it's all a lie.*

I don't leave my safe stall until the bell rings. I venture out only when I'm sure the restroom is empty.

I splash cool water on my face and stare at my blotched, hideous reflection. Meadow and her mom are so delusional. As if a haircut and her cast-off makeup can even make a dint on my ugly.

All morning the mask keeps reappearing. Taped to my locker. Slid onto my chair before econ. When it drops on my lunch tray, Scott picks it up and wipes off the chocolate pudding. "They've got to be kidding." He folds the mask up and shoves it in his sweatshirt pocket.

He gets a clean napkin and wipes off the pudding drops splashed on my neck. He doesn't try to joke about it.

An awful weight presses on my chest. "This isn't going to work—is it?" Colby made it clear today. I'll always be the Beast.

Scott pats my shoulder. "Just sing, Beth. That's all you need to worry about." His words bore a tiny hole in that weight and let out the pressure building up in my heart. I'm not flying. The sky is still impossible, but I know he's right. That is one thing I can do. Sing. All the Colbys and their ugly warty witch masks can't steal that.

chapter 5

BRIGHT LIGHTS

Don't let anybody tell you lasers aren't painful.

You know when the dentist says it's going to pinch a little, and then he jabs a needle into the roof of your mouth, and it feels like it goes right up your nose and out the top of your head? From what I found on the Internet, laser treatments are kind of the same deal.

Mom says childbirth is like that on steroids. I don't know if I'm brave enough. All that pain? It would be worth it, though, for a baby, a sweet, beautiful bundle cooing in my arms. Anything would be worth that. But even with all of Meadow and her mom's interventions, no way a guy will ever get *that* close to me. I'm so delusional about the blind, fat old guy in my fantasies. *I'm too ugly to mess with.* Colby's right about that. Look at all this time I've been friends with Scott and the most that's ever happened between us is he touched my lips with his fingertip. I don't think any of that stuff means anything to Scott. How could it? I'm so gross. He's being nice. That's all it is to him, but it makes me overheat if I just think about it. Or is that the big lamps overhead and the technician standing next to me armed with a laser wand?

The chair I'm sitting in echoes dentist, too, but it is massive, cushy, and smells like burned meat.

"Just relax." The technician waves her magic laser. I think she's smiling to reassure me. Her eyes seem to be. I can't see her face because she's got a pale-pink surgical mask covering it. "We're going to gently burn away the damaged skin." All my zit scars. "You'll have some oozing for a while. Nothing to worry about. You'll notice a huge difference when it heals. Two weeks, and you'll be a beauty queen." Not a princess?

Hold it. *Gently burn? Burn gently?* How is a burn gentle? I can take this woman. I'm bigger and stronger, but I lie here and nod, the perfect picture of cooperation. I do that at the dentist's, too.

"Would you like something to help you relax?"

Yes. Of course. Yes. Please. "No, I'm fine."

She turns on some waves crashing to the shore set to music, gives me sunglasses to shield my eyes from the dental-like light she shines down on my face, and pushes buttons that lean me way back in the chair. "Okay. Let's get started. Try to hold very still."

I hold my breath. I hate this. I hate all of this. Everyone looking at me. Trying to figure out how to fix me. I hate being reminded how pathetic and broken I am—seeing the disgust in their eyes. I hate that I need an industrial-strength makeover complete with lasers instead of a mere trip to the salon and a killer outfit. I'm not a person to these people. Especially Meadow's mom. I'm her latest obsessive project. She let her daughter give up her solo spot for me. Now she's taking everything that used to be me and turning it inside out, cutting, dicing, disguising. And I have to let her. I should even be grateful.

"You need to breathe, hon." The technician rubs goo with a touch of anesthetic all over my face.

I exhale and fill my lungs again.

"This is the same process we use to remove tattoos. You may want to close your eyes."

Okay. Closed.

It is gentle. At first. But when she gets down to the raw epidermis it stings like crazy. *Burns.* My eyes water. I'm glad I've got the sunglasses.

"There. That wasn't so bad. Let's move on to the next one."

Crap. She's just getting started. There's something wrong with me. I'm getting kind of dizzy.

"Breathe, Beth."

Right. Breathe. I take another gigantic breath in and blow it out.

"Not quite so huge, though. Keep it shallow so you don't move."

She starts on another scar.

I need to swallow. Can I? The liquid is collecting in the back of my mouth, pooling. I can't breathe through it. Nose. Right. I've got a nose. I suck a tiny bit of air in through my nose and exhale the same way. I can't stand this spit in my mouth. If I swallow it lying back like this, I'll choke. I know it. She's got me almost upside down. Can you drown in your own spit? Damn, that hurts. *Damn.* I hate that word. Why did I think of that word?

No, no, no, no. Blackness builds in me. I need to breathe deep, sit up, and swallow, but I'm stuck here. What will she say if I shove her aside and run out? My mouth is full of spit. Completely. I breathe through my nose, so careful. Concentrate on that. Don't think about the—DAMN!

I must have made some sort of noise.

"Do you need a break?" She sits the chair up.

I swallow all that drool. So gross. "Are we about done?"

She shakes her head. "Here." She pops open a couple of individually wrapped capsules, hands them to me with a glass of water.

I gobble down those drugs. I don't care what they are.

"Relax for a while." She turns off the glaring lamps and lights a couple candles. "I'll be back in half an hour." She leaves.

The waves crash against the shore, and I scan the place for a mirror. Nothing. Smart folks.

Right on cue, Meadow walks into the room. "I'm supposed to keep you company."

"Do you have a mirror?"

She looks at my face. "I don't think that's a good idea."

"I need a mirror." Wait. I have one. In my bag. On my first visit—the one Scott was going to hold my hand through—they decided we needed to clear up my face before they could laser me. They started me out with a new zit treatment, some secret, European spa stuff. They applied it here and sent me home with a supply. Morning, noon, and night. You wouldn't believe my skin. I need to tell Dr. Namar about this stuff. He kept me from being totally engulfed in acne like Aunt Linda says bio-Dad was in high school, but there were plenty of break-throughs—especially on my back and chest. So nasty. So . . . ugly.

The team also gave me secret, European spa cosmetics, hypoaller-genic and noncomedogenic, i.e., they won't give me a rash or break me out. The sleek compacts and tubes look too beautiful to use. I got a les-son in brush technique. I've messed around with it some. The lip-gloss pots are all flavored. Mulberry Lane. Cinnamon Candy. Watermelon Ice. I can't bring myself to wear it too much at school yet. But the pressed-powder compact comes in handy. And it's in my purse, sitting over there on that counter.

I stretch my arms, yawn, bend my head from side to side to crack my neck. "Hey, can you hand me my purse? I need to text my mom."

Meadow tosses me the bag.

It's not really my purse. I've never had a purse before. Backpack. Music bag. Purse? Meadow has a closetful.

She tossed this squishy, brown leather bag at me before we went shop-ping. "You can't go to *these* stores with a backpack on your shoulder."

I was going to leave it in the car. Really.

I search through the big belly of the thing and come up with the compact. I take it out and flip it open fast.

"No." She tries to grab it away from me.

I hold it way, way out of her reach. I stand up and go over to the door where there's still a soft light on. Four oozing wounds mar my face. Crap. What if this doesn't heal like it's supposed to? What if it makes bigger scars? My whole face will be one hideous wound.

"What? It's not as bad as it looks."

"Easy for you to say."

"My mother looked way worse than you do. When it all heals up, it's like you have brand-new skin. And you're young. It will heal fast for you."

At that moment I decide Meadow is almost human. "Really?"

"Yeah." She slips the compact out of my hand. "Let me put this away for you."

I watch her ditch it in the purse.

"You go lie down awhile, and I'll take care of this."

She leaves with the purse. She's way more into Project Beth than she ever was into singing that solo. Maybe I'll give it back to her and go crawl in a hole somewhere. That would be better than this, wouldn't it? Is my world debut worth all this? I sit down, sink back into the cushy chair, and that's the last thing I remember.

Ooze? Yeah. Gooey, oozy, weepy, pussy mess. And I have school. I'd stay home, but my group is giving a presentation in AP history and if I'm not there, they'll screw it up totally. My GPA needs the solid A I've got in that class.

I wash off the crusty crap that dried on my face overnight with warm water and the special medicated cleanser they gave me and survey the tube of medicated concealer for the wounds and the beautiful array of cosmetics spread out on my bathroom counter. I've got no choice—the face magnified in the makeup mirror Meadow loaned me resembles a car-accident victim in a driver's ed film.

I smooth on a pinch of the concealer. It must have an anesthetic in it. That little wound feels so much better. I spread it on the rest of my battered face. Smooth on another layer for good measure. Then I brush on the base powder, hit my cheekbones with the blush like they showed me. A touch from the Watermelon Ice pot of lip gloss. I even try to get the eyes right. Concealer. A natural-beige shadow with a tinge of shimmer. Just a touch of brown mascara. Bronzer for a sun-kissed glow to go with my new hair color.

I put on my glasses and stand back. The effect isn't so bad. As long as my face doesn't start oozing in history, I'm good. I'll ditch after that. I don't care.

"Is that you?" Scott started saying that when they dyed my hair blonde. It's getting old. And the hair isn't pale blonde. No Madonna act here. It's actually only a couple of shades lighter than my natural light brown. Meadow's guy at the salon did an amazing job with the highlights. When Sarah and Leah help me blow-dry and straighten it, it looks nice. Sarah says with my height I could be a model. Until I turn around. For school, I've been letting it frizz out to keep Colby from attacking again, but today I need it away from my face, so I go with the ponytail and straighten my bangs. I made it through the hall without Colby seeing me, but Scott doesn't let up.

He walks up beside me with his books under his arm and leans against the locker next to mine. "I thought you said the makeup was just for choir. That you felt weird wearing it."

"I do feel weird. Does it look that bad?"

"What are you trying to prove, Beth?" He flicks my blondish hair with his finger. "Every time I turn around you're a different person."

"The laser treatment made a mess." I throw my backpack in my locker. "I have to cover it up. Do I look that bad?" I force myself to turn his way so he can examine my face.

He takes his time. "You look good." His voice is low again. I can't read what's in his face. He drops his eyes, stares at my knees. "I didn't think you liked the whole makeup scene."

"It always made me break out. Makeup is kind of fun. I know I'll never be pretty, but I'm starting to like being less repulsive." I pull some lip gloss out of my sweatshirt pocket. "What do you think of this color?" I smooth on my soft-pink, shimmery Watermelon Ice.

"It looks tasty."

I hold it out to him. "You'll never guess what flavor it is."

"I'd rather try it on you."

He's doing it again, making me crazy. I hope my face is sweat-proof. The makeup can't totally hide how red I'm getting.

This time I'm brave enough to tell him the truth. "You really should get yourself a girlfriend." I'll miss the time he spends with me, but I'm his friend. He needs to hear this from someone he trusts. Someone he'll believe. "You're turning into a babe, Scott. Really."

He cuts me with the coldest look and stalks off. He's so touchy these days. I was trying to be nice. Self-sacrificing. Heroic. He gives me heck for every little thing they do to me. It's not my fault. I just want to sing. And then he teases me. Flirts almost.

He still doesn't get how much that hurts. We're not in third grade anymore. I have feelings like any other girl. And he's the only guy in my world. No wonder he turns me on. I'm so desperate—all these hormones really want to unload. But he's my friend. My best friend. He won't ever think of me as a girlfriend. I don't want him to. Really. I don't. His friendship means everything to me. The little snot.

My phone buzzes. Meadow. Great. She loves playing stage mom. I guess that's what she's been trained for all her life. Like mother, like daughter. Her mom wanted a superstar diva and all she got was Mini-Me.

My mom called hers last night. She's not all that comfortable with this woman she hardly knows playing stage mom with her daughter. Mom started off thanking her for taking such a keen interest in me. "I'm concerned about the expense."

We're not rolling in cash like they are, but Mom's a partner in her accounting firm. She does all right. I had braces like everybody else. We have insurance and stuff. Just because I choose to live in Levi's and baggy sweatshirts, doesn't mean I can't afford stylish stuff if I can find it in skinny, extra-tall. I have my own car. Good old Jeanette. I don't get a new one every couple of months like Meadow, wouldn't dream of staying on in Europe after the Choral Olympics and going to race car driving school in Germany so I can get a Porsche for Christmas like her, but Jeanette is my own car.

Mom paused. "But—" Another pause. "Choir sponsors?"

Another longer pause. "That's remarkable. The clothing, too? And all the girls are going to the salon? What about the cosmetic surgery? I'd be happy—"

She noticed me listening and walked down the hall. Fat chance, Mom. I followed, stood right in her face. She scowled at me.

"Well, all right then. I didn't realize the choir had such an extensive lineup of sponsors in the beauty business."

So much for Mom's scruples. Meadow's mom could have been lying. Whether Meadow's parents bankrolled or just fund-raised my transformation doesn't really matter. They donate tons to the choir. They are talking about using us at a couple of grand openings they've got coming up and recording a radio commercial. Girls' choir and luxury cars. Guess that works. All of a sudden, I'm Bliss. They like how the engine hums, but I need a lot of bodywork. They'll get their money out of me. I'm not worried about *them*.

My cell is still buzzing. "Hey, Meadow."

"My mom says don't forget the fitting tonight. Be sure to wear your new bra and put some extra in it."

Judges mark down for cleavage. I don't need that stupid bra or the padding. That thing's a killer. Give me my sports bra any day.

"And how are you today?"

"Oh, yeah. How's your face?"

"It was cemented to my pillow when I woke up this morning."

"Ick. How does it feel?"

"Right now? Mostly numb. It'll kill when the anesthetic in the cream wears off."

"Try some aloe."

I laugh.

"It'll be worth it when you're beautiful."

"That may not happen in my lifetime. Maybe the mortician will finally get it right. Unless they bury me with my glasses."

"Ugh. You are so morbid. Listen, you'll never be beautiful if you don't believe it."

"I just want to get to the point where I don't scare people when we walk out onstage."

"My mom says you need to send yourself positive reinforcing messages every day. That's how I made it down to a size one."

"I'll get right on that."

She hangs up. More calls to make. More people to boss. She's loving this, and she doesn't have to sing. I get all the pressure now. All the pain. All the misery. All the work. But it's going to be worth it.

Halfway through second period my phone vibrates. I slip it out, hold it under the desk. Meadow again. 2day's affirmation: I am a nokout. Repeat 100X. Will send nu 1 2mor0.

Knockout? Goodness.

I make it through AP history. Everyone in class is staring at me while I present. I get in a panic that my face is oozing and mess up a little, but no one realizes that but my teammates. They know I got them their best grade of the semester, so they don't dare complain. The joy of group projects. At least I never get stuck with guys in my group. Guys won't work with me. I don't mind carrying a few of the less talented girls. Even if they do sit around and talk while I do everything.

I dash down to the bathroom to try to repair whatever they're staring at. But my face is fine. I'm actually almost okay looking today. My eyeballs are still magnified to freakish proportions, but the rest of me is presentable. My lips look especially nice. No wonder Scott got giddy like that. I'm a heck of a long way from a knockout, but not beastly. Maybe I can write a song about that.

I don't manage a whole new song, but my old standby gets a new verse during econ.

> *Changes.*
> *Why do they surprise me?*
> *Can everyone see*
> *Inside*
> *That I'm still the same girl?*
> *Now who will she be?*
> *Can she be beautiful?*
> *Will she be blinded, too?*
> *Why am I anxious*
> *To leave my old shell behind?*
> *Can it be possible?*
> *Will all the people love me?*

No hopeful chorus yet. Stay tuned, though. Maybe hopeful is around the corner.

chapter 6

RUBY

Leah makes me sign up for the online network they are all on. My page is pathetic. I don't know what to do about a picture. That part is blank. Looks lame. The whole choir friended me—even Terri. That's kind of cool.

I'm going down the list, clicking "Confirm," and right in the middle of those smiling Bliss faces, there's one from a guy.

It startles me. I didn't think I'd have to deal with guys here. Maybe Scott, but not a real guy like this one. He's beautiful. Unreal good-looking. Dark hair, pale skin, moody brown eyes a girl could get lost in. Derek. Sounds kind of phony. Maybe he's the network host. Everybody's first friend.

I click on the message attached to his request.

Good day, I'm one of the ABC soloists. Heard you on Bliss's Web site. Welcome to the Choral Olympics. Chat with me?

ABC? Oh, crap. This guy is from the Amabile Boys' Choir.

Stupid, Terri. She changed up Bliss's Web site. I start singing as soon as the site launches. She must have put my name up there. Great. This babe of a guy thinks I'm some beautiful Blissette and wants to chat.

I move my mouse to "Ignore."

I know what guys who look like this one are really like. Mean, nasty brutes. This guy sings, though. I adjust my glasses and lean forward—trying to see beyond the angel face to the demon it must hide. I need to call Sarah. She knows about guys. She's a champion at guys.

No. She'd make me confirm, so I could pass him off to her. Too bad Meadow has her boyfriend. I owe her something like this. Her ethereal perfection matches this Derek guy exactly.

Leah? Naw. This is hardly official choir business.

I'll just ignore. I like that feature. I click my mouse. Crap. The arrow wandered over to "Confirm" while I was ogling his picture. There's got to be a block feature. While I'm hunting for it, the chat box pops up.

Derek: hi, Beth . . . thanks for confirming me

I type, "I didn't mean to. Can you tell me how to block?" I erase that and send a cautious, noncommittal, What do you want?

Derek: I'm our choir's designated spy
Beth: really?

Shoot. I should have called Leah. This is official choir business.

Derek: honest to gosh
Beth: you won't get anything out of me
Derek: sounds like it will be fun trying
Beth: oh, please

Yuck. Now my hands are all sweaty. I dry them on my jeans while I wait for his next post.

Derek: it's unusual for a choir to come out of nowhere like you guys
        did

Beth: you guys scared?

Derek: hardly

Beth: then why bother to spy?

Derek: are all your pieces as good as that one on your site?

I decide a strategic lie is necessary here—for the good of the choir.

Beth: better

Derek: hard to believe

Beth: it's true

Derek: your vocals are beautiful on that one

Beth: really? you think so?

He's making me blush. I'm such a wimp at this stuff. Crap. I need to concentrate.

Derek: if your other pieces are even half that strong, Bliss should do well in Lausanne

Beth: we think we can win

Derek: win? don't get your heart set on that . . . you're competing against us

Beth: and you don't lose?

Derek: not lately

Beth: but you're worried

Derek: not really

The cocky little Canadian snot.

Beth: then why spy on us?

Derek: spying on you

Me? What does he mean by that? I should just close the screen, but I don't. I can't help it. Nothing like this has ever happened to me before. I'll play along. Just to see what it's like.

Beth: that doesn't sound like official choir business
Derek: you have such a lovely voice . . . I'm curious about the rest of you
Beth: this conversation is over!
Derek: don't be like that . . . aren't you curious about me?
Beth: no
Derek: really? are you serious?
Beth: why so surprised?
Derek: most girls are . . . curious
Beth: I'm not most girls.
Derek: cool. see you in Lausanne
Beth: where we'll beat the heck out of you guys
Derek: not likely

I've had enough. I don't know how to end the chat session, so I close the whole site. I don't ever want to go back on it again. I don't care what Sarah and Meadow say.

Great. We're wasting half this practice trying on dresses. That cocky Amabile boy made me realize we're nowhere near ready to compete. To even stand a chance in an international competition, we can't sing standing in parts like a traditional choir—altos, first and second sopranos. We have to be all mixed up to get a nice blend. Judges can hear the difference. We'll be laughed right out of Switzerland if we don't.

It's tough to sing that way. The altos can't follow me. The other parts can't follow their strongest singers. Each chorister has to be able to sing the part on her own. And it's all got to be memorized perfectly. It's coming, but we're running out of time. We're going to be competing against choirs from music schools. They practice for hours every day, not a couple nights a week. Our big spring concert is three weeks away. We need every minute of every practice. Terri's thrown in a couple marathon Saturday sessions after school's out, but I'm not confident we'll be where we need to be. I don't want to just *go* to the Choral Olympics. After all Meadow's mom has put me through, I want gold. And that boy across the border in Ontario's fake excuse for a London, he better watch out.

So I hang out at practice that night, steaming. I'm also mad that I gave in and wore that dumb bra. No inserts. They creep me out, wobbly rubber things still sitting in their bag. I'm not touching them. The bra is bad enough. The underwires are digging into me, and it's just not comfortable to be pushed and squeezed like this. It's really strange to look down and see cleavage. I'm such a coward, though. I figured I better not risk Meadow's mom's wrath tonight by showing up in my sports bra for her fancy fitting.

She and Meadow put their hearts and souls into these gowns. I need to keep being a good girl, and I'll get to sing. It's all so unreal. I'll wake up one morning and it will have evaporated. I'll be the Beast anchoring the alto, and we won't be going anywhere. Each day that goes by and that's not true makes the next day less real. Less solid. Thin fabric that will tear if I do anything wrong. The only trip I'll be going on is whatever the hell Colby plans next for me.

I want to go back to scribbling lyrics on the back of the last song in my choir binder. I think I was getting somewhere, but Leah and Sarah, both armed with those straightener things, are ironing my hair again. "Ouch."

How did it go? Something about daisies and butterflies. No, it was . . .

Not quite a tadpole,
Not quite a swan.
An opening bud?
The sun at dawn?

Crap. Too embarrassing for words. I need to erase it all. Fast.

Sarah burns me again. "Sorry."

"It's okay." The lyrics in my brain disintegrate. "Thanks for helping me."

"I can't hold this steady." Sarah puts down the straightening iron. "I'm so nervous."

Leah releases the lock of hair she straightened. "Why?"

Sarah sighs. "What if the gown looks bad on me? Red isn't my color."

"But they aren't red." Leah clamps the straightening iron on another chunk of hair and slowly slides it down. "They are ruby. Jewel tones look good on everybody."

"You're starting to sound like Meadow's mom." Sarah puts down her straightener and brushes out her side of my head.

"Well—she's right. The other choirs will all be in black, white, or some nauseating blue." Leah releases the last smoothed strand of hair. "We'll make such a statement. No one wears red."

"Maybe because it's slutty." Sarah has been moody all night.

"It's elegant." Leah takes the brush and perfects my hair. "You saw the fabric. Definitely not slutty." She hands me the mirror.

"It is pretty." I can't imagine me wearing something made of it.

Meadow appears at the sanctuary door. "Beth—you're next."

"Wait a minute. I need to tell you three about something."

I fill them in about my chat with Derek. Meadow whips out her iPhone, pulls up my page, and uses my friend link to get to Derek's page. "Oh, baby. I call dibs on him."

"You can't call him. He wrote to Beth." Sarah peers over Meadow's shoulder at the tiny screen. "She gets to decide."

Meadow studies the screen, navigating around his page. "He obviously thinks she's me. I'm Bliss's soloist."

Leah puts down the brush and tries to get a look at Meadow's screen. "You have a boyfriend, don't you?"

Meadow shrugs. "He's starting to get on my nerves. Derek here is definitely an upgrade."

"Meadow!" Her mom's voice bellows up from the depths of the church.

"Let's go, Beth." Meadow drags me to the basement lair.

Downstairs her mom has transformed the dingy basement. Big lamps. Lots of mirrors. Four portable wardrobe racks glistening with ruby dresses. There's a screen in the corner. Four other girls are wearing long slips and stepping into their gowns.

Meadow's mom herds me behind the screen and hands me an extra-long slip. My tee is really tight. I set down my glasses, pull off my tee, and catch a glimpse of myself in the mirror behind the screen. Put my glasses back on for a clearer view. That bra makes me look way sexy. How can a lacey bra and cleavage transform my bony body like that? My too-long legs are waxed smooth, my stomach is flat, and there isn't a single zit to be seen anywhere on me. Maybe I can go to the beach this summer. Lake Huron never really warms up, but I love wading in the icy water on a muggy July day. I haven't done it since I was a kid.

I pull the satiny slip over my head. The fabric slides over my body like a whisper. I shimmy my designer jeans that I only wear to Bliss rehearsals and for Meadow's excursions out from under it. The soft fabric touches my skin, clings to the curves of my body. Totally luxurious. I feel like I did when Scott touched my lips.

Scott.

What would my old friend with his white teeth, clear skin, sexy-guy neck, and wispy locks of blond hair think of me like this? I can almost picture myself with a guy like that Derek. I stand there working out a hopeful chorus.

> *An awkward tadpole*
> *Turns to graceful frog.*
> *The swan can swim*
> *Beyond her deep bog.*
> *Delicate petals escaping the storm*
> *Beautiful prince who says*
> *He'll keep me warm—*

"Beth—" Meadow's mom saves me from my insane thoughts.

She pulls me over to one of a half a dozen women with tape measures around their necks and pins in their mouths working on girls in the room. This one's got a bunch of pretty ruby fabric draped over her arm. *Cranberry.* If it were Christmas we could call it that. The fabric turns into my gown when she holds it up.

I step into it, put my arms through the short sleeves that are gathered at the shoulder, puff briefly, and then gather onto my arm a few inches later. I wriggle to get into it. Meadow's mom zips me up in back.

The gown is simple. Round neck—not low enough to show my bra-created cleavage, but my lovely clavicle is exposed. Empire waist—the bodice is gathered tight under my bustline, and the full skirt flares out from there. Nothing tight across the stomach. Terri's so practical. We can use our gut for breath support and not burst our seams. Or look fat. The whole effect, from the short feminine sleeves to the soft gathers that give me more bust, to the perfect drape of the richly colored fabric broadcasts elegance. If you cut off my head, I'd look amazing. It must be good from the back, too, with my perfectly cut, dyed, highlighted, flattened hair hanging down my back.

Meadow's mom claps her hands. "Meadow, come look at Beth!"

Meadow rushes over. "Take off your glasses, so we can get the full effect."

I obey. Her mom gasps. She's an artist seeing her creation for the first time.

The seamstress makes me step up on a stool and marks my hem. She walks around sticking pins here and there where the fit doesn't measure up.

I squint down at Meadow. "Is there a way I can unfriend that Amabile guy?"

"Don't you dare do that. I need access to his page to prepare my offensive."

"What if he wants to chat again?"

"Call me, and I'll tell you what to say. Better yet, send me as a friend suggestion."

"How?"

"Never mind. I'll do it."

Sarah calls down the stairs. "Too bad, Meadow. We found him, too. Looks like he's got a girlfriend. She's all over his profile."

"What's his status?" Meadow calls back up.

Leah replies, "Complicated."

Meadow smiles. "Perfect."

"Ouch." The seamstress just poked me instead of the side seam she meant to pin. I can't believe Meadow is going on like this. Her boy-friend is so hot. "You're going to break up over this Derek person?"

Meadow rolls her eyes at me. "Not yet. Don't be stupid. When I get together with Derek in Lausanne—"

She's so sure—so cocky—exactly like him. They'll be perfect for each other.

"I can send Teddy a text calling things off."

"Won't a long-distance relationship be difficult?"

"I'll have the Porsche, silly. Maybe I'll bring him to driving school with me. I better get Daddy to make a reservation for him—just in case. What do you think, Mom?"

Meadow's mom absently agrees and sends Meadow up to get my purse and a couple more girls. They've got to get through eighty—and quickly so we can practice. The seamstress finishes and starts to unzip me.

"Not yet." Meadow's mom searches my bag, finds the untouched mulberry lip gloss—it's way too dark. I stick to the watermelon. She smears the rich wine goo on my lips, touches up my foundation and blush, goes at my eyes like the pro she is. She stands back. "The girls have got to see this. And it's only going to get better when your face finishes healing."

"We're going upstairs?"

"The girls need to see how our hard work has paid off."

Our hard work won't pay off until we're on the stage in Lausanne singing way better than those Amabile guys ever dreamed they could. "I need my glasses."

"No. I'll lead you."

"That's okay. I'm not blind." I hate that, though. Walking around in a blur. I wonder if they'll let me put my glasses on the whole time we're in Europe. The dress swishes as I mount the stairs. A few girls catch sight of me. "Look. Shhh. It's Beth," goes around the room. Meadow's mom, with a hand firmly in the center of my back, guides me up onto the stand.

Meadow appears beside me. "Well, girls, what do you think of our soloist?"

I only see their blurs, but I can feel it. The awe.

The voice of a younger girl blurts, "Can I have your autograph?"

That breaks the silence, and they mob me.

"You're beautiful, Beth."

"Look like a model."

"It's amazing."

I get giddy, overwhelmed, laugh and hug them, careful of the dress. Stressed that Meadow's mom will yell at me if it gets crushed. They can't be serious. Beautiful? Me? I really want to believe them. Believe this excitement that makes my heart go nuts in my chest. It can't be true, but the girls keep coming.

"I didn't know your eyes were that blue."

"You're going to be a star."

"You should do pageants next year."

Pageants? Get real. It's the dress. Just the dress.

After about fifty girls tell me it's true, I start to believe them a tiny bit. I just wish I could see the swan, too.

chapter 7

FIXED

Last night I had a nightmare. We are onstage in Lausanne. Everyone is stunning in her red choir gown, except me. All I have on is the satin slip. And Scott is in the middle of the audience, staring at me with that look on his face like last Thursday in the hall. If he doesn't get a girlfriend soon, I'm going to go nuts and attack him in the music room—friend or not. The Beast legend would be out of control after that.

> *Gather round little kiddies*
> *And say your prayers.*
> *Hike up your jammies*
> *And skedaddle upstairs.*
> *The Beast, she'll be prowling*
> *All through the night,*
> *Hunting sweet laddies*
> *Who look just right.*

I don't know how I can feel like this. Scott is like a brother. We've been friends forever. I can't like him romantically, but I find myself noticing strange things. Like the shape of his shoulder. It's hot out this week, and he's wearing a wifebeater today, and I can't stop staring at his shoulder. It's not zitty like it used to be. And there's muscle on it.

He catches me in choir. "What?"

"Nothing." I force myself to keep my eyes focused on the boring music we're singing the whole rest of the period. Bolt at the bell.

"Beth."

I don't stop. "See ya, Scott. I'm kind of in a hurry." He doesn't know I'm sparing him a fate worse than death.

My cell vibrates, and I pull it out of my pocket, flip it open. "What, Meadow?"

"It's your mother."

"Sorry. I'm losing it today."

"What gives? I thought your face was getting better."

Like I'm going to tell my mother what's on my mind right now. I'm sure she'd really appreciate a conversation about Scott's sexy shoulders. "I'm just tired. Practice last night went late." And then I had to drive all the way home from Ann Arbor—didn't get back until one in the morning.

"Would you like to take this afternoon off school?"

"Yeah. That would be great."

"Good. Walk to the office and pass the phone off so I can get you excused. I've got an appointment for you, and then you can sleep all afternoon."

"An appointment? Not you, too."

"It won't take long. Meet me at home. I need to drive you."

It must be major. She's taking off work. "Mom . . . "

"Please, Beth. Humor me on this one." Her voice sounds excited—as bubbly as an accountant is ever going to get.

"What's going on?"

"I thought of something they haven't."

"I feel like Frankenstein."

"You mean his monster?"

"Yeah. You and Meadow's mom can fight over the mad-scientist part."

"You may not realize it yet, but what's happening to you is big. I'm going to be a part of it."

"Clapping in the audience isn't good enough anymore?"

"I'm not going to be in Switzerland like them."

"You're jealous of Meadow's mom?"

"She's done so much for you."

"How can you even compare yourself to her?" It's tough to say this into a stupid cell phone while standing outside the office. "You're everything, Mom." My voice breaks and I have to whisper. "Where would I be without you?"

She sniffs. "I know it hasn't been easy for you. The boys—you used to come home crying from grade school." Until third grade. I had Scott to share it with after that. It made such a difference. "You hide it from me, but I can tell how they hurt you."

If Mom knew about the near-nude boy chained to my locker, that mask, a whole hall of guys howling when I walk by, all the creative ways high school boys can remind a girl she's *damn ugly*. Less than human. Worthless. The way the girls shun me, too. No one ever wants to get stuck with me. If Mom knew, it would destroy her. "I look fine now."

"What about your glasses?"

"I won't wear them when we perform."

"Not good enough."

"You find some space-age contacts?"

"Better."

A huge billboard I've driven by hundreds of times on my way down to choir unfurls through my brain. "Oh, no. Not more lasers."

"This will be easier than fixing your face. It just takes a few seconds."

"No, Mom. Please. Burning off zit scars is one thing, but that thing in my eyes?"

Her voice gets firm. "Suck it up, girl. Just one more step toward your genetic independence."

The hair. The acne. My awful eyesight. All from him. Now I see what she wants. No more reminders. No more guilt. Her daughter released from every curse he left behind. She wins. No way can I argue that one.

Monday I go to school for the first time without glasses. It's like I'm invisible. No one notices. No one says anything. Not even a single bark. I'm nuts, but negative attention is still acknowledgment.

I don't see Scott until choir.

"You trying contacts again? Not a good idea, Beth. You'll end up blind or something."

"Nope." I try to smile. "This is something more permanent."

"Did they dye your eyes now? They're really blue today."

"Maybe it's the drops. I had laser eye surgery Friday. Cool, huh? It makes me dizzy, but the doctor says my brain will adjust, and I'll have almost perfect vision."

"Whoa. You don't need glasses at all?"

"Don't lecture me, okay. I'm kind of shaky. Probably should have stayed home."

"No, no, of course not." He puts his arm behind me for support, rests his hand in the middle of my back, guides me up the tiers to our tenor seats. "This actually makes sense. It'll change your life. I can't believe the *Cosmo* team came up with it."

I don't sit yet, lean back against his hand—it feels so good. "It wasn't them. My mom kind of insisted on it. Remember grade school?"

Scott's empathetic, "Yeah," floats into my ear.

Squirrel Face. Viper. Boys stealing my glasses every recess. Four pairs got broken. The lenses were so heavy—always popping out. Scott rescued one pair from the boys' bathroom and got beat up for his trouble. "It still haunts my mom."

"Not you?" His hand moves to my elbow, and he steadies me into my chair.

"It is me."

"Not anymore, Beth." He sits beside me.

"It's not so easy to not be that girl anymore. You know what I mean?"

He nods. He's been there, too. And, snot that I am, I assumed he could shrug it off and go act like Mr. Charming to snag a girlfriend. He's a guy. No feelings allowed. He's supposed to just want action.

"Let's turn over a new leaf together." His hand returns to my back, moves up and down, gently soothing. "What do you say?"

"Remember when we were going to run away? In fifth grade? I'll make the sandwiches again, and we can take my car. How much cash do you have?"

"I was thinking we should face it this time." His hand stops moving. "Let's go to prom."

I laugh at that. "Like I could ever get a date."

He leans in closer. "I just asked you, stupid."

I stare at him. "You want to go with me?" My head shakes back and forth at how impossible that is. "I'm too tall."

"And I'm too short." He grins.

Crap, this is for real. "Will you make me dance?"

"Can you?" His hand, with arm attached, moves to my far shoulder. "I doubt it."

He squeezes a hug into a split second. "I can teach you if you want." Scott dances? "I've been to loads of family weddings."

"Isn't there someone else you'd like to take?"

"You're kidding, right?"

"You're sweet, Scott, but maybe this isn't a good idea." My head won't stop slowly shaking *no way*. "I don't want to muck up our friendship."

His arm drops, hangs casually between us. He frowns. "Why can't friends go to prom together?"

"It won't creep you out?" I can't look at his face. "Going with me?"

"Hardly."

"Guess I need a dress." I stick my tongue out at him. "Meadow will be thrilled."

Scott sits up as tall as he can. "This I gotta see."

chapter 8

PROM

Prom ends up being the same night as our concert. Such a pain. Scott comes to the concert in his black tux, looking way too good to be my old grade school bud. We're leaving right after. Port High has a tradition of having its proms at a country club. We're going to be way late, but that's good. The party will be hopping, and we can lurk quietly in the back for a few songs and then leave.

Meadow peeks through the side door of the sanctuary before the concert starts and spots Scott in the audience. She takes him for an Amabile spy, searches the crowd wildly for Derek.

"No, that's my friend, Scott."

"Your prom date?"

"Yeah. We've been friends forever."

"He's way hot," Sarah chimes in. "Introduce me after."

Not on your life. I'd never sic Sarah on my poor, defenseless Scott.

Terri walks in from the side and takes a bow. She's in a gorgeous black outfit. Guess Meadow's mom got to her, too. She welcomes the crowd, says a spiel about golden Olympic dreams in Lausanne, and then we're singing. The numbers whirl by. Each one gets a lot of applause. The audience is our family and friends. They'll applaud anything.

Our finale is "Take Me Home." I nail my solo. The hall goes nuts when it's over. They are on their feet, pounding their hands together while we take a bow. Terri bows. The pianist bows. I have to step forward and bow by myself. Then we all bow together. The audience still claps. They won't shut up until we sing it again.

I'm surrounded when it's all over. Mom pushes her way through and gives me a big hug. "You're beautiful. And not just the outside." It's her gift that shines through me. That is the only really stunning thing I have. She squeezes again. "I'm so proud of you."

Scott's waiting in the background. He does look nice in that tux. It accentuates his shoulders. Dang, those shoulders. Why do they get to me? He was going to get his hair cut for tonight, but I told him I wouldn't go if he did. He so liked that. I hope I can control myself this evening. I don't want to do something stupid and freak him out. He's being so nice to take me.

I finally shake the last hand, hug another old lady, and break away to change.

My prom dress is cream-colored silky stuff, almost the same style as our gowns, except the skirt hits me a few inches above my knee and the scoop neck shows more than my clavicle. Meadow insisted. I'm glad the acne all over my chest is history. This outfit definitely wouldn't have worked. I used a whole bottle of self-tanning lotion to get my legs tan. They turned out okay. My dress makes them look excessively long.

My mom's waiting around with Scott when I come out of the dressing room. She gets all teary and tells Scott we better be in by one.

One? Like we're going to be out that late.

"Sure."

"And what are you driving?" She stands close enough to whiff his breath.

I turn as crimson as our choir gowns. "Mom. It's Scott. Give it a rest." He laughs. "My dad's BMW. Don't worry. I'll be careful."

We get out of there, and I can relax into the firm bucket seat. The leather smells good. Something else does, too. I think it's Scott. Aftershave? It's kind of intoxicating. I reek like hairspray—or worse. That concert was hard work. But it's not like Scott's even aware I'm in the car. He's way into driving. Guys are so easy to please. A powerful car at his fingertips, and Scott is in heaven.

"Hey" —he adjusts his grip on the steering wheel— "grab that cooler from the back."

I'm disappointed. I didn't expect Scott to bring booze. He's so not like that. He knows I'm not. "I can't believe you—"

"Open it."

I lift the cooler out of the back, put it on the floor between my feet, and flip up the lid. There's a large, pink cloth napkin on the top.

"My mom made me put that in—for your dress."

I peek under the napkin. There's a bottle of sparkling cider, plastic wine glasses, a couple of bulging wraps encased in plastic, and six big fat brownies. "What is this?"

"Ultimate chick food—according to my big sisters. I wanted to take you out to a nice place, but with the concert—"

I get a lump in my throat. "This is so sweet."

"Dig in. You must be starving."

I start with the brownies.

We get to the hotel in time for pictures. "You better hurry." The teacher who takes our tickets pushes us down the hall. "They close up in ten minutes."

"We get pictures?" How can Scott be so stunned? Even I know that.

"I need to fix my face."

He frowns at me. "No, you don't."

I quick put fresh lip gloss on while he pays the photographer.

"So if they turn out, we can order extras?"

"Scott!"

"Just checking. My grandmother might want a copy."

"She can have mine."

His face falls.

"I didn't mean *you*. I'm hideous in pictures."

"Twenty years from now, we'll need these to prove to our kids that we actually went to the prom."

"Our kids?"

He gets pink around his edges. "Your kids. My kids. Future hypothetical miserable adolescents."

"Like us?"

The photographer motions us to stand in front of a cheesy archway wrapped in silk leaves and twinkle lights. She looks from me down to Scott. "I think we need a chair. You should sit, hon."

Scott glares at her. "No way." He points to my legs. "I want those in the picture."

"You sneaky brat."

"I've never seen them before. Who knows when you'll show them off again?"

The photographer's laughing at us now, but Scott gets his way. She has us stand facing each other, puts Scott's arms around me—adjusts them so his hands rest in the small of my back. She has me clasp my arms behind his neck, shakes her head, repositions my arms to mirror Scott's. "Now, turn your heads. Chin down, dear. Stand up straight. Smile a little. This isn't a funeral. Look here." She holds up her hand and wiggles her fingers. "That's good." The camera flashes.

I feel stiff and awkward and blink.

Scott, the little sneak, tickles me. I laugh, and she snaps another shot. "Oh," she says, "that one is nice."

Scott keeps one hand on my back and guides me into a blue plush room with chandeliers turned low. A slow song is playing. "Let's dance."

I hesitate. He knows I've never been to a dance. Enemy territory. He went in junior high. Maybe some in high school. Guys can do that—watch from the sidelines. Maybe he even danced. I don't know. I was home writing sad songs that I tore into tiny bits and threw out my window.

"Come on, Bethie." He slips off his jacket and hangs it on the back of a chair at an empty table in the back. "Slow ones are easy." He glances at the sparkly clutch Meadow loaned me. "Anything valuable in that?"

"Just my face." Who knows what that's worth? Hundreds. Thousands. I toss the bag on the table and glance around. There are a couple teacher chaperones watching stuff at the tables. One of them nods at me.

Scott grabs my elbow and pushes me onto the dance floor. He puts his arms around my waist again. I rest my hands lightly on his shoulders, barely touching him. He's staring straight at my cleavage.

"Stop looking at that."

"Didn't you wear this dress so I *could* look at it?"

"I wore this dress because Meadow made me."

"Thank you, Meadow."

"You're creeping me out. Knock it off."

"Where should I look?"

"How about my face?"

He tilts his head back, and we move around in a slow circle. "This isn't going to work. My neck's getting stiff." His eyes drop back to my cleavage.

I step on his toes—hard. "Look to the side then."

"Whoa. Everybody's staring at us."

"Crap." Heat pours up through my body and out through my face.

"Just keep dancing."

"No, let's sit down. I'm thirsty."

"You just drank that whole bottle of sparkly stuff."

I glance around the room over the top of Scott's soft-blond head. "They are not staring." I look down at him. "You are the only one staring inappropriately."

"Come closer then so I can't." He pulls me tight and lays his face on my chest, never missing a beat.

"That was smooth."

"You can learn a lot watching from the sidelines."

"So you're comfortable now?"

"Crap, Beth. Shut up and dance."

I rest my chin on the top of his head. Shoot, he smells so good. I close my eyes. We fall into the slow, seductive rhythm of the song.

> *Remember when you first held me?*
> *And I believed love could be?*
> *Your lips awoke my senses.*
> *You melted my defenses.*

I grip Scott's shoulders. It feels so good to touch them. My hands slide back and forth exploring the shape of his deltoids as we sway together. This dress is lower in back, too. He has one hand on my bare skin and the other at my waist.

> *If you love me, I'll still be here.*
> *Open your heart without fear.*
> *Come back to me*
> *And I'll be everything (whoa, whoa-oa, oh).*

I'm enjoying this way more than a friend should. I pull him even closer, caress his back, get my hands in his hair and stroke his head—kind of maternal, kind of not.

"That's nice." His breath tickles my skin.

Another blush. Does he feel the heat? "Shut up and dance."

Be my baby, and I'll be yours.
Don't say maybe, say forever more.
The truth is, babe, you're what I'm made for.

The chorus takes over, winds back, and repeats. Scott and I don't talk much for the rest of the song. We're both way too into the physicality of our bodies brushing against each other, moving together. Why is he doing this to me? Why am I letting him? The song melts into another song and another, and I melt into Scott.

Then there's a fast one, and we pull apart, kind of wake up. Embarrassed.

He looks up at the clock, almost midnight, and back at me. "Do you want to leave now?"

I shake my head. "I want to dance slow some more. I think I'm getting the hang of it."

He smiles and takes my hand. "Sure."

All this touching tonight. It's making it harder and harder for me to remember he's just my friend.

We wander back to the table with our stuff. He lets my hand go and pulls out my chair. I sit down.

"I'll go get us some punch. Now you can be thirsty."

"Make sure it's safe." I do not need spiked punch. I'm high enough already.

"Okay."

He disappears. I fiddle with my purse. My lips are way dry. I fish out my Watermelon Ice and smear some on.

"Excuse me. Can I sit here?"

I know that voice. My body goes rigid. I don't turn around. You'd think he'd leave me alone this one night. I glance to the side in the opposite direction, looking for a knot of guys watching whatever these jerks have set up. I can't find them. They must be behind me.

Colby sits down.

I don't look at him. Don't engage. The first rule of bully defense.

"So you're here with Scott? How did that happen?"

Silence.

"I mean what awful thing did a babe like you do to get stuck going to our prom with Scott? Are you his cousin? Friend of the family?"

I lose it. "Don't you have a date?" I spit the words into his arrogant, handsome face.

"She drank one beer too many before the dance." Colby nods toward a girl sleeping at the table beside ours. "So I can rescue you." He moves his chair closer to mine.

I pull away from him.

"You're supposed to be grateful."

"Get over it, Colby. Let's have the punch line."

"How do you know my name?"

I stare at him. My brain finally processes what's going on. "You don't know mine?"

"If we'd met before, doll" —he rakes me up and down, and I want to slug him— "I'd remember you. Legs like that—a guy doesn't forget." His voice is low. He's trying so hard to be sexy. He leans forward, stares down my dress. "My parents are members here. I can get into the pool." He looks back at my face and raises his eyebrows. "Do you want to go check out the hot tub?"

"You should know me. I go to Port High."

"How long?"

"Forever. I'm Beth."

"Is there a Beth?"

I stand up, unfold slowly. "You call me the Beast."

The creep's got nothing to stay.

Scott arrives at that instant, holding a cup of crimson punch in each hand. I take both and dump them all over Colby. "Thanks, Scott, but I'm not thirsty."

Colby jumps up, ready to kill me. Scott gets between us, pushes him back hard. Now he's going to kill Scott. I grab Scott's arm and pull him onto the dance floor. Colby can't attack us there in the open.

He stands and stares, teeth clenched, fists balled up, then stomps out of the room.

A few point after Colby and laugh, but most are too drunk, too busy gyrating on the dance floor, or making out in the back, to have caught the quick exchange. The chaperones conveniently didn't see anything.

Scott moves from side to side. Wooden. Scared. "He must have gone to the john to clean up."

"Let's get out of here fast."

"No way." He stops trying to dance. "I'm not letting that creep ruin our prom."

"Are you kidding? That made my night. Thank you."

"I'm not afraid of him."

"How will getting the crap beat out of you on our way to the car prove that? There are only a couple songs left."

"Self-preservation? Kind of a cop out."

"He's really drunk, really mad. We can't give him time to find Travis and Kurt."

"Okay, you win."

As we drive home, Scott says, "Promise me, Beth. Next year. Let's do this again without Colby."

I shake my head at how crazy he is.

"I'm serious."

"Sure. Whatever you want."

As we close in on my house, I start to get uptight. Everything inside me is dying to kiss him when the car stops, but will that creep him out? Sure we danced slow like that. He seemed to get off on it as much as I did. Kissing seems light years away. If I plant one on him and he's grossed out, how can we be friends after that?

We pull into the driveway.

"Don't move." He gets out, goes around the car, and opens my door. He takes my hand and helps me up. He doesn't let go of my hand. He stays there, standing so close—his lips are right below mine.

I just need to stoop—

Tip my face down—

I hug him quick, whisper, "Thanks, Scott, I loved it," and bolt for the front door.

Crap. No—Mom didn't lock it. I'm through the door and taking the stairs three at a time—all the while expecting Scott to come chasing after me and subject me to more senseless torture. I turn on my bedroom light. I can see his car through the crack in the drapes. Why is he still out there? Go home, Scott. Save yourself. I throw myself into my bathroom, turn on the shower, jam my iPod in the speakers and crank it.

As soon as I'm in the shower, I realize my iPod is in the middle of my diva playlist. I really don't need to hear throbbing, passionate songs right now. I stick my head under the water to block out the music. The third one that plays is the first song Scott and I danced to. I shut off the water so I can hear it. I dial it to repeat while I get dressed.

I sneak over to the window. He's gone. We're safe.

"Beth?" Oh, shoot. Mom. I woke her up. "Can you turn that off?"

"Sorry." I whip back into the bathroom, grab my iPod, search my room until I've got headphones, and throw myself on my bed. The song is starting again. I lie there, eyes closed, letting the music beat where my heart should be.

I roll over, grab my notebook, and start scribbling a new verse. One for me.

The scent of you on my fingers
Makes me crazy while it lingers.
Forget it, my heart murmurs.
Why do my fool lips need yours?
Could you want me? If it's a joke,
Please don't haunt me—dreams in smoke.
All we've been through . . .
We should both already know, whoa, whoa, whoa.
Can't you see how much you have changed?
Frightened to move? Yeah, I'm the same.
Insides yearning—can I walk away again?

The chorus starts. I roll onto my back, holding the notebook up, so I can try to sing my verse at the next chance.

I whisper-sing the words overtop the diva's voice blaring through my headphones. Why does Scott do this to me? I've got to tell him— put him on his guard. Explain how wild he makes me feel. If he knows ahead of time that I might lose control and attack him, he can defend himself. He'd think it was funny, right? Kill himself laughing. I'd fake a laugh, shrug the whole thing off as insane, and remind him he needs a girlfriend. He didn't get the message last time. You can't hang out with your old grade school pal forever.

The song starts to play again. I place my hand on my chest where Scott's face pressed while we danced. I want that again. I can't help it. I want his lips, too. I'm such a creep. I want my best friend.

It's his fault. He started it. Why is he doing this to me? How dare he smell that good. How dare he hold me like that while we danced. How dare he let his lips come that close to mine.

I sing my verse into my pillow, over and over, fall asleep with the music still playing, dream of bending down and pressing my mouth to Scott's.

chapter 9

TOO WEIRD

Our last Bliss practice before we take off for Switzerland is a killer. All day Saturday. Goes an hour over. All Sarah and Meadow can talk about on our breaks is Derek. Even Leah gets into it. He didn't confirm Meadow. After our chat, he's probably blocking me. Good. I'm already sick to death of him.

I'm starving on the drive home. I could use one of Scott's brownies.

Scott. It's been so weird with him since prom. I don't have the guts to bring up my issues. Don't trust myself. He acts subdued. Not talking much. Hurt? I don't know. I wish he would tell me. I'm mortified that I ran away from him, but it would have been worse if I hadn't. The last two weeks of school we sat by each other in choir and just—sang. I knew the prom thing was a bad idea. Still. Other than the night I became soloist, it was the best evening of my life.

School's been out for two weeks. I haven't seen Scott or heard from him. So weird. Last summer we hung out a lot. And we've always studied together. We didn't do that once for finals. He's working at the Save-A-Lot this summer. I'm not making milk runs. I leave in five days for Europe. Maybe he'll be normal when I get back. I hope so. I want it to be like it was.

I deleted that song we danced to from my diva playlist. I can't ever listen to it again. All it takes is a few notes and I want him all over. It's kind of exciting to feel like that—passionate like Meadow and Sarah go on about—but I can't be that way. It's never going to happen. Scott's my friend and I'm the Beast.

"Hey, Mom." I chuck my bag in the corner and head for the kitchen. I hope she cooked.

The kitchen is bare. Great. I open the fridge and rip a drumstick off a rotisserie chicken. There's a noise in Mom's study. "Mom? Did you eat without me?" I walk down the hall and push open the door.

Mom is sitting at her computer, tears streaming down her face. I'm across the room in a stride and lean over and put my arms around her. "What?"

"Aunt Linda lost her baby."

This happens to poor Linda a lot. "That's awful." Pregnancy and miscarriage talk used to make me squirm, but now it's fascinating. I gaze at Mom. She would have liked more babies—I'm sure of it.

"This was her sixth miscarriage."

"I'm really sorry." I squeeze Mom's shoulders. "Can I get you some herb tea? How about that violet kind you like?"

"I'm fine. Can you sit a minute?"

I perch on the edge of one of her wingback chairs. I feel stupid with the chicken leg in my hand.

"They did some testing on the fetus."

I'm not so hungry anymore. The smell of the chicken is turning my stomach.

"And ran some genetic tests on Linda."

"That's all she needs. They should leave her alone."

"But now she knows what's going on."

"They found something?"

Mom nods. "It's genetic." She pauses, looks at me intently. "Linda is a carrier of what's called a trisomy—a triple chromosome. Very rare."

"And it causes miscarriages?"

"Babies that have it either die and miscarry"—Mom swallows hard—"or are born with severe mental and physical handicaps. Linda's doctors told her not to try anymore."

"But Anna," my cousin, "is fine."

"She could be a carrier."

A shudder goes through me. "I'm sorry, Mom. Poor Aunt Linda. That's all she needs."

"Honey." Mom looks down at her hands and then forces her eyes back to my face. "You need to be tested. You could be a carrier."

"What do you mean?"

"From . . . him." Dad? Even gone—ruining my life, finding a way.

"That means . . . all my babies . . ." *Will die?* Be severely handicapped? I'm not sure what they mean by that. There's a kid in a wheelchair at school. He's kind of twisted and talks weird, but he's smart. I could deal with that. I could love a child like that. Even a baby who wasn't smart. I think you'd end up loving them even more. They'd never grow up. Always be with you. I'd like that. I'd never be alone again.

But all of Aunt Linda's babies *died.* Except Anna. "Did you have miscarriages, Mom?"

She shakes her head. "I just got pregnant the one time. With you."

I guess nature made me a beast for a reason. Too ugly to attract a mate and pass on the curse. Would an adopted baby love me or be frightened like those kids at the library last summer? Do they give children to single beasts?

Mom gets up and hugs me. "You'll be fine. It's nothing to worry about."

I hug her back and try to believe, but the quiver that runs through her body makes it difficult.

Over her head I catch a reflection of myself in the window behind her desk.

Dyed, straight blonde hair.
Perfect clear skin.
No thick glasses.
I'm beautiful.
But inside, I can't escape. I am what I am.

> *My world was close to change.*
> *Breaking these shackles,*
> *My bid for freedom*
> *So near this time.*
> *But chains still bind me tight.*
> *All my cries*
> *For love, for hope*
> *Fade in the night.*
> *Just run away.*

That's exactly what I'll do. I'll get on that plane, fly to Switzerland, sing to the world. Even this new curse, this awful new power my father may have over me, can't stop me.

chapter 10

INFECTED

"Oh, baby, look at that." Meadow jabs my ribs with her elbow.

Two way-hot guys wearing jeans and red and white hockey jerseys are talking to the guy who seated us. One of them is a tall guy I remember seeing on the Amabile guys' Web site and the other one—

Catches me staring—

And grins at me.

My eyes hit my plate, and I jam a forkful of pork schnitzel and buttery noodles into my mouth. I blush to the tips of my fingers. He's got a magnetism that didn't show up in his pictures online. Angel face, medium height, slim build, dark, soft hair. Pale, pale skin. I can't believe I actually chatted with this guy. I can't believe I was such a snot. He doesn't know who I am—doesn't have a clue that the awkward scarlet-faced girl staring at him with her mouth hanging open is the mysterious Bliss soloist. He's awful, right? Horrid. As bad as Colby. For sure.

"It's him." Meadow perks up. "Derek."

Poor Meadow. The trip up here this morning was brutal. Debilitating stage fright is merely one of her conditions. It's all real, too—no act. She's okay now. We're sitting in a cozy restaurant, the Crystal something or other, all windows, snow-covered peaks smack up against them, that reflect so much sunshine it makes your eyes hurt. All this balanced on top of a peak in the middle of one of the most famous mountain ranges in the Swiss Alps. The Jungfraujoch. Don't ask me how you say it. It's part of this giant installation worthy of a James Bond-villain hideout. They call it the Top of Europe. When we first arrived and saw giant peaks right in our faces, we all stopped at the same time. Staring. Amazed. Alps on steroids.

Down in Lausanne, where we started today's journey, the Alps across the lake are a striking blue granite with hints of snow at the top. The quaint old city is rich with green grass and trees, the blue lake and bluer skies, red geraniums pouring off every windowsill—perfect summer, cool and sweet down by the water. Such a relief after the heat in Rome. The place is like a fairy tale come to life compared with the humid, overcast Great Lakes summer we left behind.

Up here on the edge of the skies where clouds and birds and the very tip-tops of mountains live, it's freezing white perfection. The glaciers on the peaks are pure and lovely, like an everlasting first snowfall.

To get up here, we took train after train, and the last one went straight up through the middle of the solid granite mountain. All we could see was the rough stone walls cut a hundred years ago for tourists like us. Tunnels and Meadow don't mix.

She was breathing fast and shallow, head down, a sheen of sweat seeping through the makeup coating her face.

I remembered that awful panic feeling when I was getting my face lasered. Meadow's mom was in a different car. She always fades away when Meadow is in meltdown. Guess she doesn't like to watch her own handiwork gone wrong.

Meadow sympathized with me when I was flipping out during the lasers. On the train ride earlier today, I glanced down at myself in the picture displayed on the back of my new camera. I looked nice. She did this to me. I hated it—every second. But now? I should be grateful. At least grateful enough to help her out.

"Hey!" I shook her arm, and her terrified eyes glued to my face. "Look at these pictures from Geneva yesterday." I stuck the slim digital camera Mom and I bought after my appointment with the DNA guys under Meadow's nose. Mom got me in for testing two days before we left. Cancellation. So lucky. We both needed cheering up after that.

She focused on the screen. "Are you sure that's Geneva?"

"Yeah. There's one of you at the UN." We sang in the entrance in front of all the flags. "Let me find it." I skipped ahead to a pretty one of her.

"I can't believe we missed the Amabile guys by ten minutes." She has their schedule memorized. Guy talk works best to snap her out of it, so I kept her on the subject.

"Wasn't that them yesterday afternoon?" We had paraded en masse with all the competing choirs through the center of Lausanne, singing and waving flags. Hundreds of choirs. Thousands of singers. And a mass of guys in Canadian red and white that had to be the Amabile boys.

"Seeing them from the back, miles away, isn't what I came for."

I slowly scrolled through the shots. "You'll see them tomorrow."

"No way. We're competing. Terri will keep us tethered all day. But Amabile sings tonight. We got to get out and go."

Terri won't let us go to the opening gala. After today's long trip up the mountain, she wants us in early and asleep. Now that Meadow's had her sighting, maybe I can talk her out of sneaking out. I'm here to sing not stalk. And tomorrow it finally happens.

Not that we haven't been singing. We already spent a week in France, Italy, and now Switzerland. We sang at the base of the Eiffel Tower, flew to Rome and performed in the middle of that huge square in front of St. Peter's in the Vatican. Then to Geneva. Now we're settled in our quaint little hotel in Lausanne. The room is way tiny, but the whole place is utterly clean. Even my neat-freak mom would approve. Our hotel in Italy was a total dump. Paris was worse. My only complaint about this one is the sign outside. A giant blue mermaid who forgot her seashells. At least she makes it easy to find. And she's nothing like the saggy middle-aged women sunning themselves down by the lake that we ran into. I can't imagine being seen like that. Meadow's mom said sunning keeps them firm. Yuck. Didn't seem to help for those ladies.

When the train rolled to a stop about an hour ago, Terri came into our car. "Bundle up ladies." We tumbled out, and I pulled my coat tight. We're all wearing the same tan pants and cream raincoats with our Bliss logo embroidered on the collar, fleeces underneath for warmth up here in the mountains.

Meadow clutched my arm. "I thought it was going to get better."

We were still in the guts of the mountain. Dark, brooding stone. So cold.

"Scarves." Terri wrapped hers around her face. "Quickly now."

Meadow planted herself. "Where are we going?"

Leah got on Meadow's other side, supporting her. "We're obviously not singing in the train station."

We hustled down a stone corridor, breathing through our scarf-covered noses to protect our throats. We broke through big double doors into an open, airy space, warm and glassy. Up close and personal with mountain peaks every way you look. But that didn't cheer Meadow up.

But now, she looks like she's just had a miracle transfusion. An undocumented Amabile sighting right here in our restaurant. They aren't supposed to be up here. They must have changed up their schedule to outrun the groupies.

"Hurry up. He's getting away." Those poor guys. They will not outrun Meadow. Gorgeous guys are her element. She's excited, for sure, but possessed, ready to spring. Now I'm the one hyperventilating.

She can't expect me to go along. "No way." I know Meadow. She'll actually talk to them.

"Oh, yeah. Miss Star, you get that tall guy with him, Blake. I looked him up specially for you."

"Please," Sarah tears her eyes away from the door the guys disappeared through. "You're not giving that to Beth. She wouldn't know what to do with him."

Thanks, Sarah. I think.

"Come on, Beth." Meadow's on her feet, jumping around.

"I'm not going to make a good impression if I faint when we sing." I keep eating, slowly, pretending I'm calm, not embarrassed, not nervous. Totally indifferent. I tell myself I'm not interested in guys like that. Guys like Derek loathe me. He's the enemy. I glance out the window behind me to make sure the bright-white mountains aren't melting in the glow of Derek's smile like I am. I should be creeped out that he made me feel like this, swirled into a panic.

Meadow watches me take every bite. As soon as I get the last noodle in my mouth, she grabs my arm, jerks her head at Leah and Sarah, and the chase is on.

Just outside the restaurant, there's a stairway that leads us to a busy area directly off the entrance. There are counters where you can buy touristy stuff and racks of postcards over to one side. The rest is glass and blazing, white rugged mountain peaks.

Meadow spies the two guys looking at the postcards. "Come on." She goes right up to them, zeroes in on Derek. "Hey, are you guys Amabile?" I would be embarrassed to say something that stupid, but from Meadow it sounds like poetry.

The tall guy looks at the back of his jersey that's plastered with their logo. "What tipped you off?"

"We're your neighbors."

The tall guy gives her a blank look—guess they get this a lot.

She doesn't balk for a second, turns to her boy. "From Ann Arbor.

Michigan? You know that place just across the border? Bliss Youth Singers."

Derek grabs the hand she's sticking in his face. "You really are Bliss?"

Meadow lights up. "Yeah. That's us."

He lets go of her hand and looks at the three of us standing behind her. "Do you know Beth? The one who sings the 'Take Me Home' solo on your Web site?"

Sarah and Leah drag me forward. Meadow isn't pleased. Neither am I.

"Hey." He shakes my hand now. "That's Blake. I'm Derek. Nice to finally meet you."

I'm surprised I don't faint, but I almost throw up all those buttery noodles churning in my mortified stomach. My reply isn't an intelligible word. I can't speak or even breathe, can't look at him. I just stare at his soft, pale hand touching my rough, bronzed one.

"Sorry I was such a turd that night online." He's not smirking at me. That smile is genuine, so heartstoppingly genuine.

I manage, "Me . . . um, me, too."

"Truce?"

"Sure." He draws his hand away from mine.

Blake turns so poor Meadow gets shouldered out. "Derek's over the top with his counterintelligence duties."

Sarah laughs up at him and oozes closer. She's well-endowed with natural assets and isn't afraid to invest them. I don't know how she communicates all that to Blake with a single giggle, but he obviously gets the message.

Derek flashes me another grin. "I have a confession to make."

More heat pours into my face. Maybe it doesn't show through my foundation.

"I downloaded 'Take Me Home' from your Web site, which," Derek's smile opens up to include the rest of the girls, "really needs pictures."

Leah's eyebrows draw together. "I didn't think you could do that."

"Pictures? Easy."

"Download the song."

"You can't but—"

Sarah giggles again. "You stole our song?"

"Borrowed?" He gives me this sweet forgive-me look.

Blake tears his eyes away from Sarah to add, "So he can spy on you."

"Shut up." Derek elbows Blake in the ribs. "I've always loved that piece. We did it in chamber. And the way you do it—so much feeling. That needs to go on Bliss's next CD."

"CD?" I am so lost. Meadow and her mom forgot one thing when they remade me. I'd give anything for a personality transplant right now. I am so out of my depth.

Derek tips his head, talks low, like it's just the two of us. "Our conductor makes us listen to our numbers at night when we go to bed. Some flighty hypnosis trash. Sometimes I cheat—slip in something soothing." His deep brown eyes capture mine. "You sing me to sleep."

Blushing, sweating—what a mess. At least I keep my lunch down. Who could possibly answer that? He must be doing this on purpose, take perverse delight in reducing tall, awkward girls to puddles.

Meadow comes to my rescue. "Now you've met Beth." She maneuvers me to the side. "Here's Sarah, Leah, and I'm—" She pauses and smiles at him like he's won the lottery. "Meadow."

Blake and Derek mumble polite stuff.

Meadow keeps after Derek. "I've got your CD."

Blake says, "The new one or the old one?"

Sarah laughs at his elbow, catches his eye again. "All three. I even got the new Primus recording." Primus is the name of their special group for the older guys.

Meadow picks up a postcard. "We all do."

Derek turns to where I'm pretending to look at fuzzy gloves with "Top of Europe" and mountain peaks embroidered on them. "How about you, Beth. Do you listen to us?"

I nod. "I have all the AYS CDs, too." My tongue seems to function better if I don't look at him. "They, um, set the standard."

He shrugs. "None of them has your voice."

Meadow maneuvers to a spot on Derek's other side. "Are you guys singing up here?"

Blake puts a postcard with a guy blowing an alphorn back in the rack. "Uh-huh. We just checked the schedule." He pronounces "schedule" as "shedule." Sarah smiles at that. Blake raises his eyebrows at her. "Thirty minutes."

Sarah picks out a card I can't see and shows it to him. "You must be right after us."

"Cool." Blake looks around the rack at all of us. "We should do a piece together—in the name of international harmony."

Derek turns back to me, picks up a black velour beanie. "Are you singing your solo? I'd love to hear it live."

"No." I croak, swallow, manage to find a voice that doesn't wobble too much. "That's our competition piece. We're saving it."

"Secret weapon?" That grin again.

Dang. I'm going to die right here and now. And then they'll win for sure. A guy with his cuteness factor blended with little-boy sweet shouldn't be allowed to roam free and unprotected. He's infectious. Crap. He's an epidemic.

I can't help smiling back at him. "Maybe not as secret as we thought."

"Do you girls want to get a drink with us?" He says "girls" but he looks at me. "They've got this hot apple stuff that really clears out your throat. Great for the pipes."

Leah looks at her watch. "I don't think we have time. We're supposed to warm up in five minutes."

Blake leans over Sarah and whispers, "Your loss," in her ear—loud enough so we all hear. She keeps her cool, does this almost imperceptible cat-wriggle response.

Meadow tugs at the beanie in Derek's hand. "How about after."

Derek drops the beanie and turns back to me. "Only if you promise to sing the test piece with us."

Sing with them? Oh . . . my . . . gosh. "But we sing the treble arrangement." I'm gross sweaty again. I can even feel perspiration breaking out in the small of my back.

Derek doesn't seem to notice. "The bass piece is in the same key. It works. We sing it in our chamber choir with the AYS all the time."

Meadow shakes her sexy straight hair back out of her face. That gets Derek's attention. Blake's, too. She purses her glossy red lips. "Won't the AYS get upset if you guys sing with us?" I need to memorize what she does with her body. Head tilt, hip out, weight shift, chest movement. It all looks perfectly natural. I feel like a board standing next to her.

Blake's eyes are all over Meadow now. "They are in China."

Sarah frowns behind him.

Derek picks up the gloves I looked at. "I'll make it happen." His arm brushes mine. Not Meadow's?

The guy must be magic because five minutes later when we meet for warm up, Terri's bubbling over. "The Amabile Young Men's Ensemble performs after us. Their conductor just invited us to sing the test piece with them."

When our choirs sing together, the sound fills up the entire non-acoustical glass, chrome, and cement installation. There are eighty of us and fifty of them. I'm standing in the center in the front. I'm too tall for the risers. Derek is right behind me, singing in my ear. That means he's only a couple inches shorter than me. He shows off and sings the soprano part. I'd like to hear his tenor. I bet that would melt the glaciers out the window. Shoot, he could melt the stone underneath. I'm grateful he's goofing around. His tenor would be way more than I can handle.

Maybe I have heard it. There's this one piece on their latest CD with an aching, tenor solo. That's got to be Derek. Meadow manages to stand beside him. She sings better than usual. Guess all she needs is a little inspiration. What is she doing in an all-girls choir?

After the performance, the guys take us through the main sights, starting with the ice palace full of goofy sculptures. Meadow slips on the ice right into Derek. He catches her arm. "Take it easy, eh?"

She clutches onto him. "Thanks."

He drops her arm, gets ahead of all of us. "Watch." He runs across the ice floor and slides all the way down a narrow hall that leads to the exit, his authentic Canadianness oozing out. Maybe he plays that weird game with the stones. I can't see him in hockey gear.

Then Blake has to do it. Sarah tries and almost falls, but Blake catches her. Meadow knows she'll end up on her butt, so she just watches. I go for it and do end up on my butt.

Derek's there, helping me to my feet, touching me again. "Are you okay? I should have warned you. It's slippery."

"Slippery ice? I'll have to remember that." I stare at him. Can't help it. Is he really this nice? Really this different from any guy I've ever known? That's impossible. Best behavior. Good impression. International harmony. That's all this is. Underneath, he's a guy. They all are—except Scott. Poor Scott. He seems so far away.

We take the elevator to the very top of the peak and go out on a wild, wind-whipped viewing platform. Even with all my layers, I'm frozen in seconds. Feels kind of good. Banks my interior fires pumping up all this heat.

"We better not get chilled," Leah calls.

We all agree she's right and duck quick back through the doors.

The guys lead us to the cafeteria-style restaurant where they ate lunch with their choir while we were hogging up the nice place.

Leah glances around with the corners of her mouth drooping. "What were you guys doing up at the other restaurant?"

Blake looks at me and then Derek. "Derek heard a rumor you girls would be here. He was looking for Beth."

Derek elbows him hard. "Shut up, you jerk."

Sarah turns to me. "Oooh, Beth. You've got a stalker."

I'm embarrassed into a scarlet neck again, but Derek doesn't flush at all. He coughs like he's got something stuck in his throat and then laughs. "She figured that out the first time we chatted."

I try to compose myself while he and Blake push two tables together.

Sarah points at the table next to ours. "Look at that." Big cups of hot cocoa overflowing with whipped cream. Swiss cocoa. Banned. We can't have chocolate, either. No cream. No cheese until after we perform. That's torture in Switzerland.

The guys drool, too.

"You off dairy like us?" I take a chair.

Derek sits down beside me. "Yeah. We've got the gala opening tonight. Gotta keep the pipes clean."

Blake rolls his eyes at Derek. "What a joke that is." He slaps the menu down on the table. "To hell with clean pipes. I'm having some."

Derek shakes his head and turns to me. "Are you going tonight?"

I start to explain, but Meadow plops down beside him and pats his arm. "We wouldn't miss it."

"Great." He smiles at her but turns to me again. "I'll look for you after."

———

The three of us sneak out with Meadow. I feel a bit guilty, but the concert is a blast. Why did we come all this way if we're going to hide in our hotel room? As soon as the Amabile guys hit the stage, every girl in the audience forgets about saving her voice and starts screaming. The guys steal the show. Meaning, Derek steals the show. He's magnetic. Everyone in that giant auditorium tunes in to him and has a great time. I wish they could do more than three numbers.

"Okay, ladies." Leah's acting all official when she's just as AWOL as the rest of us. "Let's get back before somebody blows our cover."

"Hey—" It's him, Derek, pushing through the crowd toward us. "You made it."

"Great show." Meadow touches him again.

"Did you all like it?" He gracefully eludes her grasp, looks around, focuses on me. "What did *you* think?"

"That spiritual you guys sang was a blast." I can look at him if I'm talking music. "Really different from ours."

"It rocks. You can be tender. We'll bring the house down."

I nod. "Your solo vocals were totally pure."

"I can do throaty, too, if you like that kind of stuff."

"Throaty?" Meadow butts in. "Sign me up for that."

"I haven't heard that piece before." I actually elbow out Meadow— this is official choir stuff. My business. "Where'd you find it?"

Blake comes up and catches the end of the conversation. He knuckles the top of Derek's head. "Out of this guy's twisted brain."

"You wrote that?"

Derek looks at the floor. "Just arranged it. It's an old spiritual." A faint tinge of pink washes over his cheeks. "I like working with authentic tunes and lyrics."

Blake swings his arms around Sarah and Leah's necks and hangs on them. "Speaking of twisting brains, did you ladies hear that we can drink here? Just beer. Wine, too, if you're a fancy pants." He glances at Meadow. "Legal age is sixteen. Bars will serve us. How about heading uptown to see what we can scare up?" He focuses on Derek and me. "You coming?"

Derek gets a strained look on his face. "You know I can't."

"That's right." Blake winks at us. "This boy's got a drug habit to feed."

Drug habit? My eyes dart to Derek's face.

He glares at Blake. "Shut up."

"After all I've done for you, man. You could at least come hang with me. Make sure I get home safe." He whispers something that makes Sarah laugh.

Sarah looks ready to head out with Blake. "We compete tomorrow." I sound like a nagging mom, but this is serious.

Derek turns to me. "I'd rather make sure Beth and—sorry what was your name?"

"Meadow."

"Yeah. And Sarah and Leah all get back to their hotel safe. Can I walk you girls home?"

"Traitor." Blake drops his arms off Sarah and Leah and pushes them toward Derek. "That's Derek. Always looking after the women."

"Shut up!"

"If I don't make it back to the hotel, it'll be your fault."

Derek's eyes roll. "I can live with that."

Derek walks us to the metro. Meadow makes sure she walks beside him, but he keeps turning back to include the rest of us. He keeps coughing again, like he did up on the mountain. I don't blame him. He worked hard tonight. He looks tired, too. Wan, not just pale. But still he rides down to Ouchy, the part of Lausanne next to the lake, with us and escorts us to the Mermaid.

"Thanks, Derek." Meadow flounces up the steps.

Leah and Sarah say good night and follow. I'm with them, but Derek touches my arm like he wants to say something. I fall back.

"I'm glad we finally got to meet."

"Me too. You guys are great."

Derek shakes his head. "I'm glad *I* got to meet *you*." He touches my arm again, lightly like a butterfly flutter, and walks away.

I stand there, entranced by his retreating figure, and whisper, "Me too."

chapter 11

BROKEN

I catch up to the other girls waiting for the elevator in time to hear Meadow say, "I think Derek's into me."

She's perfect like him. How can he not be?

The elevator door opens, and we squeeze inside the tiny box. Leah pushes the button for our floor. "He's too charming to be real. He walked us home."

"Escorted." Sarah laughs. "There's four of us—and we have Beth. As if we wouldn't be safe."

Once an Amazon always an Amazon.

Meadow leads us off the elevator. "Obviously, he wanted to hang out with me as long as he could."

We make it down the hall and into our room without being spotted. Terri, Meadow's mom, and the other choir mom chaperones all have rooms on another floor, close to the younger girls. We've got four single beds squeezed into a room that is barely a double. We have to keep our suitcases on our beds during the day or we wouldn't be able to get through the bathroom door.

Sarah snags the bathroom first. I start to change. Meadow dumps her case on the floor, throws herself on her bed, rolls over, stretches. "Derek has the bluest eyes."

"They're brown." I throw the long tee I sleep in on and slip my bra and jeans out from under it. We weren't stupid enough to sneak out to the concert in our official Bliss wear.

Meadow sits up. "Whatever." She sighs and falls back on her pillows. "They are perfect."

I sit down on the edge of my bed. "Do you think he really does drugs?"

Meadow pitches her pillow at me. "I like him. Don't diss him."

I catch the pillow, pile it on top of mine, and stretch out. "I think he's nice, too." Massive understatement. "But Blake said he has a drug habit."

Sarah comes out of the bathroom with her toothbrush in her mouth. "Blake was joking."

Leah looks up from her suitcase at Sarah. "What, girl, do you see in him?"

Sarah turns back around and slams the bathroom door.

Meadow stares at the door. "Blake and Sarah?"

Leah shakes her head. "You're blind."

Meadow rolls on her side. "Blinded."

Leah goes back to pawing through her suitcase. "Did anybody see where I put my pj's?" She finds them and starts to change. "You know who Derek reminds me of?"

"Who?" Meadow sits up and looks around for her pillow. I chuck it back. Get her good in the face.

Leah pulls on her jams. "That guy in *Phantom*." She's way into Broadway.

I sit up. "Raoul? I don't see it." Okay, so am I.

"No. I bet under that charm he's dangerous." Leah hops onto her bed. "Drug habit. That gorgeous pale face. And he *composes*. He's the Phantom."

Meadow wriggles and sighs. "He can drag me to his lair anytime."

"But I think Beth looks more like Christine than you do."

"Beth? No." Meadow rolls on her side and studies my face.

Leah folds up her suitcase. "She's the one with the voice."

I shoot Leah a warning look. "Derek's face is way too angelic to be the Phantom."

Meadow says, "I wonder how he gets it that pale."

I sit up, cross-legged in the middle of my bed, and lean forward. "Maybe he goes back to his room and shoots up." I really don't want to believe that.

Meadow shrugs. "He probably just does a little weed."

"That's hardly a drug habit." He didn't deny it, though. Didn't offer any explanations. Behind those melting eyes and the gentle pressure of his hand on my arm, could he be dangerous? "Maybe we shouldn't try to hang out with them so much tomorrow."

Meadow sits up. "No way. If he is into drugs that means he major likes me. A guy into abusing substances needs a lot of motivation to skip a chance to go to a bar. Motivation like me."

She rolls her eyes at Leah—thinks I don't see, but I do and I get it. I'm not in the club. I don't know anything about typical guy behavior. A little weed. A couple of bars. I admit that scares me. I don't want any part of it.

I stretch and glance from Meadow to Leah. "We compete tomorrow. We need to focus." I need to focus and not think about Derek lying in bed listening to me sing—while he trips out on whatever he takes. "I don't think we should take any risks."

Sarah throws open the bathroom door. "They're doing lunch with us tomorrow after we perform. I already set it up with Blake."

"Way to go, Sarah." Meadow jumps up, hugs her, and steals the bathroom.

Leah and I groan. She plops on my bed next to me. "Now we'll never get in there."

Sarah jumps on my bed, too. Her flawless skin glows.

I hate to be a downer, but I still say, "Blake seems a little wild."

"No more than the usual guy." She pulls a face at me. "I know you've never been to a party, but—really—it's no big deal. They all drink."

I drop my voice to a whisper. "What do you think about Derek and the drugs?"

Leah shakes her head, impatient with my persistence.

Sarah wrinkles up her nose. "I don't know. He doesn't fit the average stoner profile, but artsy creative geniuses do drugs, too. He is pale."

I nod. Beautifully pale. White, white skin. Dark, dark hair. And then those brown eyes and a sensitive, fascinating mouth. It's kind of on the tortured side of the spectrum. Maybe that's where the drugs come in.

The whole gentleman, won't-go-to-a-bar thing could have been a huge act to trick Meadow. Or me. Did I frown when Blake brought up the bar? Probably. Derek could be up in that bar with Blake, chugging down a cold one—no, this is Europe, a slightly chilled, kind of warm one—at this moment, laughing with Blake about how he fooled me. How his plan is evolving nicely. How I stood frozen on that hotel step, massively entranced, as he walked away. He looks perfect, sounds perfect, but what do any of us know about him? He could be hiding anything he wants behind that heart-stopping face. I know what guys who look like Derek *do*.

Leah leans in close. "I don't know if Derek is a scary drug addict, but there's one thing we all *know*." She looks hard at me, a smile playing around her lips. "He's definitely not into Meadow."

I pull out of the cozy knot. "He was being nice. Professional." My heart starts zooming. "Guys don't get into me."

Sarah puts her fingers to her lips and whispers, "They do now."

"Get used to it." Leah tickles my feet. "You're hot, Beth."

I push her away. "You're delusional."

Sarah tickles me from the other side. "You could get anybody you want."

I squirm away from them. "What about Meadow?"

"Blake told me Derek only goes for girls who can sing." Sarah pushes aside her thick bangs.

"She sang really well this morning."

"Not like you sing that solo to him every night."

I swallow hard, shake my head. "This isn't me. I don't know how to get Derek." I put out my hands to ward them off. "I'm here to sing."

Leah and Sarah trade glances. Sarah pats my foot. "That's all you'll have to do."

I don't sleep well. The biggest day of my life is about to dawn. No pressure.

Right. I toss and turn, get up—trip over Meadow's bed on my way to the bathroom. I put the toilet lid down and perch on it, my legs pulled up under my chin, my arms clutched around them in an upright fetal meltdown.

I'm dying to sing. That's how I unwind. I fake it, quietly mouth through all our pieces. When I get to the end, I go back and lie down, close my eyes. I see Derek alone in his hotel room with a razor blade and a line of white dust, or a needle in his hand and a rubber strap tied around his arm. That picture fades, replaced by the wave of emotion that went through me when he said—

> *Sing, sing me to sleep.*
> *You can sing,*
> *Please, sing me to sleep—*
> *Tonight.*

If Derek knew the pre-dyed, pre-manicured, pre-made-up, prelasered Beth, the Beast, would he have been so happy to meet me? That's what I was when I recorded. He could be just like Colby, only smoother. A star singer instead of a star jock. Colby could be nice when he wanted to be. He managed to get all the beautiful girls at school that he wanted. If his performance at the prom is any kind of clue, maybe his brand of nice is mostly arrogance. Derek didn't seem like that. How do I know, though?

So he listened to me sing, walked us home, and touched my arm. Does that mean he isn't just as nasty as every other guy in the universe? Except Scott. But Derek isn't a short, nerdy sweetheart who's been bullied all his life. He's gorgeous, oozes talent, experience, confidence. He isn't anything like Scott. Could Derek be for real as nice as he seems—despite the drug habit? I close my eyes and find something new in my heart. A small spark of something I don't recognize.

Awake tonight,
I give up
And embrace the glow you lit
When your eyes captured mine
And I heard you whisper,
'Sing, sing me to sleep.
You can sing,
Please, sing me to sleep—
Tonight.'
All of my life
I wait for
A touch like wings brushing my heart.
Is this blush on my face
All you have to give me?
Sing, sing me to sleep.
You can sing,

Please, sing me to sleep—
Tonight.

I wake up too early. My head is pounding, and I feel like I'm going to puke. Breakfast and a couple of Advils help. Warm-ups and a run through help more. We pile on our tour bus and ride uptown to the ancient church where we'll perform.

Then I have to deal with getting ready. My face is a routine by now. Meadow's mom winds my hair up and fastens it to my head with the sharpest hairpins on earth. She shellacs it all in place. Then I'm stepping into my ruby gown. I get nervous again—hide out in the bathroom singing my solo over and over until we're called.

We file onto the risers in our swishy ruby gowns. Eighty elegant girls. I feel okay, almost confident. I know my voice won't let me down. The venue helps my nerves. No cold auditorium. A warm chapel full of wood like we sing in back home. Should be good acoustics.

I look at the audience. The benches behind the judges' table are filled with guys in white golf shirts with a fancy red "A" embroidered on the pocket. Their whole choir came to hear us. Derek is looking at me. Our eyes lock, and he smiles. At that moment I'm grateful I look so dang perfect. Drug habit or not, he's impossible to resist. I smile back at him. He gives me a thumbs-up. I take a deep breath, let it out slowly while Terri walks into the room. Polite applause. We sing the test piece. Totally nail it. More applause. We sing our technical second piece. The applause is louder for that one.

The piano starts "Take Me Home." I close my eyes. The music transports me back to the church in Ann Arbor. It's just the girls and me. No pressure. Derek's there, too, though, waiting for me to sing, wanting to fall in love with my song. I open my eyes at the cue. My voice pours out. I look away from Terri, find Derek watching me, hanging on every note, mesmerized. It sends a thrill through me. Somehow

I keep singing, but he's stolen me. Every note, every quiet throb of passion is for him. *Take me home, take me home, take me home.* I'm not sure how he's doing this, but even though I'm up here on stage with eighty girls, singing for the judges and an audience, it's way intimate between Derek and me. The intensity of it mounts when I sing, *The dark boy who said he loved me / And fills my dreams at night.*

He's the dark boy who filled my dreams last night. I want him there again, tonight and every night.

He is the first one on his feet when the last note fades. His choir joins him. The rest of the audience rises. No cheering. Decorum reigns at the Choral Olympics during the judging. But the clapping doesn't stop. We march out, our dresses swirling dramatically around our feet, with the audience still applauding. They don't stop until one of the judges makes them.

The chaperone moms herd us into our dressing area. We can't scream like we want. Or even hug. We make do with high-fiving and cheek-kissing.

Meadow's mom directs the others as they unzip us and help us out of our gowns. We all change into off-white capris and ballet pink blouses with puffy short sleeves and eyelet-lace accents. We even wear matching sandals. I dress automatically, thrilled by that ovation and the pleased look on the judges' faces and the way Derek's mouth trembled at the song's close. I wish I could take my hair down, but we're supposed to leave it up.

I wipe off the heavy lipstick they made me wear to perform and smooth on Watermelon Ice. Reminds me of Scott. Poor Scott. He's so far away from me here and now. So different from Derek. Steady. Loyal. Sweet. Friend.

Derek doesn't seem like any of those things. Especially the friend angle. But sweet? For sure. Last night showed sweet. And singing for him just now was extreme sweet. But that was in me. How did he feel?

What could he possibly see in me? Maybe it is all an act. Those guys have been around. He's had a lot of chances to perfect picking up a girl to pass the time with at a festival. I never imagined something like that happening here, but, heck, I'll play along. Why not? He doesn't know who I really am. I am free here. He thinks I'm beautiful.

We meet Derek and Blake at the pizza place across the road from our hotel. The pizzas are all named for movie stars—mostly American. The guys got us a table outside on the sidewalk. Kind of loud with cars going by but way European.

"Great job." Derek shakes my hand in both of his—holds onto it while he says, "Beautiful, Beth. Exquisite. How do you do that?"

I draw my hand back. "I heard you sing. You know how to do it."

"Not like that. I can't sing like that."

Blake leans over his shoulder and looks me up and down. "Maybe you just need the right inspiration."

He gets another elbow in the gut and, "Shut up," from Derek.

We order pizza to celebrate. Blake cheats again with the dairy, but Derek gets pasta with meat sauce. When his order comes, he takes out a handful of capsules and swallows them—notices my stare, shrugs. "Vitamins. My mom is way into macrobiotics."

I believe him. Every word. Honest.

This place serves authentic Italian pizzas—thin crust, wood fired. I stuff a slice melting with mozzarella into my mouth. It's so different from home. Fresh and chewy. And the tomatoes are sweet. I close my eyes to savor it better—can't believe I'm actually eating with him. I'm learning this guy stuff as fast as I can.

"You don't eat it like that." Derek watches me swallow from across the narrow table. He picks up a slice of my pizza, folds it over. "Here." He slides it into my mouth. Obedient as always, I bite and manage to chew without turning too pink. He's staring—looks like he's starving.

"You want a piece? This is way too much for me." Everyone gets their own small pizza here, not giant ones that will serve a table like back home, but it's too much.

He shakes his head. "Cheese."

"You guys sing tomorrow, right?"

"I hope you'll come." He looks at me the way he did while I sang.

"Wouldn't miss it." I gaze back at him and hope I'm sending the right message.

I'm lost somewhere deep in his velvet-brown stare when my cell phone rings in my bag. I'm carrying it today. Mom said she'd call to see how our performance went. She warned me that calls from Europe cost a fortune in roaming and long-distance charges, so we've made due with emails, but today actually talking will be worth it.

I find it before she hangs up. "Mom?"

"Beth?" She says something I don't hear.

I shout, "Hang on a minute," and get up, walk up the sidewalk. "I think this is better."

"How did it go, honey?"

"Great, Mom. I sang like I never have before." I glance back at Derek sitting at the table, leaning back in his chair, staring at me. He holds my eyes, makes my face hot. "We met some nice guys from Amabile—over the border in London."

"Good, dear. I'm glad you're having a nice time." She sounds down.

"You okay?" I worry about her alone.

"Sure." Her voice breaks.

"What's going on Mom?"

"Nothing that can't wait until you're home next week."

I close my eyes. No, not today. Agree with her. Hang up. Wait. You don't want to know. "Is it that test?"

She doesn't say anything, but I can hear soft crying sounds.

"It was positive, wasn't it?" Something deep inside me clenches hard against the pain that's cutting into my heart. "I'm a carrier."

"We'll go see a genetic counselor when you get home." She takes a deep breath, tries to control her voice. "I didn't want to tell you like this."

"Okay. Is there anything else I should know?"

"Don't let this news ruin your trip. Forget about it and have a great time. We'll deal with it when you're back. The doctors wanted you to go on the pill right away, but I told them we didn't have to worry about that. I'm proud of you, honey."

"Thanks, Mom."

"I love you. I'm sorry. I'm so—so—sorry." She's crying again.

"I love you, too." My voice cracks on the last word. The phone goes dead. My eyes sting. I figure I have about two minutes before I fall apart. No way can I go back to pizza. And calm, cool, beautiful Derek.

There are yellow stripes on the road in front of me. Crosswalk. Good. I step into it. A car slams on its brakes. I jump. I'd be dead in Detroit, but the Swiss stop. I look up at the leathered face of an old Swiss man, raise my hand to thank him. He smiles and waves back. A lump grows in my throat.

Now traffic is stopped for me, going both ways. I hurry across, pass paddleboats and a place selling ice-cream cones and soda, walk down to the lake. There's a ferry terminal on my right. Big trees. Benches. I find one that's mostly hidden behind a fat tree trunk and bushes.

I sit down, try to get a grip. The lake is a mirror today. Really blue. The sky, too. A few fluffy clouds and sunshine. Mountains, blue in the distance with white jagged peaks, rise up on the other side. It's so serene. I can't look at it. I need clouds. Driving rain. Crashing waves. The beauty of this place mocks me, screams *Da-amn ugly* back in my face.

I almost escaped him. Almost escaped all of them. Every guy who's ever called me a beast. I'd started letting myself hope I had a shot at something like a normal life. A relationship. Marriage. A family. I'd resigned myself to that blind guy when I was forty, but this new facade transformed my fantasies.

Look at Derek. Even Scott.

Crap. At the prom, Colby hit on me.

Somebody could love me. I'm not repulsive anymore. Meadow's painful intervention gave me that gift. Kind of amazing.

This death sentence on my unborn slams the door shut. Natural selection wins. I am the Beast. Who could love that? The risks are way too high.

Maybe I can get them to rip it out of me—all of it. Everything that makes me a woman, that makes me yearn to love somebody, everything that makes me cry right now for babies that will never be.

> *Empty.*
> *God, take all these feelings,*
> *Let me just be*
> *A shell*
> *Alone on the seashore*
> *While life swells around me.*
> *Soft tiny fingers,*
> *That sweet baby smell,*
> *Still the dream lingers.*
> *Please, take me from this new hell—*

Tears slide down my face. I wipe at them, angry. He shouldn't have the power to make me cry. My father is a faraway shadow. I never even knew him.

Hot liquid pours out of my nose. Gross. I bury my face in my purse.

Somebody sits down on my bench, hands me a packet of tissues.

Derek.

"Thank you," I whisper, rip out a soft white tissue, and wipe my nose. I try to hand the package back to him.

"Keep it. I've got a suitcase full."

I clutch the package, fumble to open it up again.

"Bad news?"

"Kind of." I get out another tissue and sop my face.

"I'm sorry."

He sounds sincere. I want him to be—desperately need him to be. "Thanks for finding me."

He puts his hand on my shoulder. "I was watching you. I can't stop watching you, Beth." He's rubbing my back now—like you would a hurt child. "I could tell the call didn't end well."

I close my eyes. The tears are coming back.

"Is your family all right?"

I nod, swallow hard. "I had some tests done right before we left. My mom got the results."

His hand stops moving. "You're not sick, are you?"

I shake my head.

"You're not going to die on me?"

"Why do you care?"

"I'm sorry. Do you want me to go?"

"No." I sit up and stare at the lake, try to get a grip. "I can't have kids." Saying it out loud, to this velvet boy, makes it real, seals my fate. I break apart, can't stop it—even with Derek watching.

"Come here." He puts both arms around me, tucks my face to his shoulder, and holds me. The sobs win.

He whispers soothing stuff, hums a tune I've never heard, and rocks me back and forth. Never once does he say, "It's okay." You could love a guy like that. Easy.

I finally get control. His shoulder is wet under my face. I raise up a little. "Crap. I made a mess of your shirt."

"I have four more just like it."

"Your pasta will be cold."

"I like cold pasta."

I manage a smile. My lower lip shakes. "I'm sorry." I smooth the wet spot on his chest.

He presses my head back down. "I'm not."

"I must look awful."

"I'm not looking."

"I guess you can let me go now."

"Do I have to?"

"No." My throat aches like the tears are going to start again. "If you don't mind, it helps."

"Good." His lips brush my forehead.

"Derek?"

Now he's kissing my temple.

"I don't really know you." Is he taking advantage of me or does he know this is exactly what I need?

His mouth drifts across my face. "Sure you do."

I close my eyes—can't breathe.

His mouth finds mine. He kisses me, soft and tender, whispers, "Does this help, too?" And kisses me again. "I've been dreaming about this for weeks—since we chatted." His lips caress and soothe as much as his hands did. "You've got me in some kind of spell. Am I rushing you?"

"I think—" My eyes drift open. "I want to be rushed."

That brings his kiss back. My lips move against its soft touch.

"You're beautiful, Beth," he breathes into my ear.

"Don't say that. Not today. If you knew the real me—inside."

He takes my face in both of his hands. "What—you're an ax murderer?"

That distracts me into half of a smile. "How'd you guess?"

"I knew it." He bites my lower lip and tugs on it. "I love dangerous women."

His kissing gets faster, more intense.

I pull back.

"Rushing?" He touches my face, kisses me slow and soothing again. "Are you feeling any better?"

I put my hand over his and whisper, "Don't stop. It's amazing therapy."

"For me, too."

"You need therapy?"

"I've had my share."

Drug habit. Therapy. Dangerous. Genius. Artist. Who is this guy I'm making out with on a park bench in broad daylight on the banks of Lake Geneva in Lausanne, Switzerland? He's no Colby. Not even Scott could be this understanding. He looks like an angel, sings like an angel. He found my breaking heart and coaxed it into a new rhythm. A rhythm so sweet, so captivating, so enticing, I can't get enough.

Who is he?

His arms wrap around me, his mouth moves to my neck—

And I don't care.

chapter 12

WHOLE

"Back off, Meadow." That's one good thing about being a beast. I know how to defend my territory—call it animal instinct.

She was on the sofa in the tiny lobby of our hotel watching for me. She's on her feet and in my face before the door swings shut behind me. Too bad there's not a window out to the street. She could have seen Derek kissing me good-bye.

"What happened to you. Your face is a mess."

"I got some bad news."

"And you had to drag Derek off because . . . ?"

"He noticed and came looking for me to see if I was all right."

"You are so naive. You should have heard what Blake said about him after you both ended up missing."

"Blake's a jerk. Why would I care what he says?"

"Derek plays this game everywhere they go. Picks out a girl before-hand, overwhelms her, gets what he wants, and then the festival is over, and he vanishes on a jet plane."

"Sounds like somebody else I know."

"You mean me? Hardly. Ann Arbor isn't that far from London. I'm after more than this week."

"Until I got in your way."

"Exactly. You need to step aside and leave this to a pro. I don't want you to get hurt."

Hurt? She has no idea what it means to be hurt. "Too late. He kissed me." We made out until he had to go to practice, and if this week is all there is, I'll do it again every chance I get. Go home to your boyfriend, Meadow.

"I made you, Beth. Remember that." Whoa. Now Meadow looks like a protective beast. She holds the dirty look long enough to make me blink.

I really want to pull this fake hair off my head, scrape the makeup off my face, and strip off every Meadow tainted thing I'm wearing. I hate that she's right. Derek may love my voice, but it was the fake me he was making out with.

Meadow crosses her arms. "So—what's this awful news?"

I'm a mutant beast and will produce deformed offspring. No way I'm telling Meadow that. "It's personal." I push by her, take the stairs up.

"Three more days," she calls after me, "and then kiss him good-bye."

The whole choir goes to the concert that night. We're in the balcony. Derek's choir has seats on the floor.

"There he is." Sarah points him out to me. Derek is standing up searching the hall. "Where's Blake?"

Leah spies him, too. "Stand up, Beth, and wave at him."

I feel so stupid. "He'll never see me up here."

Leah prods my ribs. "Stand up."

I get on my feet to shut her up, watch him searching the auditorium, section by section. Then he's waving, smiling, pointing at the exit.

"Go," Sarah whispers. "I'll distract Meadow. Find out where Blake is."

The orchestra is warming up. It would be so cool to perform with a full orchestra to back us. I tell Terri I'm going to the girls' room and slip out without Meadow tripping me.

I hurry through the exit, and he's there—pulls me behind a pillar and kisses me. It works standing up. I wasn't sure. I just have to stoop a little.

I run my hands down his arms, exploring the muscles. "Hey."

He takes my hands. "Hey."

That's all we manage. We get lost in lips, miss the opening two numbers.

"You all right?"

I bite my lip and nod. "I better go back, though, before Terri sends Meadow for me."

He grins. "Anything but that. She scares the hell out of me." The *oo* in his *out* is so delicious.

"You're not into high-maintenance hotness?"

He laughs. "Come here—one more time."

We miss the third number, too.

"I gotta go."

"Meet me tonight. I'll hang outside your hotel until you can get out. We can go back to our bench by the lake."

Is Meadow right? Does he expect that already? "I don't know if—"

"This isn't about sex, Beth. I wouldn't disrespect you like that."

I'm flaming red. "Am I that easy to read?"

"Trust me. I just want more time with you. We can walk and talk. Sarah told Blake you write, too."

I'm going to kill her. "I scribble lyrics. Bad ones. Nothing like what you do."

"I want to hear them."

"No way."

"Please." He kisses me.

"No."

He kisses me again—lingering and utterly persuasive.

"I'll go out with you, but no lyrics." I'd die if he ever heard that thing I made up last night. And no one will ever hear what I composed sitting on that bench this afternoon. But that was before. Before Derek found me and kissed me and changed me.

Derek smiles, gets ready to kiss me again. "Bet I can get you to sing them for me."

"You're welcome to try." I close my eyes, ready to get lost in him one more precious time.

"I'll bring my best tune."

"Are your lips tired yet?" he whispers into my ear.

I'm in Derek's arms, draped across his lap, knees bent, feet up on our bench. There's a fresh breeze blowing so it's cool. I snuggle into his warm hockey jersey-clothed arms, glad that he wore it. "I could kiss you all night."

He props me upright and stands up. "Let's take a walk."

I don't want to stop making out. "No." I grab his hand and tug.

He pulls me to my feet and kisses me one more time. "I need a break—or it *will* be about sex."

Why doesn't that scare me? Crap. I have a massive urge to shove him back down on the bench and see what happens. The Beast wants loose. Who knew I could be this skanky? Maybe those dumb doctors do have something to worry about.

Derek takes my hand, and we walk along the paved pathway that skirts the lake. He points across it. "Those lights are France. Evian, where the water comes from."

"How do you know?"

"I looked it up to impress you. The lake is a thousand feet deep."

I stop walking. "I don't want a tour right now." I try hard to sound sexy. Me. Sexy.

He turns and points to three large tufts of feathers, bluish white in the moonlight. "Those are swans—should I wake them up?"

I shake my head and let him tug me forward. "Why are little boys like that?"

"I'm a little boy?" He glances sideways at me and frowns.

"No. Most definitely not." We come to a grayed statue and turn our backs to the lake to look at the frozen woman. "I'm trying to figure out what you are."

"Dazzled." He brings my hand up to his mouth and kisses it. I'm surprised the statue doesn't melt. I am. So melted.

We stand like that, breathing each other in, eyes sinking, sharing the miracle of feeling like we do. I think he's going to kiss me again, but he turns away, coughing, gets out a fresh packet of tissues.

I sigh. The evening is cool for summer, especially here by the lake. This air can't be good for his voice. "I don't like the sound of that. Are you getting a cold?"

He coughs again.

"You're singing tomorrow. You should get back."

"Don't worry." He tugs on my hand, and we wander toward our bench. "I'm allowed to sleep in."

"Star treatment?"

"This from the diva."

"I'm so not a diva."

"I know." He wraps his arm around my back without letting go of my hand—so my arm goes with it, and he can pull me in close. "I can tell from the way you sing." He speaks quietly, his breath warm on my earlobe. "A diva couldn't come up with the purity and emotion you get. You're an artist."

"Coming from you—that's huge. Thank you."

"Simple truth."

"I like the way you see the world."

"I'm seeing it differently today."

"You make it sound like I'm the first girl you've said that to."

He stops walking. "I've had a huge crush on you—" He bends his arm and holds me tight to his chest, buries his lips on my neck.

I stroke his soft, perfect hair and whisper, "With my voice. You don't even know me."

He raises his face, lets go of my hand, so he can cup my face between his palms. "I know your soul. It's there in every note." He brushes my lips with his. "You can't fake that. You can't hide it." He holds my lips a long time. "I was dying to meet you." He's breathing faster.

It all gets too unreal. I pull away. "Sorry to disappoint."

"Very funny. You know what the guys back in the choir call you?"

I can imagine.

"The goddess."

His eyes are so full, so deep—I drop mine, stare at the chipped pink polish on my toenails. "I've been called a lot of things but never that."

He puts his index finger under my chin and gently raises my eyes back to his. "Thanks for hanging out with a mere mortal." He tucks a sticky hair-sprayed dyed-blonde lock behind my ear and moves in to kiss me again.

"You know how fake I am?" I turn my face away. "This hair. My face. If you saw me back home—"

"But we're not back home. We're here. We don't have to be who we are back home." There's a fierceness in his voice that frightens me. Is he running from the realities of back home as much as I am? That is what I'm doing—with him, to him—substituting how I feel when he kisses me for the empty desolation that tries to creep back as soon as he stops. I cling to him. Need him. He grips me tight. Can he need me, too?

We stand there holding on, trying to stop time, compress it into this moment so we can drift on this feeling forever.

I raise my head off his shoulder. "What is it—for you—back home?"

"Let's walk."

I keep expecting him to start telling me, but he's silent.

It gets uneasy—at least for me. I want to ask him about drugs—is that what he's in therapy for? Or is it something else? Musicians aren't particularly stable. Even perfect ones like him. Instead, I just say, "When did you start composing?"

He swings my hand then, ready to pretend with me. "I've been arranging for the choir a couple years. I play the piano—guitar, too. Of course, there's the choir stuff, but I like Marley, and folk. Jazz it up sometimes. Not much pure pop or rock. But sometimes I can get down. Guess I'm a musical omnivore."

I look out at the black lake and the lights winking on the other side. "Me, too. I'm no expert on Marley, but the folky stuff works for me. And then, I do listen to most of those divas."

"Do you play?"

I shake my head. My dad played the guitar in his band, left an old acoustic behind. Mom still has it. Strange. I don't know why she didn't burn it.

We stop walking, stare out at the lake. A ferry goes by, all lit up with music playing. Derek squeezes my hand. "Let's hop on one of those. Run away."

I like that idea. "But it's a lake."

"A big lake."

"We need to go back. You've got to go to bed."

"Sing me something you wrote first. I need a lullaby."

I shrug my shoulders. "You first."

He puts his arm around me and starts to hum, breaks into *Ooohs*.

This voice is rich with texture—not that pure choir voice he used at the concert. The melody is entrancing, winds into my heart, makes me want to smile and cry at the same time. It fades away. "That's all I have."

"I love it. What do you call it?"

"'Beth's Song.'"

chapter 13

ROCK STAR

Derek keeps his eyes on his conductor all through their competition performance until he starts his solo. His delicious chocolate eyes find me in the fifth row breathing in every note. Somehow he turns an "Ave Maria" into a love song. I'm lost in the power of it—overwhelmed by the intensity of the emotion that pours out of him. Tears form in the corner of my eyes. What is this? How can I feel like this?

I take everything back that I said about divas and love. If love is anything like the way I feel this moment, sign me up. Singing makes me happy, alive, but this is unbelievable.

His solo finishes, and the rest of the choir joins Derek. He focuses intently on the conductor again. We stand and applaud with everyone else when they're done.

Leah frowns. "I think they beat us."

Meadow stops clapping. "They're kind of professional. It's not really fair."

I'd forgotten that we were competing with them. Gold medal. Right. Best youth choir in the world. I'm sure we're looking at them.

Sarah watches Blake step down the risers. "Even with you, Beth, we're not in their league. No one is."

I lose the thread of their conversation as the next choir files onto the risers. I get up and go outside. They are in the foyer, shaking hands. Derek sees me and starts to head in my direction.

When he gets to me, he takes both my hands. I stare at him. What can I say after that?

He squeezes my hands, leans forward and whispers, "When's your free time today?"

My throat is so dry I have to swallow. "Two hours, after lunch."

"It's mine."

We wander, slowly, around the center of Lausanne, holding hands. Derek seems tired. He jerks away when I put my hand on his forehead to check if he has a temperature. "I thought I wasn't a little boy."

The rest of my choir is touring the cathedral. We avoid it. Too many stairs, according to Derek. There's a big market set up in front of the tiny shops in old stone buildings. Tables of fresh fruits, veggies, honey, and carts selling cheese make the narrow winding streets even narrower. Derek buys some nasty dried-up sausage and makes me try it. So salty. I buy some fresh strawberries to get the taste out of my mouth—and his. The city center is a maze. We get totally lost, head downhill until we pick up the metro signs. We take it down to Ouchy and end up back on our bench.

He sits down, and I take up my position. Instead of kissing me, he pulls me into a hug.

I bury my face in his neck. It feels like coming home. "One more day and the fairy tale ends."

"Don't remind me. I want to stay here with you forever."

"Sign me up."

"Okay. The guys and I are staying on a couple weeks—backpacking, trains. Stay."

"Two solid weeks with no distractions?"

"Blake would be around."

"Even that would be so much better than" —emotion catches at my voice— "saying good-bye Monday morning." I curse the bane of non-refundable group airline tickets.

He strokes my hair. I washed it three times to get all the gunk out of it and hot oiled it before breakfast. It's gorgeous today. As long as it doesn't rain and spoil the flattening job the girls did on it. Keep touching it, Derek. Please, keep touching it.

He does. He's wearing a short-sleeved polo like the one I cried on. I notice small red scars on the inside of his arm. Tracks? I don't want to see them. All the drugs in the world won't change how I feel about Derek. I close my eyes.

His fingers comb through my hair. "It won't be *good-bye.* Just *see you later.*"

My eyes fly open. "Really?" Take that, Meadow.

"Like Meadow said, we're neighbors. London is only a couple hours from Detroit. How far is Ann Arbor?"

An amazing, tingling sensation goes through me. I tip my head back and laugh.

"What?"

"I'm up in Port."

"You're kidding? That's like a half hour from my house—if you go fast."

Then I'm afraid. This can't be real. He can't be saying this. I clutch the front of his shirt. "You really want to keep this—happening?"

"Of course. Don't you?"

I nod my head.

He frowns at me. "What did you think?"

"I don't know. That you were passing time. Being nice. That it doesn't mean to you what it means to me."

"That's cold."

"I'm sorry. I don't know how to do this. Nothing like you has ever happened to me before."

"Good." He shifts his hold so he can kiss me. "Let's keep it that way."

We get lost in lips and hands and hair and faces. It feels different this time—now that I know it will last. Less physical. More emotional. With every kiss, the way I feel about him deepens. With every touch, he is more and more precious. I'll be his high. I'll be his therapy. If he has me, he won't need anything else. I so want to take care of him.

His lips flow over every inch of my face, promising me.

Hundreds.

Thousands.

Of moments like this.

My official Bliss Tour Itinerary is fat as a book. The gala celebration tonight, the awards-ceremony thing tomorrow morning, shopping all afternoon, and our flight home the next morning are all that's left. The schedule says we have to board the bus at 5:00 a.m. Derek and I better say our *see you later*s the night before. He doesn't do mornings.

We, meaning me and eighty girls, not me and Derek, arrive at the sports arena, where the closing concert will be held. We're lucky it hasn't rained. Clouds rolled in this afternoon, but so far it's been dry. They didn't have to move the concert indoors. Terri hands the usher the plastic card with our seat assignments. Instead of leading us to nosebleed seats in the rafters, they take us to a couple of long, empty rows on the field.

The orchestra starts the evening off. Derek told me they are all Hungarians. The Choral Olympics couldn't afford the Swiss. After a couple of stirring classical pieces and a piece from a recent movie soundtrack, a Hungarian tenor comes out and sings. He's good-looking for a guy in his thirties.

Meadow flips out over him. "Next summer—Hungary." Give me Canada. Just across the border. And soon.

An adult choir from the Philippines sings "The Circle of Light" from *The Lion King.* They sit in a giant circle with one side open to the audience and make all those animal sounds using only their voices.

The evening wears on. Lots of choirs. I love the Scottish men's chorus—especially the kilts. The Amabile guys need to get some of those. Derek would be so hot in one. A Hungarian soprano sings a striking aria. I wish I knew how to make my voice do that. The tenor joins her. Standing ovation. The first of the night.

Leah nudges me. "They're next."

I glance down at my program. I knew the Amabile guys were closing the show, but I didn't realize it was so close to over. A shiver goes through me and I'm not cold. I'm hyped to see Derek on the stage, but when this is over, we're that much closer to going home. I hope they sing all night.

They file out. There's Derek in his tux again. My Derek. How can that gorgeous creature be with me? He held me, kissed me, and wrote me a song. Me. Maybe it isn't real. At dinner Meadow was eager to confirm he has a girlfriend in the Amabile Girls' Choir. Meadow said his online relationship status is single now, but the girlfriend's profile picture is a pretty cozy one with him. Her status is "Complicated." I ignored Meadow. My lips were soft and pink from making out with Derek. My head full of his promises.

They start to sing and a nasty voice whispers inside me, *He didn't promise you anything. He just wants to see you again. No commitment.* The thought consumes me. I barely hear the two numbers they perform.

The lights go down. A spot shines on Derek walking out, lots of girls squeal. He sings the opening lines of "We Are the World." It's a tradition to sing it at every Choral Olympics. The real Olympics are about peace through sports. We're about peace through song. Derek sings, slowly with lots of feeling. My heart jumps around inside my chest. I struggle to inhale.

A half dozen of the older guys, the core of Primus, follow him off the riser to the edge of the stage. More screaming from the audience. The other guys join Derek's voice. The tempo picks up. Derek and the guys clap over their heads, getting everyone on their feet. Thousands of voices from all over the world sing about brighter days. Derek leads, in the center of it all. A total star.

So far, far away from me.

The place goes pretty wild after that. Choral decorum out the window. And it's all because of him. He made that number the highlight of the night. He truly is infectious. Intoxicating. I'm not the only one who feels him. He managed to get to everybody in this sports arena.

When the audience calms down, Derek takes the mike. Major screaming. He smiles and waves. Then he announces, "Ladies and gentlemen, fellow choristers, families—we've got a unique treat this evening to close the show." The orchestra starts playing the tune of a guy-girl pop duet—way romantic, way popular last winter. I've sung it to my mirror with my eyes closed a thousand times. I can't wait to hear him sing it.

But he's still talking. "I'd like to introduce you to a new voice that made this festival heaven for everyone who heard her sing. Will Beth Evans, the soloist from Bliss Youth Singers, please join me on the stage."

I am so glued to my chair. Leah and Sarah get me on my feet and push me out into the aisle. I have to force myself to stand up straight and fake a confident walk. A spotlight follows me up the stage. Derek hands me a mike and whispers, "You know this one right?"

"Remind me to kill you later."

He sings, *I gotta be, I gotta be about you,* in my face.

I, *You—oooh, ooh,* back at him.

Onstage, in front of the entire choral world as we know it, he puts his hand lightly on my waist and draws me close, so we're singing mike to mike.

The way you walk, your golden hair. He touches my hair. *The way I see you everywhere. / Babe, don't be afraid—hold out a hand to me.* He takes a hold of my hand before he's done and I have to sing.

My verse is kind of raw, and it comes out that way. *Your breath that drifts across my face.* He squeezes my hand. *A fire ignites when we embrace.* I flush, barely get the next line out. *Your lips on mine promise what I don't dare.*

I take a deep breath and close my eyes. The chorus starts with me.

> *And now—our love is so true,*
> *I won't take a step without you.*
> *Thank God, you came. If you love me, please don't ever let me go.*

I mean every word. Does he? Is that why he chose this song? He comes in and our voices wind together.

> *All my life I gotta be about you.*
> *Can't sleep, can't dream without you.*
> *It's a fairy-tale vision for two. It's you. It's you.*

My eyes open. I get a break while he sings.

> *I raise a kaleidoscope up to my eye,*
> *Twist it once and watch the bright colors fly,*
> *And the picture is so clear—*

He cups my cheek with his free hand. *It's gotta be you.*

He gets me swaying with him during the orchestral interlude. I probably look like a tree. We sing, *It's you, you,* back and forth to each other. And then he does a run.

By the second verse, we're moving in sync with the music, touching each other. Honest, passionate, Derek sings—

> *The way you kiss, the way you sing,*
> *The way you tell me everything.*
> *Will you take my heart?"*

He puts my hand on his chest and holds it there. *I'm offering it to you?* I feel his heart pumping. The spotlight makes him glow.

> *I feel your love—it beats so strong,*
> *I'll walk with you until the dawn.*

He smiles. I slide my hand up to his face and trace his lips while I sing, *Now I love only as long as I sing you, you.*

Derek takes my hand and swings it with the beat. *You, you,* I echo him. Then we're singing the chorus again together. The Primus Amabile guys back us up. I'm totally into it. Instead of fearing the audience, I'm drinking in their appreciation. Major rush. Powerful. It twists with the feeling that's pouring off Derek, and I'm ready for the dramatic second refrain.

Derek and I don't worry about the words. The guys have it. We improvise runs up and around, chasing each other's voice. Derek singing, *Oh, baby, you.*

I get, *Whoa-ooh, you-oo.* At the end it all comes together. Our back up Amabile guys drop out. My voice blends with Derek's in the final throbbing phrase. *It's gotta be, it's gotta be about you.*

Applause washes over us. Derek kisses me, and the place goes nuts.

chapter 14

WINNERS

Derek and the rest of the Amabile guys shred whatever decorum was left after the concert last night before the closing ceremony can even get under way this morning. It starts out with all the choirs waving flags and trying to outsing one another's national anthem. Derek and his friends notch it up to raucous when they get up and run around the arena waving a giant Canadian flag. That bright-red cloth with the red maple leaf in the middle is like a matador's cape. And the bulls can't resist coming after it.

The Aussies get up. Then the Chinese. The Russians, Italians, Irish. Soon a mini UN pours onto the floor. Leah and Meadow pull me with them. Sarah and about fifteen other girls follow. We plunge into the craziness, get swept into the current of choristers and national pride. Leah and I have our big flag. Everyone else has the small flags from the opening ceremony. Major red, white, and blue.

The national anthem singing continues, gets louder. The running wilder. Lots of pushing. A total rush. Nothing like the rush I got onstage with Derek last night, but running in a crazy mob of happy humanity is cool. The only thing better would be Derek beside me in this sweaty, pulsing mass. That would make it hot. I sort of amaze myself. Who knew I could think like this?

"The judges have made their decisions," blares on max over the sound system. "TAKE YOUR SEATS." After three tries, our competitive natures get the better of us, and we flood into the rows.

The announcements start with the mixed-voice youth choirs. SATB—guys and girls. A choir from a music school in Poland wins.

One of our judges comes to the mike. "The bronze medal choirs in the single-voice youth category are . . ."

I hold my breath. Terri has her head down. We're all like that— united in tension. In the Choral Olympics every choir gets a bronze, silver, or gold. It would be so humiliating to get bronze. Phew. He's announcing the silvers now. I see Terri relax. Her head comes up. Silver would be respectable.

Meadow squeals out loud when the judge says, "And now for our gold medal choirs," without announcing Bliss Youth Singers of Ann Arbor, Michigan, USA. Terri shushes her, but she's smiling all over the place and giving us two thumbs-up.

Gold. We got *gold.* Terri's counting so she can figure out what place we end up. In addition to the medal category, they announce in order— from worst to best. If we break into the top ten, she thinks we can get funding from an arts commission for a CD.

As the judge continues without calling our name, we're having a hard time containing ourselves. Squirming, crying, suppressed celebrating. Another choir. Still not us. Another choir. Still not us.

Meadow bends over with her arms wrapped around her stomach, chanting, "We won. We won. We won."

The judge pauses and looks around the room. "The top three choirs are Amabile Young Men's Ensemble, London, Ontario, Canada; Expressly Haiku from Kyoto, Japan; and Bliss Youth Singers, Ann Arbor, Michigan, USA." Applause and cheering. We're going crazy jumping up and down, hugging each other, screaming.

"Will a representative come forward from each of these choirs?"

Meadow starts to head out, but Leah and Sarah tackle her. Terri nods at me. "Beth, get up there!"

I follow a tiny Japanese girl onto the stage. Derek comes forward for his choir. The judge recognizes us from the previous evening. "You two behave yourselves this morning." My face gets as ruby red as our gowns. The crowd laughs. A couple of wolf whistles.

The judge holds his hand out for quiet. "A gold medal and third place go to . . . Bliss Youth Singers, Ann Arbor, Michigan." The audience claps as I plaster on a smile and move forward to get our medal and special plaque for placing third. I step back.

The Japanese girls get second.

The Amabile guys win. Of course they do. No one has a chance against them. They are too good. Way too good.

Derek goes forward, gets the medal and trophy. Major clapping. He turns and waves and the screaming starts. The guy is chick bait. No doubt about it. How can he want to be with me? He could have any girl he wants. As many girls as he wants. Does he really want just me? Or am I one of the many?

The judge calms the audience, introduces the next presenter, and leads us offstage. Derek walks behind me, leans forward, whispers, "It should have been you."

His voice wipes out my jealous doubts. I lean back so he can hear me. "Third in the world? I'll take that." I wish we could escape to a corner for a steamy make-out session, but he goes off to his choir, and I return to mine.

Terri's losing it. I put the gold medal over her neck and hand her the plaque. Massive hugging moment. We're both laughing and crying. Shoot. We have to sit and be quiet while the adult and children categories' results are read off.

When the announcements are finished, we all sing the test piece in a mass performance, and then it's done. Over until next summer.

The adults start to file out, but the youth choirs pour onto the floor. All kinds of kids congratulate me. The Amabile guys get mobbed. A knot of sweet, nerdy guys that remind me of Scott asks me to sign their programs. I can't see Derek in the chaos.

The craziness starts to subside. Terri and the moms begin rounding us up. I look around. Sarah is kissing Blake. Derek is still surrounded by about twenty girls. He sees me—excuses himself. Okay, he breaks away from them.

We're drawn together. I'm desperate to hold him, kiss those lips that are smiling so big at me. We come together in a rush. Then I am holding him. I am kissing that delicious mouth. It is real. He is mine.

"We're going to miss lunch, ladies." Terri's got everybody together but Sarah and me.

Derek lets me go. "This afternoon?"

"We have to go shopping."

"Come with us."

Sarah and Blake join us. "Yeah, Beth. Sarah says she'll do it."

"What?"

"It sounds really cool. Come with."

I look at Derek. "What?"

"Time we had some adventure."

Adventure Park. That's what they call this place. It's ropes and nets in trees. And zip lines.

I'm wearing my fleece—it's cool up here—heavy leather gloves, a helmet, and, get this, a harness. A ring clipped to a rope is supposed to keep me from falling. Derek and I are on a tiny wood platform built about thirty feet off the ground in a massive tree. I wish we could just walk through this ancient forest with its whispering foliage, holding hands and staring at each other, but no—adventure calls.

I'm standing in front of the first zip line, freaked right out. Derek is behind me. "You're hooked in, right?" He reaches under my arm, brushes my ribs, and tugs on the ring to reassure me that it will hold.

I don't jump and slide down the line. Partly because I'm totally scared and partly because I like the way this feels, him behind me, reaching his arm around me, looking after me. I lean back into him. "Kiss me for luck."

"Go Beth. There's a bunch of people waiting."

I don't jump. He pecks my cheek and pushes me off the platform. I scream and close my eyes as I zoom down the line. Halfway down, though, the scream of terror turns into a jazzed squeal. Zip? They aren't kidding. I actually catch the net at the other end and pull myself onto it. I unhook the metal gadget, so Derek can follow me. He launches himself off the platform—glides way faster than I did.

I'm giddy and laughing. He's happy that I'm not wimping. We scramble through the rest of the course. It's way fun. By the end, I leap off the last zip line and take it with my eyes wide open.

Derek's ready to go again. We have a couple more hours here and can go down any of the courses through the trees that we want as many times as we can get our butts down them.

We bump fists, and he says, "Let's take the high course. You rock."

I slow down. "That wasn't the high course?"

He points to a couple of his friends on a platform at the very top of the extremely tall, massive like a skyscraper—no way, nohow I'm getting up there—tree we're standing next to. "That's the high course."

Jelly knees. Total wimp. "How about I watch?"

He hesitates. "Are you sure?"

"Just don't kill yourself. I haven't had enough of you."

He laughs—like I made a joke, but it's got a bitter edge to it that takes me by surprise. "What?"

But he's gone.

I follow and watch him. Not a good idea. Even the lower course looks scary from the ground. The high course is bloodcurdling. I know he's hooked in—but he's way, way, way up there. And he just goes for it. No hesitation. No fear. At one point, there is a younger Amabile singer stuck in front of him. Derek *unhooks* completely and scrambles around him. *Unhooks.* He slips—

"Derek!"

He catches himself instead of splatting at my feet. He hooks in again and focuses down until he finds me. He reads the flipped out terror expression on my face from all the way up there. "Maybe you shouldn't watch."

I go looking for Sarah, but she and Blake have disappeared.

I could go back and do the same route I went through with Derek, but what a drag doing it by myself. Aren't I spoiled? All of a sudden, I don't want to ever do anything by myself again. It's him or nothing. That makes me sad. Tomorrow morning I'm on a plane, flying away from Derek. He'll be home in two weeks, and then we'll squeeze every minute together we can into our lives, but it won't ever be like this again. How can he waste a minute?

The duet we sang together last night keeps running through my head. I hum the chorus as I wander through the trees. . . . *Our love is so true . . . won't take a step. . . . Thank God, you came. . . . It's you. It's you.* As long as there isn't a giant tree to swing from.

I make up my own verse, get lost in the trees as I work out the lines. Finally get it to say what I can't. I sing first.

> *I want you near, all night, all day.*
> *I need to believe the things you say*
> *You say it's me—*
> *But how can that be true?*

I imagine him singing back to me.

There's no one else, I'll be so true.
Trust me babe, and I'll love you.

I get stuck on his last line. By the time I find the wood building where all the courses start, Derek's already there—waiting for me, chugging a giant bottle of tepid Evian.

"How did you finish so fast?" How many more times did he unhook to pass somebody? "You're a maniac."

He shrugs his shoulders. "Gotta get that adrenaline any way you can."

"You scared the heck out of me."

"That's so sweet."

"Not particularly pleasant—for me."

He clears his throat and takes a swig of his water. "Probably a good thing you won't be around for the next couple of weeks." He's sweating, pulls off his hockey jersey. His T-shirt underneath rides up and exposes a Band-Aid on his lower stomach on his right side.

"I thought you were touring." I walk over to him, run my hand over his stomach, find the Band-Aid. "What did you do to yourself?"

"Mosquito bite. Look at this one on my arm." He holds up his arm. "I swell way up." There is a nasty, swollen, scratched bite on his arm.

"You're not supposed to scratch at it. Do you have another Band-Aid?" The spot on his stomach wasn't red like this mess on his arm.

He slips one out of his pocket. I dump some water on his arm, pat it dry with a tissue, and plaster the Band-Aid on it.

"Now that itches like crazy."

"Stop trying to distract me. Why did you say that about me not being around?"

"We're not going to be hanging out in museums. Did you know there are glaciers in the Alps you can ski on all summer?"

Shoot. I need to call my mom and see if she'll buy me a new ticket home. He'll kill himself.

My face must look desperate. It gets to him. "I'm sorry, Beth." His eyes fill with a pain I don't understand. "I shouldn't have forced myself on you like this." He makes it sound like tomorrow will be good-bye. "It's not fair."

"Don't say that." Now I'm scared. "I'd still be crying on that bench by the lake if it weren't for you. Force yourself? You rescued me."

"But I haven't been totally honest with you." His hand rests on his waist, covering the spot where the Band-Aid is.

I don't know if I want to hear this. Is it Blake's drug-habit tease or Meadow's girlfriend theory? "I'm listening."

"I have—um—"

Whatever it is, we'll work through it. At least he's going to tell me. I can help him. He doesn't realize it, but I owe him. Every time he touched me—all week long—that stupid test and my wrecked genes did disappear. And last night, for those few minutes onstage with him, I was a star. I can't believe he did that for me. I dreamed the applause all night. Nothing can hurt with him in my life. I never want to sing with anyone else.

It's bittersweet, though. Here's a guy I could imagine wanting to have a baby with someday. At least trying. Or practicing. That makes me sweat. Maybe I will need that pill prescription. He says it's not about sex, but the way I feel when we make out is overpowering. I'm pretty sure it has something to do with sex. Isn't he feeling that, too?

Whatever it is that haunts him—whatever he needs me for—I'm there.

I step forward, close, so I can speak low. It comes out in a rush. "You can tell me, Derek. It's not going to make a difference in the way I feel about you."

He starts to cough, takes another long drink of water, coughs again.

I put my head on his shoulder. "Admitting it is the first step."

He shakes his head. "Not applicable here." He puts his hockey jersey back on.

"Of course it is."

He drains off the rest of his water bottle, pitches it, and grabs my hand. "Let's go. We're wasting time."

Stubborn.

Frustrating.

Foolish.

Intoxicating.

He scares me. Thrills me. Totally confuses my sense of direction. Up in the trees. Down on the ground. In the spotlight. In his arms. I have no idea where I am.

There's a backup at the zip line, and we have to wait. He's in front this time. I slide my arms around his chest and lean over to ask, "How good a skier are you?"

"Boarder. Maniac level."

I let go of him—jab my finger in his back. "Now you're doing it on purpose."

"I won't tell you what we're doing tomorrow."

"Jumping off a mountain?"

"No—that's Tuesday."

chapter 15

SO RIGHT

"We're so boring." He met me outside my hotel again tonight. It's darker. More clouds out. Maybe it will rain. "Last night in Lausanne, and we end up on this same bench."

"I love this bench." I don't want to bore him, though. I nerve myself and let my lips slide down to his neck. He catches his breath. He tastes sweaty. Salty. Savory. Sexy. I suck harder, move my mouth, and do it again. I'm so not bored. He pries my mouth off his neck so he can administer some lip action.

"Uptown is just the bar scene at night." His words tickle my lips.

"And we're not into that."

"I'm just into you."

I laugh at how delicious he is tonight. "That sounds like a corny pop song."

"I think it is." His lips explore the side of my face. "Or you could write it."

"That's you." I pull back so I can see him better. I like him in the dark. Somehow he's softer, safer. I caress his face. "Did you finish my song?"

"Nope." He frowns at me. "This beautiful angel distracted me."

"Uh-oh." I lean back against his arm. "I don't want to come between you and your art."

He grins. "Who said it was you?"

I pummel his chest. He defends himself. He bears down on me, trying to kiss me. I whip my head back and forth. When he finally gets my lips, the kissing is crazy and fast. Eager and desperate. More tongue. More passion than we've let loose before. His hot mouth moves to my neck, my shoulder. He sucks on my prominent collarbone. Now he's kissing my sternum. His mouth slides lower. His hands creep higher.

I should be nervous and freaking out, but all I want is for him to keep going. I'm aching for him to touch me. I want his shirt off—my hands on his skin. His hands on mine—

But he stops.

He pulls his face away, props me up, bends over with his face in his hands. "I'm sorry." His breath comes out in spurts.

I hang over him. "I'm so not offended." My fingers go to my blouse buttons—undo the top three, and all I'm thinking is I'm glad that underwire bra pushes most of me into view.

Derek looks up. "Beth. Don't. I'm trying to do what's right here." He turns his back to me.

I stroke his back. "I've never felt this. I like it."

"It's not right."

It's dark. No one can see us here. "Is there a right or wrong about it?"

"Of course there is. There are things you don't understand."

"It feels right."

He slides to the far end of the bench so I can't reach him. "Trust me. It isn't. You don't get it."

"Come back, Derek." I glance down at my bra peaking out of my shirt and whisper, "What don't I get?"

"You know how hard it was to stop?" He glances at me over his shoulder, his eyes linger. "How hard it is for me not to jump you this second?"

I swallow. "Would that be so awful?" Something crazy and powerful has me, and I don't want it to let me go. Enchanted? Naw. This is stronger than any magic.

He turns his back to me again. I slide down the bench to him and kiss the back of his neck. I lift his shirt from behind, try to slip it over his head.

"Knock it off." He gasps as if he can't breathe and tears out of my grasp, gets up, and walks over to the edge of the lake.

I go after him, wrap myself around him from behind and chew his ear.

He turns around and pushes me away. "I told you—this isn't about sex."

"Maybe it could be." That doesn't come out how I wanted it to sound—sultry and inviting. I sound scared. Pleading. Desperate.

He turns and can't keep his eyes from drifting down my shirt, pulls me close, puts his face on my chest, murmurs, "And you've got condoms in your purse?"

"No." I groan. "I'm not a—I mean, I don't . . ."

He lifts his face, his eyes lock onto mine. "Exactly."

"You don't carry—I mean," I'm not ready to give up, "shouldn't *you* be prepared?"

He lets me go. "No. I'm prepared to control myself."

"But . . ."

He's looking down my blouse again, practically shaking. "You're not making it very easy."

"What if I never see you again?" I choke on the words. "What if this isn't real? That I wake up tomorrow, and you've evaporated out of my life? I don't want it to be too late."

"Evaporate?" He tears his eyes away from my cleavage. "You've got my email, my cell." We exchanged on our way home from the ropes. "You already know me online. What more do you want?"

That seems kind of obvious, but I don't answer. Red-hot

embarrassment catches up with me. "I'm sorry." I fumble around with my buttons. They came undone so easy. Now my fingers are sweaty and awkward. "I'm so stupid when it comes to this stuff."

"It messes you up, Beth. It'd mess us up. I won't treat you like that. I've been there, babe, trust me." He brushes my hands away, buttons me up. His fingers are trembling, too.

I'm such a fool. Maybe it would have gotten to a point where I got uncomfortable and tried to stop him, but there was absolutely no resistance in me. If he hadn't stopped—

Crap. Shouldn't I not want to give in to him? Isn't it supposed to be the guy who wants sex?

Respect. Have I lost that? "So now we know. I'm a slut." He's right. It isn't what I want.

"It was my fault, Beth. You're a nice girl."

"I wanted to feel you touching me." I look down at the dark water softly lapping the rocks. "Still do."

Derek clears his throat, puts his arm around me. "I don't think that's slutty. That's how you're supposed to feel when you love someone."

Love? He said "love."

"Acting on it, though." He leans over and kisses my cheek. "That's trouble."

"Especially when we're dealing with my DNA." Guess I need to get a backbone or carry protection.

"I know what you mean." He's sweet not to dwell on it. Not to force me to examine all the nitty-gritty details.

He takes my hand, and we walk toward our statue. The clouds have dropped low enough to obscure the lights across the lake. A cool breeze wafts around us. It feels good. I'm so hot.

I want to get Derek back on the topic of love, but I don't know how. He dropped it so casual. Maybe he didn't mean it. I'm aching to hear it again. I realize that before I let him go tonight, I need some words.

I want him to tell me he's my boyfriend. That I'm his girlfriend. Not some chick touring China. All the email addresses and cell numbers in the world mean nothing if he's not really mine. But that's not what I say. I get really, really stupid.

"This afternoon you were going to tell me something."

"It's not important." He pushes his dark hair out of his eyes. His forehead is wrinkled with concern that I can't fathom.

"You said it wasn't fair."

"It isn't."

"Then Meadow's right. You have a girlfriend in the AYS? That's why you won't—"

"*Had* a girlfriend." He turns and leads me back to our bench. "Let's not waste tonight like this."

I stop walking. "You're not going back home to her?"

"She didn't like my obsession with you."

My eyebrows draw together. "You broke up over me—before we even met?"

"What kind of creep do you think I am?" He walks away from me.

I hurry after him. "All guys—"

"That's stupid." He takes my hand. His voice loses its edge. "You know me. Do you think I'd be going after you like this if I had a girlfriend? Even if she is in China. You must have dated a bunch of jerks."

"Dated? No."

"I'm not like that."

We get to our bench. "But if it's not about sex, why *are* you going after me?" I sit down, bring my legs up on the seat, and wrap my arms around my knees.

Derek settles next to me. "I'm addicted." I tense when he says that word, but he doesn't notice. "I can't get you out of my head. First it was your voice. My ex saw it before I did and dumped me. Then I met you—"

"You like the pretty wrappings? It's all fake. Everything you see—hair, face, eyes, clothes—even my teeth."

"Your voice isn't fake. And your lips," he barely brushes them with his, "feel incredibly real."

I freeze, hoping he'll kiss me again, but he puts his head on my shoulder like that little boy we joked about. "I like your heart, Beth. When I found you on this bench, you opened it and swallowed me."

I stroke his hair.

"I like that you have no clue how good you are, how gorgeous you are, how fresh and open you are."

He's so convincing. I almost like myself. But then I say something that reminds me I'm the Beast. "That Amabile girl, did you sleep with her?"

"*No.* And we went out a long time."

"Do you regret—"

"*No.* Listen, Beth. I'm not going to pretend it's going to be easy when we get back home. You've got your choir. I've got mine. We do a ton of gigs, and we're getting more and more sponsors. I have to spend a lot of time—" He pauses, searching for words.

"What?" Shooting up? Snorting? Popping pills? No, Derek. You don't need time for that.

"—With my family."

I don't believe him. He knows it.

He bends his forehead to touch mine. "I've got stuff going on back home that—please—I never want it to touch us. I want something pure, untainted. Be that for me, Beth." The agony in his voice cuts into my heart.

I sit up and hold him. "Of course, of course. I'm sorry. Of course." It's my turn to soothe, my turn to rock. I hum my solo and sway gently.

Something awful has him. He's running away as much as I am. I should leave right now, but then I would be the Beast. He needs me. I'm here. No way am I letting go of this. I kiss his hair and sing,

Oh, the glory of that bright day
When I cross the river Jordan.
The angels playing banjo
And the good Lord on the fiddle.

He starts to cough.

I stop singing and place the back of my hand on his forehead. "Are you coming down with something?"

He doesn't jerk away this time. "Only you." He tips his head so he can kiss my palm.

I pull him to his feet. "I should walk you home tonight."

"I'm just whipped from this afternoon." He steers me in the direction of the Mermaid.

"You're still not telling me what you and Blake are doing tomorrow?"

"Classified."

We cross the street to the hotel. Great. Leah and Meadow are sitting on the steps. I don't want to kiss Derek good-bye with them watching. If we're alone, he might slip up and use "love" again.

They jump up and run at us. "Thank goodness you're here."

"What?"

Meadow glares at Derek. "Sarah's AWOL with Blake."

Derek curses. "He was going to the bars."

Leah nods. "We got a weird call from her. She was definitely drunk. Didn't make a lot of sense. Told us not to wait up."

Meadow puts her hands on her hips. "She's a big girl. She can do what she wants, but she's got to get back here before our wake-up call. If they're in your room—"

"In our room?" Derek gets upset. "She can't go in our room." He realizes how weird that sounds. "Amabile rules. Besides, I've got the key. I'll go find them."

I don't let go of Derek. "I should come with you."

"No." He squeezes my hand and lets it go. "Stay here in case she shows up."

He flags a passing taxi and is gone.

I sit down on the steps, resign myself to worry. Stupid Sarah. Stupid Beth. Stupid, stupid me. Poor Derek. He has to save everyone tonight.

Half an hour later a taxi pulls up to the Mermaid. Derek gets out. I jump up. "You found her?"

"She's in rough shape. I need some help." He opens the door. Sarah was leaning heavy against it. I catch her before she kisses the pavement. Derek helps me lift the rest of her out and stand her up.

I look at him over Sarah's head. "Thank you."

"Blake's a good guy most of the time. Not when he drinks, though."

"I don't mean this."

He gets what I'm saying. "Don't mention it."

"Where's Blake?" Sarah puts her face into Derek's. "You're not Blake." She stumbles from Derek to me. "I promised Blake tonight."

Derek lets go of her. "Blake was even more soused than she is. He was trying to unlock the door with his car keys. At least they didn't do it in the hall. Can you girls manage her from here?"

"Yeah. You better get back. Kick Blake in the shins for us, okay?"

"He threw up and passed out in it on the washroom floor."

"Gross for you."

"Maybe waking up with his face glued to the floor by crusted vomit will make an impression."

Sarah wobbles and groans. Crap. We better hurry. I turn away from Derek, and Leah helps me get Sarah into the elevator Meadow has waiting.

"Bye, Beth," Derek calls after me.

Stupid Sarah. She ruined our *see you laters*.

The elevator doors close. Crap. Derek said, "Bye."

Sarah puts her hand over her mouth.

Meadow says, "Hang on. Not here. Or we'll all be banned from every future trip."

Sarah sways.

Leah steadies her. "And Blake was drunker?"

I take Sarah's head and arms. Leah and Meadow each take a leg, and we carry her down the creaky old hall to our room.

She makes it to the bathroom—barfs in the bidet.

We clean her up and get her undressed, and she barfs again. This time in the sink.

I'm brushing my teeth in the shower stall tomorrow.

It's after one by the time we get settled. Our bus leaves at five. I'm pumped full of every hormone my body can create. It seems useless to try to sleep. I lie down anyway and try to relax. Stupid Blake. Stupid Sarah. I didn't get to say good-bye to Derek.

> *But it's not good-bye. It's just . . .*
> *Later, babe—*
> *Don't say good-bye, love,*
> *So I can dream of*
> *The day you'll hold me close again.*
> *Close my eyes,*
> *And you will be there.*
> *I swallow my fear*
> *That you will fly too far from me.*
> *I can hold on now*
> *To your promises.*
> *Forget all my questions—*
> *Just believe. . . .*

chapter 16

SEE YOU LATER

Next thing I know, there's a choir mom outside the door, pounding hard. "We load in fifteen minutes."

I roll off my bed and into our travel clothes—pink track pants and a white T-shirt with my comfy old choir hoodie if it gets cold on the plane. I dash for my turn in the bathroom. The place still reeks of puke. "Gross, Sarah!"

I do what I need to and brush my teeth, using the shower faucet, then hand the place over to Leah. I stand over my bed, grab an elastic, and harness my hair. I stuff my nightshirt and toiletries into my suitcase. My makeup is in my purse. I can put my face on later. Who cares? We're eating breakfast on the bus. I zip up my bag, and I'm good to go.

Sarah is a disaster. I get her bag packed while Leah dresses her. Meadow hogs up the bathroom.

Terri pounds on our door. "Let's go girls. The plane won't wait."

A curse on 8:00 a.m. flights to Paris forever.

I grab my suitcase—give up on the elevator—haul the bag, bumpety bump, down the three flights of stairs. I dump it by the bus, turn to go back for Sarah.

And he's there. Derek. Looking paler in the brisk morning breeze, huddling in his Amabile hockey jersey, trying to suppress that cough of his. It sounds worse. He's holding a pink rose. He looks at my track pants. "I figured you like pink."

I pull a face. "Meadow likes pink."

He frowns. "Sorry."

I take the rose and breathe it in. "But I love this."

"I wanted to—"

"Thanks."

"Last night—"

"Yeah."

We move together, kiss for the last time in wonderland.

He whispers, "See you later."

I drink him in. Our bodies wind together, and our lips move in harmony. I don't let him go until the bus honks. "Later."

The girls are whoo-whooing at me when I board. Crap. They all watched that exquisitely private moment. I realize how awful I must look. Derek didn't even flinch. I make one of the younger girls move so I can have a seat by the window on his side. I press my face up to it and search for him.

He waves. Coughs. Waves some more.

Shoot. Shoot. Shoot.

I hope he's not getting sick.

I eat a nasty packaged croissant with plastic chocolate in the center as the bus rolls down the Swiss autoroute. It winds along the lake and passes by vineyards. The girls start counting how many castle-like places we go by.

I hang over my music binder, tuck the rose into the rings and scribble. I keep scribbling at the Geneva airport while we wait for our flight, scribble all the way to Paris.

My heart's yours
And yours is mine.

You are what I crave—
I won't live until I'm kissing you.
With your love,
I can change my fate.
I circle the date,
When my new dreams will spring to life.
You'll drop from the stars.
Happy evermore
Like old stories say.
You can believe.

We land at Charles de Gaulle with plenty of time to make it to our flight, but the place is so confusing. We get off their stupid bus at the wrong place, stand forever in a big passport-control line that isn't going to our gate. Terri's almost crying by the time all eighty of us are running down the concourse to our gate. This French woman behind the desk screams at Terri because we were supposed to be here early. And then the plane is delayed for some mechanical thing, but everyone acts like it's because of us. We miss our connection in New York and get rerouted to Detroit through Chicago. We get stuck at O'Hare all day. When we arrive in Detroit, I have no idea what time it is—what day it is. I just know it's dark out. Humid.

I see Mom.

Her hazel eyes water. Her graying brown hair sticks to the sides of her face.

Crap. I can't do this now.

I fall into her arms, and she starts to sob.

"Stop it, Mom." I pat her back, fight to keep myself from dissolving like she is. "My life is great." I've got a huge lump in my throat that makes me croak the words. I sniff and give her a little shake by the shoulders. "I mean it."

"Oh, honey, you need to face this."

No. No. No. I've figured out how to escape it. Derek.

I got him online in Chicago. We've worked out a plan. Every morning, 8:00 a.m. to 9:00 a.m. Swiss time, is mine. That's two in the morning for me. I glance at my watch. I don't have a clue when I last reset it. "What time is it, Mom?"

"Half past midnight."

"Great—we're going to make it."

"Make what?"

All the way home she gets the gushy Derek dish—as much as I dare tell her. None of the private stuff, or my suspicions about his drug habit. She'd go ballistic. "You're going to love him. I can't wait for you to meet."

She smiles at me and nods along as she focuses on the road. "I saw Scott at the Save-A-Lot. He mentioned he's got something for you."

Scott? The prom. How badly I wanted to kiss him that night. It all rushes back in HD-quality vision. But, I've got Derek now. I'm safe. Scott and I can be friends again.

I'm too tired to carry my suitcase up to my room.

"Just leave it, Beth. Get some rest."

I kiss Mom good night. "I'm okay." I look at her, and she gets what I'm talking about. "Let's not make it a big deal."

She shakes her head.

I haul my tired butt up the stairs. My alarm clock reads 1:50 a.m. Ten minutes. I fall into the shower and throw on a fresh nightshirt. Clean feels delicious. I can't remember when I showered last.

I sign on. Derek's there, waiting. Early. That's delicious, too.

Derek: where are you?
Beth: home

Derek: you should go to bed
Beth: I need to talk to my new boyfriend

I send it before I realize what I wrote. Boyfriend? I wanted him to say it first. Thirty plus hours of travel will do that to you.

Derek: about time you owned me
Beth: you've never said it to me
Derek: uh-huh . . . three times.

Like I would have missed that. I yawn and shake it off while I type.

Beth: you are delusional
Derek: girlfriend . . . girlfriend . . . girlfriend
Beth: now I can sleep

I stretch and yawn, get ready to sign off. I'm not sure what to write. I don't know how he'll respond if I go on the gush side. I feel overheated, romantic, and so into him even though he's so far away right now.

Derek: you're not going to grill me again over my plans for today?
Beth: I don't want to have nightmares
Derek: my poor little Beth . . . relax . . . we decided to take it easy
Beth: good
Derek: we rented mountain bikes and took them on the train up a
          mountain . . . a small one . . . we're in a wired café having that
          fried potato stuff with eggs and cheese and ham all over it . . .
          it's pouring out

I take a perverse delight in Derek's ruined day. Good. He won't be able to risk breaking that neck I left my imprint on. I'm hungry for it again. These two weeks are going to be way too long. I'm major possessive.

Beth: rain? YES . . . we can chat longer
Derek: the guys are done . . . I gotta go
Beth: INSERT BLOODCURDLING SCREAM HERE
Derek: get some rest . . . girlfriend
Beth: what about your cold? don't make it worse

He's gone. Definitely no gush. I fall on my bed, imagine him riding a mountain bike full tilt down a mud-slick mountain path. He starts to cough and wipes out. I fall asleep. The vision is worse in my dreams. I'm there riding, too. I wipe out *into* him—cause the crash. He's lying in the rocks—bloody, muddy. I crawl over to him, and we get it on in the mud. I wake up way too soon.

chapter 17

FRIENDSHIP

The doorbell rings.

I roll over, crack an eye at my alarm clock. It's almost 2:00 p.m. I've given in to jet lag. It's summer. Who cares? It's been overcast and humid nonstop since I got back to Port. I wish it would just rain already and get it out of its system. I want it to be nice out by the time Derek gets home. I want to get him to the beach, get him some sun, make out in the sand. We've never kissed lying down. Or in the water. These past couple weeks I've imagined every possible place we could make out. I've compiled quite a list.

Derek was stuck in the Amsterdam airport last night. We chatted until almost 4:00 a.m. my time. Then he got on a plane. I didn't have the guts to tell him about the list. I'll show it to him when he gets here.

The doorbell rings again.

Crap. How many hours is that? Could it be him?

I fly out of bed. Sloppy oversize T-shirt. No makeup. Wild hair. Total wreck. Race down the stairs. Throw open the door, and there's a guy walking away.

"Hey. Stop. I'm here."

He turns around.

"Scott?" I can feel the flush that's running up my face.

"So you are home."

"Yeah."

"I thought maybe you'd call." He takes a step toward me and stops. "I told your mom—"

"I've been out of it. Total jet lag." And I've been avoiding you. Still.

He nods slowly. "Did I wake you?"

I realize I'm not dressed for visitors. "Sorry. I must look awful."

He eyes my bare legs. "I don't mind." He gets his naughty grin on. "Honest." He walks up the cement path that leads across our scorched lawn to our white-painted porch—still looking at my legs. "It's nice to see the real you." A car zooms by behind him.

"Don't be morbid." I slap at a mosquito on my thigh.

He comes up the porch steps and hands me an envelope. "I brought these—if you still want them." He's wearing a short tank top and cut-offs. He must be doing the weightlifting thing with his legs, too. Nice. His neck is even thicker now. And I can see real abs beginning to form on his stomach. And those shoulder muscles are even more defined.

I take the envelope from him, slide out a dark brown folder, and open it. There's Scott looking sharp in his black tux with his arms around a tall blonde stranger. "This is me?"

He nods his head. "One of you." He stares for a moment. "I think I like this one better."

I manage an embarrassed smile. "That was the best night. You were so sweet. Thought of everything."

"What did you like best?"

"The brownies—no, the dancing." I get redder remembering how we slow danced.

"Too bad Colby is such a creep."

I lean against the doorway with one leg bent up, like a stork. "It did make it exciting."

"But we didn't get to dance again."

"That's right—you owe me a nice long slow dance." I can say that now. I have Derek. I can tease Scott. We're friends.

"Okay." He doesn't look at me like a friend. He looks at me like Derek does. He seems taller. Could he finally be growing? And he's been at the beach. His hair is blonder, and he's got a great tan. Scott messes with his iPod, moves in really close, hands me an ear bud—the first slow song we danced to plays. He puts the other end in his ear. "Dance with me, Beth." He smiles like he's playing around, but the intensity I read deep in the blue of his eyes says something else.

His arms go around me. He pulls me tight and lays his face on my chest. Shoot, he's wearing that same aftershave he had on prom night. I can't resist touching his shoulders. His bare leg brushes mine while we move to the music.

I close my eyes, and the lyrics take me back to that night:

> *Remember when you first held me?*
> *And I believed love could be?*
> *Your lips awoke my senses.*
> *You melted my defenses.*

"You need to tell me something, Bethie." Scott raises his face. "I'll never bug you about it again, but it's driving me crazy. Promise you won't get mad?"

"At you? I'm never mad at you." I stroke his head like at prom. Derek won't mind. Scott's my friend.

"Why didn't you let me kiss you good night? One kiss. What's so awful?"

Man, it's hot out. Sticky. "You wanted to kiss me?" I really need a fan. How can he still do this to me? I have a boyfriend. I'm not starving anymore.

"Wasn't that obvious? Why did you run like that?"

I don't answer. Whispers of the words I wrote after my escape float through my memory.

> *Can't you see how much you have changed?*
> *Frightened to move? Yeah, I'm the same.*
> *Insides yearning—can I walk away again?*

"Bethie?" Scott stops moving and takes me by the shoulders. The little boy is gone from his face. He's a full-fledged guy—not cute anymore. He's handsome.

I bend down and whisper, "I thought it would gross you out." It feels good to finally say it. "All night I wanted to attack you."

"Attack me?"

I nod. I need to let go of him—get away from his mouth too close to mine. And those shoulders. I need to run from those shoulders.

"I don't understand." His voice is low—sexy—irresistible. "Do you think you can show me?" He closes his eyes and presses upward on his toes, reaching his lips to meet mine.

I forget everything. We're back at the prom. He wants me. He always wanted me—even when I was ugly. He's not grossed out. He's turned on. I inhale him, clutch his shoulders, close my eyes, and let my lips brush his.

> *Could you want me? If it's a joke,*
> *Please don't haunt me—dreams in smoke.*

Crap. I'm kissing my best friend.

And he kisses me back. Major kisses me back. It's not smooth and tender like Derek. Scott's lips are hard on mine—way intense. Too much teeth. But I ache for more when he finally releases me.

He traces my lips with his fingers. "Virgin lips meet virgin lips. I've been waiting since fourth grade to do that."

I bend my head to kiss him again and then pull back with a start. Derek. I have to tell Scott. I try to start, but he meets my mouth more than halfway. He's better at it this time. I try to push him off, but he fights back, presses his body to mine. I stop resisting. Get way too into it.

He finally lets me loose.

"Scott, Scottie." I'm breathless from kissing him and feeling so bad at what I'm going to say. "We need to stop this."

He smiles and hugs me. "Yeah. I had late lunch break. I gotta get back. But I'm off at five. I'll come over, and we can do that some more. Maybe it won't rain, and we can go to the beach."

"Just shut up a minute. My lips—aren't—virgin lips."

"Not anymore." He tries to kiss me again, but I pull back this time, pull his arms off so he's not holding me.

"I met a guy at the Choral Olympics."

"Wait. What?" He grabs me by the shoulders and glares. "What happened? What are you saying?"

I shrink back from him. "I got some bad news. He was sweet and . . . it just happened."

"But I'm your—"

"Friend."

"No. Beth. No. Not anymore. I'm sick of that. I've loved you forever. This creep—whoever he is—doesn't care about the real Beth. Not like I do. You don't have to fake it with me. I want to be your boyfriend. You want it, too. I can tell." His hands slip from my shoulders to my back, and he draws me closer.

"But what about—"

"I don't care if you kissed a thousand guys in Switzerland." He starts to lay his face down on my shoulder but jerks back up. "That's all you did with him, right?"

"Scott!"

"It doesn't matter." His arms tighten around me—brick hard. "Right now it's you and me. Today. Tomorrow. And the day after that and the day after that. It's always been you and me. It's just taken us a while to grow into this part of it." He kisses me, and he's got so much love on his lips that it makes me cry.

I pull away from his mouth, sniff, and wipe my eyes. "The thing is . . . this guy and I are—" How can I do this to Scott? I have to, though. I'm with Derek. I want to be with Derek.

"Over. No big deal. I'm not upset." His arms relax, and one hand moves up to stroke my hair.

I need to get away from him. We're both sticky and hot. It's so gross out. But I can't let go. I clench my teeth and say, "We're sort of involved."

"Crap, Beth." Scott's hand freezes. "What are you saying?"

"I'm in the middle of this. I care, Scott. I really do, but—"

My cell phone rings. The sound floats out my bedroom window and coats us. I know it's Derek. And even with Scott holding me, giving me his heart, a thrill of Derek desire shoots through me.

Scott looks up, curses. "I'm here, Beth. I'm real. That isn't." His mouth is on mine again. Warm. Hungry. So vulnerable.

But my cell keeps ringing.

I pull myself free of Scott.

"Please, Bethie. Don't."

I whisper, "I'm sorry, Scottie," and race for my cell phone.

I get to my room too late. I look out at the cracked sidewalk with grass dying in the gaps. Scott's car is still there. I pull down the window blind. The doorbell rings. I don't answer.

I take my cell phone into my bathroom, shut the door and lock it, perch on the seat of my toilet like a giant bird roosting, staring at the phone.

Ring.

Ring.

Ring.

I'm so stupid. I flip open the phone, pull up the missed call, and hit the green button.

"Beth?" I close my eyes at the sound of Derek's voice. "Were you still asleep?"

I can't answer. The resonance of what I just did to Scott gets a hold of me.

"Beth? Are you there?"

I finally manage a weak, "Where are you?"

"Waiting for our bags in Toronto."

"I can't believe you got home so fast." I pick at the last sliver of pink nail polish on my big toe.

"Direct flight from Schipol."

"That isn't fair." My voice is too high, wobbles at the end.

"What's up? You sound—"

"We're on the same continent." Can he tell what I did?

"Same time zone."

I need to see him. He'll figure this out. He always knows what to do. "Do you have any nice park benches in London?"

"I think we can find one."

"I really need to be with you again. Something crazy just happened." I blurt the whole episode with Scott out to him. "I don't know what got into him. I'm so sorry. It won't happen again. I told him all about you. We've been friends forever and ever. It's so weird."

Derek doesn't say anything. Crap. I'm so stupid. Why did I tell him?

"It's okay, Beth. I get it. At least I get him." His voice is smooth and reassuring. He's not mad at all. Shouldn't he be a tiny bit mad? "What about you? What do you want?"

"What do you mean?" I hold myself still as I can and press the phone hard against my ear.

"I'm glad you have somebody solid like that. Maybe you should dump me. You obviously have feelings for him."

"What? Dump you?" I feel dizzy. "For Scott? No. What? No."

"I don't want to hurt you."

I take a deep breath so I don't fall off the toilet seat. "The only way you can hurt me is to keep talking like this."

"Beth, I—"

"Why are you so understanding?" A hint of suspicion creeps into my voice. "You should be livid. And incredibly jealous."

"I didn't say I wasn't jealous."

"That girl. That's it. You want to get back with her. No, Derek. Please. I'm really sorry."

"You're insane."

He's right, but I can't stop myself. "She wants you back. I know it. Have you seen her yet?" The dizzy returns. I force myself to breathe.

"At the baggage claim in the airport?"

"Could happen."

"I called you first—even before my mum. I want you, Beth." His voice goes deep with intensity. "The question is do you want me?"

"Crap." I stand and stretch my legs.

"What now?"

"That means you've got to go. Call your mom, you idiot. Then call me back and tell me you can't live without me."

"I can't live without you."

I'm swirling in Derek deliciousness. "And you're insanely jealous over Scott?"

"Insanely. No more getting it on with old kindergarten buddies."

"Preschool." I glance in the mirror. I can be Bliss perfect in an hour.

"Thanks for telling me. It's so—"

"Stupid?" I plug in my hair flattening thing.

He laughs. "You. No pretense. No games."

I turn around and lean against the sink, focus on what he's saying. "Games? Don't play them with me. My heart can't take that."

"What can it take?"

"Seeing you tonight?" If I leave in an hour, I'll be in London in time to meet his bus home from Toronto.

"I'm dead on my feet."

He wants sleep instead of me? "Tomorrow?"

"I'll get back to you on that."

How can he stand not seeing me? We're so close. "I'll come to your place. I've got a car—"

"Not a good idea."

"You can come here then." If I work all night I can have my room clean. Him in my room? Thinking that makes me crazy. "I'm going to be a wreck until I see you again."

"I'll try to borrow some wheels."

"Call me."

He misses his beat.

"Derek?"

"Are you sure, Beth?" He coughs. His voice takes on the twist of torture it held when he broke down on our bench back in Switzerland. "I can't guarantee getting tangled up with me won't be rough on your heart."

Why, Derek? How will you hurt me? When will you tell me everything? I cover my questions with a shaky laugh. "You do want to dump me. Crap."

"Just think about it. That other guy—"

Doesn't he remember those words he sang to me in Lausanne? That promise?

> *The way you kiss, the way you sing,*
> *The way you tell me everything.*
> *Will you take my heart?*
> *I'm offering it to you. . . .*

I do. I sing my reply, *It's gotta be, it's gotta be about you.*

chapter 18

PILLOW TALK

I spend the rest of the day trying to get my cell to ring. I call back twice. Leave a message once. Send two texts.

I even call Sarah. "Hey. They're back. Have you heard from Blake?"

"Blake's a jerk. Why would I want to hear from him?"

"Do you have his cell?"

She gives it to me. Memorized. Jerk, huh?

I enter it in my cell's phone book, dial, but hang up before it rings. Calling Blake is over-the-top desperate. I write Derek an email just in case his cell phone got flushed down the toilet or something tragic like that. I finally put on the Amabile guys' new CD, fall asleep listening to Derek sing, clutching my cell phone to my heart.

It goes off at 2:00 a.m. I startle awake—not sure what's going on. I sit up confused. The phone is jumping around in my sheets.

Derek. Yes. Derek.

"Hey."

"You awake?"

"Sure."

"I fell asleep on the drive from Toronto. I don't even remember walking into the house."

What happened to, *Can't sleep, can't dream without you?*

"Sorry I didn't call back." His voice sounds thick and scratchy. Exhausted.

At least he's sorry. "That cold of yours is back. You should get some more rest."

"I'm wide awake now. Don't you want to talk?"

I'm wide awake, too. "How about we do more than talk? I'll get in my car, and you guide me to your place. Just don't hang up." I get out of bed and search through the pile of clothes on my floor with my foot. Designer jeans, where are you? I get silly and start singing him the chorus of our duet.

> *And now—our love is so true,*
> *I won't take a step without you.*
> *Thank God, you came. If you love me, please don't ever let me go.*

He doesn't come in on his cue. "It's almost an hour drive. You can't do that at 2:00 a.m."

With him as the prize, I could do anything. "Meet me halfway then." I sing, *I'll walk with you until the dawn.*

He sings back, *I don't have my own car.*

"That was so not romantic. Swipe your parents' car." I unearth the jeans. They are clean—enough. "You'll be back before they know it."

"My dad works the night shift. I'd get busted."

"Don't be such a baby." I hold the phone with my shoulder and squirm into my skinny jeans. "You're almost eighteen—right? What can they do?"

"Actually," he pauses, "I'm nineteen."

"Really?" I sit back down on my bed. "You don't look that old."

"Too old for you?"

"No." I won't be eighteen until next spring, but that hardly matters. "I didn't picture you starting college this fall. Are you leaving?" That's not really a *fairy-tale vision for two*, is it?

"I'm not going."

"What?" I assumed Derek was an AP student, straight-A guy like . . . Scott.

"University isn't going to work out for me."

"But it has to—" I get up and paw through my laundry, looking for something to wear on top that isn't an ugmo sweatshirt.

"I'm looking forward to working full-time on my music. And I've got some other issues to work out."

I stop hunting. "Like what?"

"Nothing important." There he goes again. Evading me. He can even do it with jet lag.

"But eventually—if you ever want to support a family—you'll need to get a degree and a job."

"So now you're my guidance counselor?"

"Sure." I pull a deep-blue clingy V-neck I bought with Meadow out of the pile. Price tags still on. Yes. "Get a music degree. Study composition."

"Dissect it?" He sounds miffed. "Pick apart the music that flows out of me and try to put it back together? No thank you."

"Don't be such a prima donna. I bet even a genius like you could learn a lot." I find some toenail clippers in the clutter near my bathroom sink and snip the tag off the shirt. "What about a voice major or directing? I can see you doing that."

"I'm not enjoying this conversation."

"Because you know I'm right."

"I never said I didn't *want* to go." He clears his throat. "I can't. Not this year."

I hang the top on a hook so I can slip it on as soon as he hangs up. "Don't they give scholarships and student loans out in Canada?"

"It's not the money."

Is it the drugs? That's what I want to ask him. Are you not going to college because of your *drug habit*? I don't want those suspicions in my brain. I sing in my sexiest voice, *Your breath that drifts across my face. A fire ignites when—*

He breaks in. "Can you be serious for a minute?"

I was being serious. I stop singing. "Sure."

"I need to tell you something you're not going to like." Shoot. It's her. She wants him back, and he's going to dump me over the phone.

"You already did that. Tell me something I'll like instead—how about, you're walking out the door, getting in your mom's car, backing it up, and driving out of town to meet me in the middle of the highway?" I examine myself in the mirror over the sink. Five minutes for makeup. Trap my frizzed out hair in a ponytail and iron the bangs. Ten minutes and I can be on the road. It'll be dark. I don't have the time or patience for the work true beauty takes tonight. I sing, *Your lips on mine—*

"Gosh, Beth. You've got a one-track mind."

I give up the song. "I need to touch you. I'm not sure you're real."

"You're talking to me on the phone. That isn't real?"

"Not real enough for me. Don't you want to be with me again—like in Lausanne?" That sounds whiny. Am I turning him off? I need Boyfriend 101. Where is Sarah when I need her? I'm not dumb enough to ask Meadow for help. She'd sabotage me for sure.

"I went back and took pictures of our bench. I'll email them to you."

"I'll come see them. I guess I can wait until tomorrow." Then I could wash these jeans, shower, straighten my hair, put on full makeup—dazzle him. "Tell me how to get to your house, and I'll be there. Is 7:00 a.m.

too early?" I wish Meadow had set me up with sexy perfume. It's not like I can swipe some from my mom—she's an accountant.

"I can't." He starts to cough again. When he stops he says, "That's what I've been trying to tell you."

I'm silent. Afraid. It is her. Crap. I knew it.

"My mum rented us a cottage up in lake country. She's always wanted to do it, but we never had the cash, or Dad couldn't get off, or I was too . . ." Wasted? I don't want to hear this. Stop, Derek. Just stop. Sing to me instead. You know the song. You picked it.

He doesn't. "We couldn't ever go before. She met this woman who gave us a great deal on her cottage. She can't use it this year. Doesn't normally rent it. We've got it for the rest of the summer."

I blurt, "Can I come, too? What happened to, *I won't take a step without you*? I'll sleep on the couch." I leave the bathroom, pace around my room.

"It's tiny—one bedroom. I'll be sleeping on the couch."

"We could share. We're both pretty skinny."

"You really think my mum or yours would go for that?"

I spy the pink rose he gave me when we said our *see you later*s. I pressed it in my music after we left Paris. I had to hide it from the customs guys just in case they decided it was a fruit or vegetable. It's lying on a bookshelf next to my choir binder. "I'll buy a cot, bring a sleeping bag. I could even sleep in my car." Desperate? Of course. "It's true for me. *I gotta be, gotta be about you.*"

"No." The gruff in his voice turns coaxing. "My dad's got all this vacation time saved up." His voice gives out. He clears his throat. "I have to do this with them."

"Okay." Fine. I pick up the rose—hold it up to my nose and inhale. It still smells sweet but holds a touch of decay. "How many days do we have until you go?"

"We leave in the morning."

I wave the dried rose like it's a magic wand and chant, "*No way.*"

"I'm sorry."

Rats. I set the rose carefully on my nightstand. "I'm getting in my car right now."

"Please, Beth. Don't. If you show up here at 3:30 in the morning, my mum will go ballistic."

"That's stupid. I'll be quiet." I grab the shirt. To heck with my face and hair.

"She's an incredibly light sleeper."

"Then I'll get to meet her." I head out of my room. "Isn't she curious about me?"

"She doesn't know about you."

That freezes me halfway down the stairs. "Why not?"

"I just got home."

"Stop lying to me, Derek. It's her, isn't it? Your old girlfriend. You're not going anywhere." It's not about me. It's about her. I hate myself. And I hate him.

"Please, Beth. Don't be like this."

I sink onto the step and lower my voice to a whisper. "If I could see you again, I wouldn't be such an idiot."

"Try to understand. This is major for my mum. This fall isn't going to be easy."

"What's happening to you this fall? Just tell me the truth."

"The truth?"

"From your heart—spill it. I can take it. I'm used to guys disappointing me."

"From my heart?"

"Straight." I close my eyes, clench my teeth tight, hold my breath.

"I fell in love in Switzerland with this beautiful girl whose every move makes me crazy. I want to be with her twenty-four/seven. Right now. Today. Tomorrow and every tomorrow after that. My mum planned this trip all year as a special surprise. You want me to break *her* heart?"

"What about my heart?"

"It's in good hands—trust me."

"That's not what you said this afternoon. When will I see you again?"

"I'll get to your place as soon as we get back."

"You'll call me a lot?"

"There's no phone or Internet in the cabin—but I'll use the cell whenever I can get a signal."

I stand up and hang on to the handrail. "It's going to be a long five weeks."

"Even longer for me."

I turn around and tiptoe back to my bedroom. "Did you really mean that—what you said?"

"I promise—I'll call." He starts coughing again. Definitely that cold. I should let him go.

But I don't. "No. That you fell in *love* in Switzerland?"

He doesn't even hesitate. "I thought that was a given."

"You are so frustrating—delicious—but frustrating." I'm absolutely dying for him all over again.

"What about you?" He stops, struggles a minute. "Did you fall in love?" His voice catches.

My eyes go to his rose on my nightstand. "I'm not sure I even know what love is, but I've got my hands full of something beautiful." My voice quivers. "I don't ever want to let it go." I lie down on my bed, curl around my pillow, wishing it was him.

He slowly says, "Mind if I take that as a *yes*?"

I'm melting again. "Not at all."

"Hang on, Beth. We'll get it together this fall. I'm working on a plan for you."

I roll onto my back. "For me?"

"For *us*."

"*Us?* I like the way that sounds coming out of your mouth." I reach out and touch his rose.

"Us. Us. Us. Us. Us."

"I'll miss you like crazy." My voices cracks, and I have to sniff.

"I love you, Beth. Say it back to me—it's easy."

And now—our love is so true, singing that to him makes me cry. "Oh, gosh, I do love you. I really do."

I curl up in a ball, staring at his rose, trying to hold on to the intensity of the way he makes me feel. I should be angry, suspicious, hurt, but I'm mushy and devoted. I totally adore him. I don't entirely believe him about the cottage, but he said he loves me, twice, no, three times. He even got me to say it.

No guy has ever told me he loved me.

Certainly not my father.

Scott, though. He said it this afternoon. What was it? *I've loved you forever.* That made me want to cry, too. Do I love Scott? How can I when I feel like this about Derek?

Crap. Scott. I kissed him today. And then ripped his heart out. Poor Scottie. I don't think I can ever face him again. I'll have to transfer schools or something.

Derek was so cool about it.

I close my eyes. I can't sleep. There's too much spinning in my brain.

Derek hasn't even told his parents about you. Saying he loves you came too easy, too fast, too smooth. You'll never see him again. He will evaporate. How can a boy that perfect exist? He's some kind of spirit or ghost. Or he is a haunted artist with a bad drug habit like those crazy poets my English teacher is mad about.

I hear Sarah joking about Derek back in our hotel room at the

Mermaid. Phantom? No way. That guy was twisted. Derek's not—crap, how do I know he isn't? He said he wanted to be with me, but he's avoided me ever since.

I fall asleep and dream I'm Christine and Derek is the Phantom. I'm in white voile and lace and look like that beautiful girl with Scott in the prom picture.

Derek holds out his hand. I take it and beg him—

> *Take me to your dungeon.*
> *Bind me in your chains.*
> *Keep me*
> *With you forever.*
> *Alone there's only terror.*

He pulls me along dark corridors, singing in dusky romantic tones.

> *Trust me in the darkness*
> *Give me time—you'll see*
> *I'm not*
> *Your mad enchanter,*
> *An elusive encounter.*

I move into his embrace. His lips are on my face, and I sing back to him.

> *Hold me closer,*
> *And I'll keep my eyes closed.*
> *We can hide forever from the sun.*

I nestle my head against his neck. In the dream, I'm short enough to do it. Petite. Tiny. He presses me to his heart.

Stay beside me, love, and ask no questions.

He just gets the one line. I gaze up at him and drop my song to *pianissimo*—

> *I'm afraid—how can your love be real?*
> *Is it true or am I dreaming still?*

The music gets wild. Scott's in the dream—running after us, but we lose him. Derek drags me to his lair, and we stay hidden forever. No crystal-shattering screams. No chandeliers crashing. Just Derek and me and the song we sing. It's not a nightmare. It's the best dream I've ever had.

chapter 19
REALITY

Back to school today. It's raining out. The gray clouds go great with the gray-metal lockers that line the halls. People I sort of know come up to me. A couple of girls from last spring's AP history class stop and talk to me. They can't get over how great I look. I got up early and made myself beautiful. I didn't bother with flattening my hair—not in this rain—but I did my face almost as well as Meadow's mom does it, wore that slinky top I was going to wear to see Derek, and my styling skinny designer jeans. Why not show the world what I've become?

School is definitely going to be better this year. Colby isn't here. All of his drones are gone, too. Still, I'm jumpy. Derek's supposed to call. He gets home Friday. Again.

I thought he'd come home before school started, but then he reminded me, just before he lost the signal, that school isn't starting for him. I jumped into my usual argument about that, and the line went dead. He probably hung up. He doesn't like that argument. He knows I'm right. When he tries to explain, he always gets stuck at that place he won't go beyond. I know it. He knows it. It makes me so mad. I don't want to be an angry girlfriend always attacking him, so I bite my tongue and remember holding and rocking him like a little boy.

I never want it to touch us. I can still hear the pain in his voice. *I want something pure, untainted. Be that for me, Beth, please.*

And then I feel creepy for wanting to know what's behind the lies. He wants to be a/different person with me. If it is drugs, that's a good thing. He could be off at a woodsy treatment place to detox. Maybe he'll tell me Friday. He'll be clean, cured, and we can be happy hanging out with each other. Every day. All the time. Nonstop. No more of this.

Gosh. I miss him.

Scott didn't make the waiting any easier.

I got my old summer job at the library back. They even let me help with the kids' program this year. The kids aren't afraid of me anymore. They like me. I ran a toddler story time, and they crawled all over me. The moms just stood there, happy to have their kids pulling someone else's hair out for a few minutes. I loved it. Every second.

I hated those moms. How they took what they had for granted. How they had what I could never have.

My mom made me see the genetic counselor. He talked about sterilization options, the pill, and gave me a discreet plastic case full of condoms. He mapped out the genetic odds for me.

I wadded up the paper and threw it in my purse with the condoms. "What if I just took a chance?"

He was aghast that I'd even consider it. "You're too young to take any chances."

"But, someday." I looked down at the gleaming tile floor. "I think I want a baby."

"Adoption is your best option."

But I want a baby with Derek's hair and Derek's eyes. Derek's voice. Can I adopt that?

On the tail of that pleasant interview, Scott started stopping by the library—every day. Sometimes twice. I thought he'd be weird and hurt.

He kind of was at first, but then he was just good old Scott, my friend, but not. I think he grew two more inches before the end of summer. Talk about a late bloomer. He kept asking me out. I almost kissed him again—twice. I came close to giving up and going to the beach with him.

He never brought up Derek. I did—every time I turned him down.

"I have a boyfriend. His name is Derek. Why do you keep doing this?"

He'd move in close, drop his voice all sexy like it was on my front porch and whisper, "I haven't seen him around. Are you sure he remembers you're his girlfriend?"

"How do you know he hasn't been around?"

"I have my sources."

"You're stalking me?"

"You wish."

He's so annoying. He knows he's hot now. He knows I think he's hot now, and he won't let me forget it. I've got to get Mom to quit telling him the pathetic details of my lonesome existence every time she goes grocery shopping.

It's going to change, Mr.-Scott-nosey-pants-won't-leave-a-girl-alone. Derek's coming home. Friday. This week will go fast. School will keep me busy and my mind from wandering to Scott's muscular, available shoulders and the tender way he stares at me.

Bliss practice starts again Thursday. Today's Tuesday. It's almost Friday already.

"Hey." Scott stops at the locker next to mine and opens it.

"You've got to be kidding."

"The polite reply would be 'Hello,' 'Good morning,' or even a simple 'Hey back.'"

"How'd you manage that?" I close my locker and lean against it. Great. Now he's got stubbly blond beard all over his face, and it's way sexy.

He pushes his overgrown sun-bleached blond bangs off his forehead. "The Prince Charming lessons are paying off." He opens his new locker. "The office ladies were putty in my hands. I told them all about you and me—how we hung out in grade school, how we always had each other's back, how our friendship was flowering into something more." He grins at me with all his straight, white teeth.

"You little liar."

"One lady was almost in tears." He chucks his backpack into the locker.

"He's coming back this week."

Scott shrugs. "I'll believe that when I see it."

"I don't want to hurt you."

"When this jerk breaks your heart, I'll be here. Right next door. All year long."

I stand up straight. "He's not like that. He's so different."

"I'm different, Beth. I wasn't lying in the office. You want me as much as I want you. I can tell." He moves close—into my space. "You're the liar." He touches my hair.

"Okay." I draw back. "I admit it. You're really appealing—I'd be a stone not to notice."

"It's more than that." He moves in on me again, puts a hand on my waist.

I close my eyes and whisper, "I know."

"You admit that, too?"

"Of course, but—" I open my eyes.

He puts his warm fingers on my lips. "Leave the *but*s out—for once just shut up." He's so much taller now—can reach my lips with his if he wants to without me stooping. He smells good. Like he did prom night. I want him to kiss me. I'm dying to kiss him back. Right here in the hall with the 8:35 warning bell about to ring.

Derek. Friday. Derek. Friday.

But Scott—

My cell phone rings.

I pull back, away from Scott's lips.

"Don't answer it, Bethie." The way he looks at me—stripped, vulnerable, alone—tells me exactly how much my relationship with Derek hurts him. "Bethie, please."

I flip open my phone. "It's just my mom," I lie.

Scott touches my face. "See you in choir." He leaves me to my phone call.

I put the cell to my ear. "Are you sure you can't come home today? I need you."

"I'm on my way."

"Don't tease me."

"Serious. Mum has an Amabile board meeting she forgot about. I'll call you when I get there."

Now I'm mega-jumpy. I keep feeling my cell vibrate, but when I slip it out, it's not going off. I check the battery life a hundred times. I barely notice Scott in choir.

He can tell I'm jazzed. "What's up?"

I shrug my shoulders. "Nothing." It's easier to lie to him. It's really none of his business.

I'm packing my backpack at my locker, head down, avoiding Scott, when my cell goes off for real.

"I'm here."

"Cool. I'll take off as soon as I can. Email me directions, okay?" I'm down the hall, pushing out the front door. Shoot, it's pouring out.

"I don't think you'll need them. I'm pretty easy to find."

"Just do it. Don't mess with me."

"Whatever you say. Hey—how do you get your hair to do that?"

"My hair?"

"It's hot—wavy like that."

I look up and squeal like a cheerleader hugging the QB after a touchdown.

Derek sits in front of the school steps on a sleek black motorcycle with two helmets dangling from the handlebars. Dang. He looks good in leather.

I fly at him—almost knock him off the bike. I don't care if it's raining and I'm getting soaked. My lips are all over him. He doesn't even have a chance to say hello. I hear a cell phone clatter, don't know or care if it's mine or his. Nothing matters—as long as he's here. Solid. Real. Kissing me.

Then there's a tap on my shoulder. "Excuse me." Scott? How can he do this? "You're making a scene. PDA on school property." He's standing under one of the school's giant blue and yellow umbrellas.

I bury my face in Derek's black leather jacket.

Derek chuckles. "Hello." He holds out his hand. "I'm Derek."

"Scott." They actually shake hands. "Do you have a minute?"

Derek looks down at me. I shake my head. "It's raining." Scott hands me his umbrella.

"Come on, Beth. Scott's a friend." Derek gets off the bike and walks a few feet away with Scott. They turn their backs to me.

When they come back, they are both drenched. Derek's smiling. Scott's not. "Bye, Beth. See you tomorrow."

"I'm sorry about that. What did he want?"

"He told me if anything happens to you, he'd kill me."

"Scott couldn't kill anything."

"Just me. He doesn't like my bike. Called it a death trap. If he only knew—"

I glance down, examine his bike. It bristles with chrome and a major engine. "If anything happens to *you* on this thing, I'll beat Scott to it. Where did this come from?"

"I needed a way to get over here—often."

"I have a car." I point out Jeannette, glistening in the rain at the back of the parking lot.

He pulls a face. "You don't expect me to ride around in that? Come on—hop on." He hands me a helmet. "I'll take you home."

"It's raining."

"We're already wet."

"What about my car?"

"It'll still be here tomorrow when I drop you off."

"You're staying" —I swallow hard— "the night?"

"If your mum will let me sleep on the sofa."

I punch his shoulder. "Don't do that to me. Feel my heart." I put his hand on my sternum, so he can feel how he makes it race.

He slides his hand up my neck, caresses my cheek with his thumb. "Don't do that to me."

I unzip his jacket and press my ear to his chest. His heart matches mine—beat for beat.

He takes the helmet from me, slides it slowly onto my head, does up the chinstrap, kisses my nose, then kicks his bike to life.

I climb on the back, slide close so my legs are hugging him, wrap my arms tight around his waist, bury my face in the wet sweatshirt hood sticking out the top of his jacket. "So far, so good," I holler over the engine.

He laughs. "Hang on."

We tear out of the parking lot.

"Slow down. There's kids."

He obeys—senses something by the way my voice catches, even manages to touch my hand without losing control of the bike.

I lay my cheek against his shoulder blade and think about him and me and kids all the way home. "Left here. Now right. Okay. You can let it out. This is an open stretch."

He gives it gas, and we're flying. I see the appeal. Huge rush. Loads of adrenaline. He thinks he's going to ride this thing all winter? Maybe I need to get a better car. Poor Jeanette. I wonder what I can trade her for.

When we get to my house, I don't want to get off the bike, can't let him go. He twists around and kisses me—our helmets clashing together.

He is real. I didn't make him up. No ghost. No phantom. Just this endangered boy I'm learning to love. He unlatches my helmet's strap, slowly pulls it off my head. Dumps his, too. Puts the kickstand down on the bike—I think. I don't know. I'm too lost in his hands smoothing back my wet hair, his breath on my temple. His mouth closing in on mine again.

I pull away for a second. "I need you to promise me something."

"Anything if you'll kiss me again."

"You aren't riding this in the snow."

His grin says everything. "Shoot, Beth. That's what makes it fun."

chapter 20

MY GUY

We make out on the back of Derek's bike in the pouring rain until my mom pulls up in the driveway.

Derek is so cute with her. "Hi, Mrs. Evans, I'm Derek." He shakes her hand and unloads all the groceries out of the trunk, helps her put them away while I change and dry my hair. I throw down an old pair of Levi's and a dry hoodie for Derek.

"Beth, honey," Mom calls up to me. "Bring that pillow from your closet and some sheets and a blanket when you come down. I'll make up the pullout in the den for Derek. I don't want him riding all that way tonight in this weather."

I am so tempted to call down and tell her not to bother, that he's going to sleep in *my* room, but she knows me. Knows my room is trashed—knows how squeaky that old den sofa bed is. Gosh, do I know her? How did she get so devious?

If Derek wasn't determined to keep me a nice girl, I'd rise to her sneaky challenge. Maybe even clean up my room. Next time he comes over, I will. Just to flip her out. Just in—I don't know. Better not go there. I'm still at—*Your lips on mine promise what I don't dare.*

He *cooks* dinner with Mom while I do my homework.

I can never get her to cook.

Mom's got work to do. She leaves Derek and me alone in the kitchen with the dirty dishes. I clear the table while he loads the dishwasher.

"You made a good impression." I put our three dirty plates on the counter so he can scrape them down the disposal. I turn to slide a platter of oven-roasted potato wedges into a Ziploc.

Derek moves up behind me. His arms go around my waist. "I always do."

I drop the bag of potatoes on the counter and twist to face him. "Thanks."

"My pleasure."

I close my eyes—can't breathe. He kisses my eyelids. Each one, lightly. I will my lips to be patient. His mouth moves to my left temple, my cheek, now it's on my neck. I bruise easy. I should warn him, but I want to wake up in the morning to find his lip prints on me. I wrap my arms around his head, don't let him off my neck. He sucks harder and harder, moves his mouth, and does it again.

Then I can't stand it. I bend my knees and get his lips. I'm so hungry. Starving. No matter how much I ply his mouth with mine, I want more and more. I get my mouth on his neck like in Lausanne. "You been working out?" He looks leaner than he did in Switzerland. "You taste sweaty." I find a fresh place on his neck to chew.

"Do you like the way I taste?" There's a deadly serious note in his voice that wasn't there before.

I stop biting him, caress the spot on his neck that's already turning pink. "Yeah."

"My sweat's kind of salty."

"What causes that?"

He pulls me close. "Don't stop, Beth. I didn't want you to stop."

I hold his eyes for a moment. We're both trembling by the time I slowly bend my head and place my lips lightly on his neck. I run my tongue along his skin. I love the way he tastes. Salty-sweet mystery boy. I lick his jaw, suck on his chin, chew on his ear.

I want to be the first to say it face-to-face. "I love you."

He picks me up and sets me on the counter. I wrap my legs around his waist.

"You're crazy, Beth. You shouldn't love me."

"That's not what I expected to hear."

"I love you. A thousand times I love you, but you shouldn't love me. Love Scott."

I feel like he slapped me. I let go of him, slide off the counter, turn around, and hide behind my hair. "Is that what you came to tell me?" My eyes are burning. "That you want to call it quits? You're dumping me?"

"No—don't be dense—no. I want you to dump me. You could be happy with him. I'm—"

"Who I want. You did this to me. Made me feel this. You're stuck with me."

"Are you sure?"

"I thought you had a plan. I was hoping for something more substantial than a motorcycle."

"How about we run away together on the back of it."

"That's your plan?"

"Plan A."

"Okay. Let's go. As soon as my mom hits the hay. I've got about $5K saved for college. How far will that get us?"

"We could go to Nova Scotia and learn to fish. Have a bunch of kids and raise them up to the trade."

I crumble inside when he says that about the kids, hunch over with my hands pressing hard against my gut.

"Oh, Beth. I'm sorry. I forgot. I didn't mean it."

"I'm such a beast."

He guides me to the table and into a chair. I lay my face on the table. He squats down and strokes my head. "No you're not. I'm the beast. I really do have a plan. I'm working out the details. It's coming together. I should know by Friday."

"Maybe we should discuss it. How come you're doing all the planning?"

"We'll talk about it when I come back on Friday. You're going to love it."

I sit up. He takes a cup out of the cupboard and nukes me up some chamomile tea. I watch him clean up the rest of the kitchen, polish the sink and counters, sweep the floor. He hands me the tea. I take a sip and add more honey. "I have a plan."

He dumps the dustpan in the garbage and turns around.

"Why don't you move into the den, permanently? You can visit your parents on holidays and every other weekend."

He sits across from me and weaves his fingers through mine to stop how I'm drumming the table. He gives me a cautious grin. "You wouldn't stay a nice girl very long if I did that."

I snort. "Oh, I'm prepared now. I had to go to the doctor because of that test. They wanted to laser me, but I settled for a box of condoms."

"Beth, don't—"

"I need to talk to somebody. Please. I'm going to go nuts. I can't talk to Mom. It reminds her of my father—and that's so painful. She feels guilty, like she should have known better. Chosen a guy with better genes for my sake."

He strokes my cheek with his free hand. "Then you wouldn't be you."

"I've never thought of it that way." I look up at him. "I'm supposed to see a counselor in a couple weeks. It'll take me months to get over that doctor's appointment."

He frowns and stares down at the table. "Doctors can be idiots. They aren't all like that. It sounds like you need a new one. Find someone you're comfortable with." He looks back up at me. "Someone you trust. You don't want a lot of bull and false hopes, but you don't need a bully, either."

"You're right." I nod my head. "I'm never going near that man again."

"But find a counselor." He squeezes my hand. "A good one."

"How do you know so much?" I sip my tea.

"I've been around doctors a lot, used to want to be one until—"

"You started to compose."

He stares past me at the two of us mirrored in the dark kitchen window. "I'd really love to be a researcher. The guy who finds cures."

"Do it, Derek. Cure me."

His eyes return to mine. "Don't give up, Beth. They are working on unbelievable stuff. Especially with genetics. You'll have as many babies as you want."

His voice sweeps hope all through me. Then I remember that doctor. "He told me I have to disclose my condition to any—what did he call them? Oh, yeah, *potential partners*."

Derek plays with my hand, lets me rant.

"And they should *all* be screened. Like I'm shacking up with half the football team. Good thing this isn't about sex. If you ever decide to stop respecting me, you'll need to get your cheek swabbed first."

He doesn't say anything.

"I'm sorry. I'm grossing you out now."

He stands up, comes around to my chair, and pulls me to my feet. He holds me like I'm going to break. "When it's right, Beth." His voice is husky. "You and me. I'm your guy. I don't care what that idiot doctor says."

"You love me that much?" I press my face against his cheek.

"Of course. Any decent guy would." He pauses. "Scott does, too."

"Why do you keep bringing him up?"

"If you and I don't make it," he strokes my hair, "I like knowing there's a good guy there who knows the real Beth—the Beth I love—who will love you better than I can."

"How can we not make it?"

"I hope we can, but—"

"Whatever it is, Derek. You can beat it. I know you can. For me. I love you. Do it for me."

His hand drops away from my hair. He lets go of me.

I wrap my arms around his shoulders and press my face against his neck. "Tell me, Derek. I need to know. Where were you this summer?"

"I was at the cottage."

"No, you weren't. I'm not stupid."

He kisses my hair. "I was at the cottage."

"Please, Derek. Let me help."

"You want to help?"

I nod.

"Then don't ask me any more questions. And kiss me again."

He gets his way—like the Phantom in my dream.

He always gets his way.

chapter 21

PLAN B

Derek parks his bike behind a teacher's minivan, so we can say good-bye without an audience. Especially Scott. We don't want to be in his face.

I walk through the hall, keep my eyes down. Scott's leaning up against his locker with his arms crossed, glaring at me.

"What the hell, Beth. He spent the night?"

"In the den. My mom was there. And what business is it of yours what I do with my boyfriend?"

Scott gets in my face. "What are you going to tell our daughters when they want to sleep around? Go ahead—as long as he's good-looking. I'm not having that."

"What are you talking about?"

He realizes what he said. "I mean your daughters."

My daughters? The sons? They'll die in utero. All those miscarriages Aunt Linda had—they will be my children. The doctor said if an afflicted baby survived, it'd be severely handicapped—would spend its life dying. The other children will be carriers like me. Like my cousin. Like my dad.

Scott's bracing for me to scream at him, but I don't. I slump against my locker and touch his wrist. "You've got it all planned out, don't you?" Scott comes from a big family. "Oh, Scottie, you still want to play house."

He was so sweet when we were in preschool. He always wanted to feed the dolls. The stroller rides he gave would have made any real baby puke its guts up, but even that was sweet.

"That's kind of impossible now."

He looks away from me. "Because of Derek."

"No. It has nothing to do with him."

"I'm supposed to believe that?" The pain of seeing me all over Derek leaks out with his words and splashes around us in tiny bitter drops.

I look away from his face. "I should have told you sooner. I've been busy running away from you. Resisting you isn't easy."

"Then stop."

"That's what he said." I make myself face Scott. "Derek told me to dump him and go out with you."

"He's not as dumb as he looks." Scott recrosses his arms.

I take a deep breath. "This summer—"

"Doesn't he want to play house?"

I shrug. "I don't think he's the kind of guy who plays house."

"But you are—Beth—you're a house-playing girl."

I nod. "But I *can't* play house."

"Sure you can." He relaxes his arms. One drifts toward me. "We'll get married and play house as much as we want." He cradles my elbow, gently strokes my arm.

"It won't work with me."

"Of course, it will." He takes hold of my other arm, too. "When Derek self-destructs, you'll come to your senses and come back to me." He leans in and whispers, "Just don't sleep with him, okay? I was ready to run him down with my pickup when I saw him dropping you off this morning."

I swallow hard. "Like I'd tell you."

"You don't think I'd figure it out? You're a crap liar. You told me just now that you didn't."

I push away from him. "Our relationship isn't about sex."

"Good—because ours will be."

I put my hand on his chest. "Shut up and stop sidetracking me. This is important."

"I'm sorry." He takes both my hands in his and squeezes them.

I let him. I even squeeze back. "I probably can't have babies." My head drops.

He touches his forehead to my drooping head. "Who told you this?"

"A doctor and a genetic test."

"When?"

"I got my cheek swabbed right before the tour."

He starts, pulls back. "That was the bad news?" His voice sharpens. "You never said a word to me about this and you told a perfect stranger?"

"Post-prom things were all weird with you." I flush. That was all my fault. "And he wasn't a stranger. We have a connection you wouldn't understand."

"Right." Scott lets go of my hands. "Him all over you. Making a play when you're falling apart."

"It wasn't like that."

"You are so naive." He turns back to his locker and starts slapping his books around.

"This isn't about him." I grab his arm and jerk him back. "It's about you. I can't be that girl in your daydreams rocking the baby while you play catch with our son. That's what you want. Find someone who can give you that."

He takes me by the shoulders, squeezes really hard. "Is that what you think of me? That I care about some stupid fantasy more than I care about you? The dream can change, Bethie. As long as you're in it—that's all that matters."

"I'm sorry, Scottie." My eyes sting. "I really am. I'm not in it."

"You can't know that."

"Find somebody cute and sweet who adores you."

"Don't make me retch."

I sniff. "Please, Scottie, stop torturing yourself. Stop torturing me."

"No way." His face gets hard. "I'm here, Bethie. Every day. Loving you. Wanting you. I'm not going to run off into a hole and lick my wounds. I'm going to bleed in front of you. I'm not going to fake it with somebody else. I'm going to be right here in your face—until the day I die."

"You following me to college?"

"Yep."

"What if Derek and I decide to get married? Will you walk me down the aisle?"

"You won't marry him. He won't last. I will. You're going to marry me."

I pry his hands off me. "Your crystal ball needs a tune-up."

He stands in the hall, his face full of pain. "I love you, too."

"I don't—"

"Don't lie to me, Bethie. You do."

"I'm sorry, Scottie. If I make you bleed, I'm so sorry. I can't help it. I love him. I'll love him forever."

Scott won't talk to me the rest of the day. Every time I see him, I want to hold his hand and tell him it will be okay, but it won't. I can't.

Thursday he's the same, but at least I've got choir to look forward to. I play Derek's CD all the way down to Ann Arbor. Terri plans to tell us her ideas for this season. I used to always love the first practice when she introduces new music. The challenge of sight-reading the parts and making sure all my altos get it right. But Bliss can't hack the really challenging stuff.

The Amabile girls sing some hyper-hard, atonal modern pieces. I would so love to do that. I've only ever seen one other choir do those—and it was crap compared to the AYS. I wish we could sing pieces like that. Maybe in college I can.

I haven't decided on a major, but it's going to be music something. I don't have the bucks for an elite school. I'll have to stay in state, go public. If Derek stays in London, maybe I better stick with Ann Arbor and go to the University of Michigan. But that would be so far from him. There's a big university in London. Maybe I could go there. We could start together next year. Major in music together. It seems weird he wanted to be a doctor, but he's composing now. That's a gift he can't waste. Somebody else can cure me.

Friday is twice as long as Wednesday and Thursday combined. Scott is twice as grumpy. I need to move my locker. When the final bell buzzes, I race out of school and speed home.

Derek's there.

Waiting in my driveway.

Just like he said he would be.

I can't get out of the car fast enough. He opens my door, gives me a hand. I can't kiss him here—too like Scott and prom night.

I step all the way out of the car and push the door closed with my butt, lean up against it. Derek comes at me hard, pins me there with his body, greets me with his lips. We make out for about ten minutes, then he pulls away. "Hi." He drills me with his chocolate-brown eyes and plays with a piece of my frizzed-out hair that he said was hot.

"I missed you." He's turned me into a puddle again. I'm sloshing in the driveway.

"We need to talk."

"Plan B?"

"Ready to execute."

"Should I pack a bag? I've got my bankbook in my purse."

"That's Plan A."

"Right." I lead him into the house. We both eye the stairs going up to my room. "We can talk in my room if you want." I cleaned it up—just in case. I want to be ready when it's right.

He shakes his head and tugs me in the direction of the family room. He sits on the loveseat and makes me take the couch. "If you're any closer, we won't talk much."

I lift my eyebrows.

He looks at his watch, then me, alone in the middle of the couch.

I run my hands over the leather cushions. "We've never made out lying down." I want him to lie beside me, feel his weight on me, even if it's just kissing.

"First, you must agree to Plan B."

"Right. I'm sorry. You are distracting."

He leans forward, rests his arms on his knees, and clasps his hands together. "I spoke with my director, and she talked to the AYS conductors. They want you. You're in."

"The AYS?" I shake my head, stunned. "What are you talking about?"

"The Amabile girls' directors listened to your rendition of 'Take Me Home.' Auditions were last spring, but they'll make an exception for you."

"How does this get us together?"

"They practice Tuesdays. We can hang out before and after. On Friday nights we have chamber, the best girls and guys. You and me sitting together and singing. We can go out after. Every Friday like clockwork. We'll be together at festivals and extra practices."

I tense up. "Why can't we just hang out on the weekends?"

He leans back on the couch and stares at the blank television. "My weekends are pretty full. After our Choral Olympics win, everyone wants us. It's going to be a head rush. I want you there for as much as possible."

I wrap my arms around my torso. "Can't I just be a groupie in the crowd?"

"No. I want you part of it. Don't you want to sing with me again?"

I close my eyes and remember those amazing impromptu moments with him on the stage. The taste of the mike. The magic of the crowd screaming our names. The elixir of his lips on mine. Who wouldn't want more of that? I open my eyes and nod. "I do want to sing with you."

"My music."

"Yeah."

"We'll do it together."

"Sure." I nod my head.

He's nodding along with me. "And you'll get to sing with the AYS. We're touring together next summer. Think what that would be like."

Touring together. An international flight together. Days and days. It sounds so good. But . . . "Me? Singing with the AYS?" I can't get my head around that one.

Derek smiles and keeps me nodding.

"But my choir practices Tuesdays. I can't—"

"Do both."

"I have to leave my choir?" I feel guilty for being impatient with them last night. Feeling like I was too good. Terri planned our entire season around me. I've got four pieces with solos this year. Not just one.

"They aren't good enough for you. You owe it to your talent to sing in the best choir you can."

"The AYS are the premier choir in the world."

He leans forward and clasps his hands in front of him, so earnest, so handsome, so devastating. "And they want you."

I turn my back on him. I can't decide if I keep looking at him. "I'm going to have to think about it. The drive—"

"We're way closer to Port than Ann Arbor is."

"What's it like in the winter? You guys are on the snowbelt side of the lake."

"Brand new highway. Always plowed. I don't want you driving through Detroit anymore."

The protective note in his voice doesn't make me angry like it should. It makes me want to go over to the couch and tell him I'll do anything he wants. Then I remember Bliss. He wants me to leave them. "Terri will die. I'm her only star. She invested in a lot of great stuff for me to sing."

"She'll get over it. She should be happy for you."

I hate that his answers are all so true. "The AYS are going to hate me."

"Certainly not."

"Don't be stupid. First, I steal you. Then I barge into their choir and steal the solo spot."

"I didn't say they were giving you the solos. Those you'll have to earn on your own. They have about six soloists. The competition will be tough but good for you."

"So I'm going to sit by your ex every Tuesday? She'll let me have that spot beside you in chamber?"

"She'll like you as much as I do. They all will. I'll tell them they have to."

I turn around and pull a face at him. "You have that kind of power over an entire choir of mega-talented women?"

"Of course." He manages not to smirk.

"You're full of it."

He sits up and gets all innocent looking. "They want me to be happy. When they see how happy I am with you, they'll welcome you like a long-lost sister."

I shake my head. "I can't do this. I can't abandon my choir."

He stands up. "Get something to eat. Chamber practice starts in an hour and a half and you're coming with me."

"Tonight?" I don't follow his lead. "Now?"

"Yes." He nods.

I'm glued to the couch. "No."

"I already told them you would. Kind of an informal tryout."

"Great." I lean back on the couch and stare up at him, finally starting to get steamed. "No pressure there."

"Pressure is a good thing. It makes you stretch."

"I'm tall enough already, thank you."

"Three more inches and you'd really be sexy."

Three more inches? I'd be a skyscraper. "Let's stay around here tonight. Go to a movie. Watch TV. I cleaned my room."

He shakes his head. "I have to go to practice. And I promised you'd be there."

"I wish you would have discussed this with me first."

"I didn't think it would be an issue. I thought you'd be falling all over me with gratitude." He comes over and sits beside me on the couch. "Please, Beth." He cups my face in his hands and kisses me long, slow. "I want to be with you." He kisses me again. "This is the best way." He pulls me close against his chest. "Come sing with me."

"This kind of persuasion isn't fair."

He keeps kissing me, presses me down on the couch with his body. My womanly senses go berserk. He kisses me once like that and gets up. "You coming?" He gives me his hand.

Of course, I take it.

I hate that he's so confident.

I hate that he takes for granted I'll agree to whatever he comes up with.

I hate not knowing his secrets.

"If I come tonight, you have to tell me—"

His eyes get pained. "Don't go there, Beth."

Then I hate myself for prying, probing the tender spot, hurting him, but I do it anyway. "What are you on?"

"We don't have that kind of time."

"I do."

"Stop this, Beth. It's not going to work if you keep asking me."

That scares me. I'll put up with anything to make this work. Even drugs. Even not knowing. Even going along with this crazy plan.

We get sandwiches, I call Mom, and we launch into the night, Derek on his bike, me in my car. I follow Derek over the Rainbow Bridge that crosses the Saint Clair River before it dumps itself into Lake Huron. We only have to wait at the border for about ten minutes. Once we get into Canada, we're on that new freeway Derek bragged about. It is well maintained. This is Ontario. Nothing like the broken-up mess we drive on around Detroit. Not much traffic. Perfect for Derek to kill himself on. I can't keep up with him. I don't try. I'm not going to encourage him with even a hint of a race. He keeps circling back to find me and racing off again. Jeannette has a hard time over seventy. He's going a lot faster than that. I couldn't race if I wanted to.

The buzz of his bike turns into the drone of an organ, and I'm back in that dream. This time it is a nightmare.

I'm in my lacey white Christine dress again, kneeling by the side of the freeway, cradling Derek's broken body in my arms, headlights beating against us. The organ gets loud and screechy, the orchestra comes in, cymbals crashing, violins on hyperdrive. I look up at the sky and sing, but I don't sing like Christine this time. My voice is tortured madness.

No, God, you can't have him.
You gave him to me.
He's mine.
He's all I ask for.
This boy I can adore.

I imagine ambulances arriving and paramedics rushing toward us. I put out my hand and screech—

No one else come near him.
He sees only me.
My love
Can never harm him.
My touch will ever warm him.

Derek's eyes flutter open. They fill with terror. I'm not Christine anymore. I'm the Phantom, and all those Amabile girls—especially his prissy ex—better get this straight. I won't ever let him go, no matter how many chandeliers I have to take out.

Derek's headlight cuts into the night. He flips a U-turn, catches me, passes me. I sigh in defeat and turn on Jeannette's crackling old radio to keep the ghosts at bay, getting more and more uptight about this whole situation. What am I doing? Amabile? Who am I kidding? I'm not even Canadian. I need to run back to my own kind with my head down and my tail between my legs. Crap. He's gone again.

It's getting darker. What if he's nowhere around when I get to the turn. What if I don't see any signs that say London? What if I slam on the brakes and flip my poor, rattling, ugly old car around. Head for home. Now. Jeannette stutters. I agree and ease up the gas to give her a break.

Shoot. He's back. No escape. That lone headlight bearing down on me has to be him. Mind reader. The guy's got some sort of powers. He's certainly got control of me. Yes, Derek. Whatever you want, Derek. Please, Derek. Keep me in the dark—that's fine with me. I'll just sigh and let you kiss me again. He's too perfect to withstand. It's so not fair.

And now he's Evel Knievel on his motorbike. I've got to sabotage that thing. What if he got high and went out on it?

Self-destructs. Scott saw it as soon as he laid eyes on Derek. Stupid Scott. If Derek dares to self-destruct on me, Scott won't have to carry through with his dumb macho caveman threats. I *will* kill Derek myself.

chapter 22

CHAMBERS

Derek slows down when we get near London. He puts on his flashers and rides smack in front of me like a police escort for a pop star. I so don't miss the exit. And he's right there as we wind through the city to the church where they practice.

He parks his bike beside me. I get out. "I'm never following you again."

"What?"

"Every time you disappeared, I was sure I'd find your crumpled body in the middle of the road. Don't do that to me." I stalk away, push through the door into the church before he can make excuses.

He introduces me to all the directors. There's two from his choir and two from the AYS. I smile and shake their hands, thank them for letting me sing with them tonight.

She's here. His ex. I recognize her from Derek's profile. He took her pictures with him down, but she's still all over his wall. Great. She's even tinier than she looks in her picture. She's standing in a spot in the center of the choir next to an empty space that's obviously Derek's. She moves—quietly finds a new spot. Our eyes meet, and she smiles.

Crap. She is a nice girl.

My face heats up, and I look back at the tall conductor with a wispy beard that I'm supposed to be talking to.

"Why don't you try the solo on this first piece?" He hands me the sheet music.

Derek's name is in the corner next to *Arranged by.*

"Derek wrote the solo for one singer—"

"Back when I could still hit the high notes."

"We split it alto/soprano—which line do you feel comfortable with?" The guy waits for me to answer.

I don't. Derek butts in with, "She can sing it all."

"Derek." There he goes again. I flip through the music, sight-reading in my head and checking the lows and highs. He's right. As usual. I can. "I'll try it."

Derek maneuvers me through the choir to our places. "Don't be nervous."

"You are the only thing that makes me nervous. Singing calms me."

"Then we better get started before you bite my head off."

One of the AYS directors leads the warm-ups. No back rubs—guess that's a girl choir thing. Derek tries to stick with me on the high notes, gets screechy, and gives up. On the low scale, I can go way past the lowest note in this solo. Derek is impressed.

"I sing tenor at school."

He laughs.

We both have to drop out when it drops to bass range. I notice Blake is a bass. Figures.

Now tall guy with the wispy beard takes the wand. "All right, ladies and gentlemen. Welcome. It's good to be back with you. We're going to get right to work on Derek's arrangement. He's found us a soloist who can sing the impossible range he wrote. Everyone say hello to Beth." He pauses while people turn and nod to me. I half raise my hand and wave a couple fingers. "She's joining us this season. Please make her feel welcome."

Wow. Done deal. I look sideways at Derek. He's so avoiding me. He's supposed to keep his eyes glued to the director, so am I for that matter. Still. No excuse. He must know I'm fuming. I open my music, hold it so I can watch the director, too, and smash my foot down hard on Derek's toes.

He winces.

Now I can sing.

I fall in with the altos. This is their first run-through of the piece, and already the sound is amazing. The basses are really good, mellow and rich. Their low vibrations ground it. Derek's pure voice beside me leads the tenors. The altos are all getting the part—not just me and my perfect pitch. And the sopranos don't balk at the harmonic descant Derek throws at them on the second page.

The first verse and chorus is SATB. Then an instrumental interlude with piano and strings, and I come in. It's not perfect, my first shot at that solo, but it's pretty good. At the end of the piece, several of the girls turn around, lightly clap. Not haughty. Friendly. And Derek's ex is smiling at me again. It's nice. These girls are nice. It's all overwhelming, Canadian nice.

Derek's hand on my back and brief, "Way to go," is knee-melting nice.

Derek tries the tenor solo in the next piece. He muffs it a couple times but makes it through. Another girl sings the soprano on that one. It's short but poignant, and she sings it well.

All of them, the girls especially, have a real beauty to the tone of their voices. Nobody is weak. And the blending is flawless. No one tries to stick out. I can't say it isn't a total rush to meld my voice with that group. It would be amazing to sing with them all the time. I can't believe Derek talked them into me. He obviously has everyone here wrapped as tightly around his baby finger as I am.

How does he do it? Why do they let him? Maybe they know. Whatever it is that he won't tell me. Everyone here could know every little nasty, sordid detail. Maybe I *should* get chummy with all these nice girls. Especially Derek's ex–nice girl.

After practice, Derek introduces me to some of them. His ex included. She really is nice. "We'll see you Tuesday, then." No hint of anger at me in her voice whatsoever. "Practice starts at 6:30."

"I'm not sure—"

"She'll be there." Derek decides for me again. "Save her a seat, okay?"

She gives him a dazzling, perky smile. "Sure, Derek. I'll look after her."

One of the AYS directors hands me a heavy binder of sheet music. "We'll be doing the first ten on Tuesday." Ten? Whoa. "Know your part, okay? Derek says you're happy to sing alto."

I nod.

"Great. We had to retire a couple of our best last year." She makes it sound like her singers are racehorses not girls. You can compete in the youth choir category until you are twenty-two. Then retirement? I hope not.

I can't make it Tuesday. I have to go to my choir. The words are there, ready to escape my lips, but I just nod.

We leave Derek's bike and drive Jeannette to a nearby Tim Hortons. I'm starving. I get soup and a big sandwich on a croissant. Derek polishes off four pink-frosted, candy-sprinkled donuts.

"That's not a very manly choice."

"You're so sexist." He picks up his last donut and bites into it. "Pink? I thought you'd get it. In honor of Meadow. She'll get to be the soloist again."

"Poor Terri."

"She'll get over it."

"Poor Meadow—and her parents." I put down my spoon and lean forward. "They invested a lot in me last spring."

"And you delivered in Lausanne. You don't owe them anything."

"That's easy for you to say." They counted on me for radio spots and their Christmas party this year.

Derek nods at my choir bag. "Go home and take a look at that music, and if you can honestly tell me you'd rather sing the baby stuff Terri's got for you instead of what the AYS are doing, plus my fantastic creations in chamber choir—fine."

I lift a spoonful of soup and pour it back into the bowl. "You know it doesn't compare."

"Good. How about we meet back here—Tuesday at 5:30 for a quick dinner before your practice."

I glance around and frown. "Is this the only place to eat in London?"

"That I can afford?"

"Now who's being sexist? I can pay—especially for better food."

Derek wipes his sticky fingers on a napkin. "You don't like the ambiance?"

"I don't like the soup." It's even worse than the Dunkin' Donuts by my house.

"Can't beat the donuts."

"If you get fat—"

"Me? Impossible."

He's right. I look at him closely. It's not just that he's leaner than in Switzerland like I thought on Monday. He's thinner—probably by at least ten pounds. Drugs make you skinny. Even I know that. He slips out a few pills and swallows them—like in Lausanne. Right in front of me. Who takes vitamins at night?

"Do you think that's a good idea? You have to ride your motorcycle home."

"They're for my stomach."

I study his face. "Not vitamins?"

"Vitamins for my stomach."

"I'm worried about you."

"Don't be. My cold is cleared up for now."

"But—"

"I'm fine." He takes off for the guy's restroom.

When he comes back, I smile truce at him and say, "Hey, why is your ex-girlfriend being so nice to me? She caught me staring and smiled. It's weird."

"She's dating somebody else. We're friends. She's cool with you and me."

"She's too nice, though. There's something kind of creepy about it."

He shakes his finger at me. "Now that isn't nice."

"I live next to Detroit where people shoot you if you cut them off in traffic."

"Here, people stop and wave you in."

"I could see your ex doing that." I stir my soup.

His eyes follow my movements. "I told you. She wants what's best for me, and she knows that's you."

"How can she know that?" I drop the spoon and lean back, get his eyes. "Why isn't she best? I think I'm best for you. But she should think she's best for you."

"It's complicated. Ancient history. I don't want to get into it tonight."

"Of course not." I dig a spoonful of soup out of my bowl and stare at it with distaste. I can't eat it.

Derek clears our tray. I follow him to the door. He holds the door open and says, "Just let *me*—let *us* be nice to you. I want this to work. We need it to work." He takes hold of my hand and strokes the back of it with his thumb while he talks low in my ear. "I love singing with you. I want to write with you."

I shake my head at that. "We can always go back to Plan A."

"I don't want to be a fisherman."

"Pack your guitar and we'll head for Nashville."

He takes my keys and unlocks my car. "With Motown in your back-yard? You've got diva pipes. You could be the next Mariah." He opens the door for me.

"Not Whitney?"

"You could be any of them."

I get in and wait for him to go around and get in on the passenger side. "Motown is too close. It wouldn't be running away."

"I can't run away. I've got—"

"Too many ties? I'm not enough? I'm not sure if I like your Plan B. I want you to myself. Too many Derek groupies back there."

"You're the only one I kiss good night."

My eyes are drawn to his lips and heat pours through my body. "Prove it."

Derek pushes his seat back as far as it can go. "Come here." He holds his arms out.

I shift over the parking brake in the center console and onto his lap. I hold his face between my hands and kiss him.

He kisses me back. "I want what's best for you."

"And that's you?"

"Probably not. But if I can get you singing with Amabile—that's something. The best I can give you."

I shake my head—press my lips to his chest. "Your heart. That's all I want. That's the best thing you can give me."

"You stole that before we even met."

"I don't want to be a thief. I want you to give it."

His arms tighten around me, and his mouth presses on mine again. "It's yours, Beth." His words flow into my soul and twist me into knots. "You know it's yours."

chapter 23

QUITS

You say that you're mine.
You say that your heart is true.
I believe every line,
When you look at me the way you do.
And even though I doubt you,
I can't live without you.
Your lips made it right,
Holding me tonight.

I close my eyes and say, "Yes."
Say, "Yes," forever after.
If I'm part of your song,
Nothing, love, will ever go wrong.
Our tune will hold laughter,
Soothe my fears of disaster.
I'll leap and fly with you,
Fly with you forever after.

I couldn't sleep after I got home last night—wrote that to my favorite song from junior high. I got groggy before I could finish it. It needs two more verses and a bridge. In the cold light of this morning's cold cereal, I reread my scrawl, try to make sense of the crossed-out lines, and remember what he wants me to do. Derek's Plan B is unbelievably great. Really. But I so don't want to call Terri. Awkward times a zillion. It takes three tries dialing her before I have the guts to let it ring. She doesn't pick up. I force myself to let it ring five times, get ready to hang up before her voice-mail comes on.

"Hello?"

Crap. "Hi, Terri."

"Beth? Is that you?"

"Uh-huh." I sit down on a kitchen stool and then stand right back up. "Sorry to bug you."

"Don't think of it."

"I just wanted . . . I need to—"

"You sound upset. Is there a problem?"

"Um—not really." I walk around the counter.

"Do you need help?" She pauses and her voice gets intense. "Are you safe?"

"Oh, yeah. No. It's nothing like that."

"You scared me. I know your parents are divorced and—"

"No. No. Nothing like that."

"Well, what can I help you with?" Her voice lifts. "I hope you like the pieces we're doing." Excitement comes through our static-laced cell connection.

"They're all great. I appreciate you showcasing me." I lean my elbows on the kitchen counter. "But, um, maybe the other girls don't."

"Nonsense."

"I've been thinking . . . maybe I should . . . " I trail off.

"Don't worry about it a second. You'll be off to college next year. We wasted so many seasons hiding you in the altos. I'm making this last one count."

I realize I have a chunk of frizzy dyed hair clutched too tight in my hand. "I've been listening a lot to the Amabile CDs."

"The guys or the girls?"

She caught me. "Both."

"If you go to the right school next year, you'll be performing pieces like that. Where are you applying? We should talk."

"Okay. Thanks. We should." I try to start telling her about the AYS, but she's way ahead of me.

"Have you heard from Derek? Since Lausanne?"

"Yes."

"How's that going?"

"He's intense." Why do I make him sound like that? I should say that he's amazing, says he loves me, wants to look out for me.

"Smooth?"

"Very."

"Be careful, Beth. I know you're new to guys wanting your attention. You shouldn't do anything you're not comfortable with."

"Really?" I know she's talking physical, but maybe her advice applies to more.

"Of course."

"Thanks."

"You're sure you're safe?"

"Very. Bye."

I hit Derek's number.

"You talk to Terri yet?"

I grit my teeth. "Uh-huh. Just."

"How'd she take it?"

My face screws up tight. "She hasn't got the pill yet." I don't say it very loud.

"What?"

I sink onto a stool and tip my head forward so my hair falls around my face. "I couldn't do it."

"You can't just not show on Tuesday. Call her back. She deserves that much."

"I can't quit over the phone. Never see them again." I sound defeated. "They're all going to hate me."

"Who cares? They're using you."

His confidence makes me sit up straight. "Amabile won't be using me?" My voice has an abrupt edge to it.

"No." Unyielding. Harsh. Commanding. All in one solid negative.

That gets me up on my feet. "And you're not using me?"

I'm glad I can't see his face. "What does that mean?"

"Terri asked about you—about us. She said I shouldn't agree to anything that makes me uncomfortable."

"That's rich."

Mom's head pops around the corner. "You okay?" Guess I'm getting screechy.

I wave her off and run up the stairs hissing into the phone. "Maybe I'm not comfortable with quitting my choir. Maybe I'm not comfortable singing with all those nice AYS girls. Maybe I'm not comfortable with you planning my life."

Silence. He starts saying something and stops. Clears his throat. Twice. "Comfort is highly overrated. Joining the AYS won't be comfortable. It'll be loads of hard work. I didn't think you'd be afraid of work. I thought you'd eat it up."

"It's not the work." I make it to my room, shut the door, and lean back against it.

He's saying, "Are you afraid of spending more time with me? Does that make you uncomfortable?"

Does it? I don't know. I thought that's what I wanted. All I wanted.

"Sometimes I am afraid." I sink slowly to the floor. "Not *of* you—*for* you."

"Don't worry about me." His tone cuts.

Crap. He's angry. But I keep pushing. "Back in Lausanne—Blake said—"

"Blake's an idiot."

"It's eating me up. When we're together, you're overpowering. I can't think. But when I'm alone—that's all I do." I'm talking too loud again.

"Then we need to be together more." I'm on the verge of dissolving into the sexy, coaxing thick in his voice.

I bang my head back against the door to clear it. "You're sidestepping me again."

"You've got a lot of music to learn. That should keep you busy until Tuesday. No more worrying."

His bossy tactic gives me backbone. "I'm not coming Tuesday."

"You have to."

"No. I don't."

He heats up. "You'll be way behind. It's tough to miss even one week of practice. They started this week. If you don't go Tuesday, you'll be two weeks behind. You'll miss solo auditions."

"If they want me to solo, they know how I sing." I get on my feet and glance around my cluttered room for that folder of music.

"But you have to compete for it."

I laugh. "Are you saying there are claws under the nice?"

"Hardly. They give everyone a shot."

"So I don't solo on those ten pieces." I uncover the folder on my dresser and flip through the pieces. Some of them look really good.

"I vouched for you. My rep's on the line here. Get over yourself and call Terri."

I slam the folder shut. "I don't like being told what to do. I didn't ask you to risk your precious name for me." My room is too hot. I go over to my window and open it. Muggy out. I pull it closed, stand staring out at the overcast afternoon and the cars going by on the cracked asphalt.

"Please, Beth. I miss you." His voice is slinky again. "Let's not fight over this."

Crap. We're fighting. The defiance drips out of me. I don't want to fight with him. "Isn't there a Plan C out there?"

"Amabile will be so good for you. Please. Come sing with me."

"It's going to break Terri's heart."

"If she cares about you, she'll be pleased." He's right. Again.

"I can't tell her over the phone."

He exhales. "Go Tuesday, then. I'll email the AYS directors and tell them you're winding up your commitment with Bliss."

"Thank you." Relief washes through me. "I'm sorry. I guess I'm scared."

"Don't be." That's easy for him to say. He's never been scared in his life. "I'll see you Friday then."

Friday? That's way too long. "How about I drive over to your place tomorrow afternoon? You're not busy on Sunday are you? Can't I meet your parents?"

Too fast, he says, "Sorry. No can do."

"You met my mom. You blew her away."

"Good to know. The way you're talking tonight I may need an ally in this. What does she think about you joining Amabile?"

I turn away from my window. "I haven't told her. I didn't know it was all so definite until last night. No sense getting her hopes up for nothing." Is that the truth? I don't know.

Derek doesn't believe me. "The only one undecided here is you. Let me talk to her."

"No way."

"You *are* quitting Tuesday?"

"Of course."

"Then commit. Tell your mum or I will."

"You'd make a good Central American dictator."

"Not big enough for me."

"Total global domination?"

"Now she's talking."

I sit cross-legged in the middle of my bed. He's got me smiling again. "Are you sure there's no Plan C churning in the maniacal recesses of your genius?"

"Talk online. Text. Get an international calling plan. I got my cell bill. The calls to you wiped out my entire college savings account."

"But you're not going."

"This year. I didn't say I was never going."

My smile fades. "You mean I sacrifice my choir and join Amabile so I can be with you, and you're going to take off on me?"

"You're more likely to take off on me."

An exasperated huff escapes me. "I don't have the bucks for that."

"And I do? School or no school—I have to live at home. Right now, I just want to make it through this fall."

"You keep saying that. I don't get it. What's so tough? All you're doing is sitting around composing, singing with your choir, and pulling my puppet strings."

"I don't want to get into it on the phone."

"You never do."

"I need to go."

"Wait a minute."

"Really, Beth."

"Stop." It hits me that I finally have bargaining power on my side. "Let's make a deal. I quit my choir Tuesday, and you tell me everything on Friday."

"Please, Beth. Don't put me in a corner like that. Trust me."

My phone goes dead.

I scream words Derek's nice ex-girlfriend doesn't know and pitch my cell across the room. It hits the wall next to my bed and disappears down the crack.

Dang. I'm toast if it broke. I get down on my belly and start pulling crap out from under my bed so I can get to the phone. When I cleaned it up last week, I avoided under the bed. Actually, I shoved a bunch more dirty clothes, magazines, and random junk under it.

There's my binder from the Choral Olympics. I was supposed to turn it in last week. I sit up, cross my legs, open the binder, and turn slowly through the music. I'll miss them. Terri. Leah. Stupid Sarah. My altos who follow wherever I lead. I'll even miss Meadow. They're no longer just girls in the choir who barely speak to me. They are friends.

I never had girlfriends before. Normal girls at school wouldn't ever have anything to do with me. And the other outcasts—the fat ones and mutants like me—kept to their own lone selves. Dumb. I know. I should have reached out, formed a powerful alliance of the forbidden, and taken over the whole school. It will be so hard to walk into the church Tuesday night and tell them I'm joining the Amabile Youth Singers.

I open the sheet music for "Take Me Home" and find two of Derek's tissues with the imprint of his rose between the pages of my solo. I get up on my knees, find the flattened flower on my nightstand, breathe in its faint sweetness. Why can't we go back? Spend our lives on that bench on the banks of Lake Geneva, watching the clouds drift past the Alps across the smooth blue sheet of water, discovering each other.

Those moments were magic. When I think back, it feels like I'm watching a play. It's someone else crying on Derek's chest, someone else singing that sexy pop duet with him, someone else kissing him good-bye in front of the bus, someone else watching him cough in the cold morning light as we rolled away.

He should be with that girl at Amabile. She knows her lines, has the stage business down. She won't trip and take out all the scenery. She'll bat her eyes and nod her head. "Yes, Derek. Of course, Derek. Whatever you want, Derek."

He's in love with her. Not me. I'm a shadow. Leftovers. Hungry and grasping—wanting more than he's prepared to give. Afraid to give him what he wants.

It should be easy. Most guys would want my body and that's it. Use me up and then split—like bio-Dad did to Mom. All Derek wants is to sing with me. He's on an entirely different plane of existence. If this *was* about sex, it would be so much easier.

But that's not what he wants.

He wants my soul.

chapter 24

CREEPY

I spend all day Sunday learning the AYS music. I sit down at the piano and pick out some of the trickier parts. Four of the pieces are on their old CDs that I've got uploaded on my iPod. I make myself a practice playlist and walk around school Monday and Tuesday with my head-phones on. There's a killer solo in one of the new pieces that I want.

I still haven't told Mom what I'm doing. What if she doesn't want me to quit Bliss? She's clueless about the youth choir world. She doesn't get how big an opportunity this is. I mean, I could be on one of those CDs. If I wasn't so gutless, I'd be singing with them tonight instead of driving all the way down to Ann Arbor again. If I wasn't so gutless, I'd get to see Derek again. We connected online last night for a few exchanges, and then he had to go, with a "good luck tomorrow night." I'm going to need more than luck.

"Hey." Scott bumps my arm as he sits down beside me in choir.

"Not today, please."

He puts both hands up. "Excuse me."

"Sorry. I've got a big decision to make tonight."

"Don't."

"Honestly—is that all you ever think about?" I wiggle my butt over to the far side of my chair. "Did you ever think there could be more than one type of big decision in a relationship?"

"Good to hear."

"The Amabile Youth Singers has offered me a place." Why am I telling Scott? "I have to tell Terri tonight."

"And you're not sure?"

"No. I am. It's an amazing opportunity and—"

"Derek's making you."

"No."

"Then why is it a 'big decision'?"

"You're twisting what I said."

"No. You're denying what you said. Gee—" He rifles his hands through his hair. "Don't let him control you like that. It's creepy."

"Shut up. You don't know what you're talking about." I turn my shoulder to him and focus on the music we have to sing.

As I drive down to Ann Arbor, Scott's words hum in the drone of the freeway. *Creepy.* A weird shiver hits me. I try to shake it off. I remind myself that this drive to Ann Arbor is ninety minutes—on a good day. London is a lot closer. And the drive is pretty. All those trees and fields. When the leaves turn this fall, it'll be like driving through a postcard. And then I'll get there and get to see Derek—on Fridays we'll sing together half the night. Make out the rest of it. That makes me almost turn the car around and head for the bridge to Canada. He would be so happy if I called him and told him to meet after the AYS practice. I could be in his arms again tonight. I'll go Thursday and tell Terri. No big deal.

Crap. I've gone too far south. I just passed the sign to Windsor. I'm a full two hours away from London. And the AYS start way early. If I try to change course, I'll end up missing both.

I need to pull myself together. All I can think about is making out with Derek. It seems to drive my decisions more than anything else. How shallow is that?

I will do this—swallow my cowardice, misgivings, my craving to get behind Derek's perfect facade to the trouble he refuses to share with me, and silence Scott's voice saying—

> *He doesn't treat you, babe, like I do—*
> *He doesn't meet you babe, like me.*
> *I'll be your rescue on the horizon,*
> *Your prince on bended knee.*
> *I'll climb your walls,*
> *The dragons fall,*
> *If you'll stay here, babe, with me.*
> *He's creepy, so creepy, stay with me.*
> *You're the beauty to my beast.*
> *If we kiss, the spell will release.*
> *It's midnight, girl, the ball has passed,*
> *Wake up, and you'll see*
> *Whose love will last.*
> *He's creepy—*

No, he's not. Shut up, Scott. You can't even sing.

I march into practice ready to tell the world I'm joining Amabile.

Terri is in the front with a smile bubbling from ear to shining ear. "Good, Beth. I didn't want to make this announcement without you."

I squeeze through the altos and take my seat next to Sarah. "What's up?"

She shrugs her shoulders.

"Okay." Terri takes a big breath and fans her face. She's pink. Whoa. Maybe she's met a guy. She's getting married and leaving us. She's going to introduce a new director that I will have absolutely no loyalty to. Bliss will fall apart without Terri. Lucky I'm leaving.

"Is everybody ready?"

"Get on with it." Meadow echoes what we're all thinking.

"I went to the mailbox this morning and look what I found." Terri waves an off-white envelope in the air. "Any guesses?"

"No!" we all shout back.

"Now, girls, girls, remember—your voices." She slowly slides out a letter and shakes it open. "Dear Miss Bolton, Thank you for your grant application. The commission is impressed with Bliss Youth Singers' achievement on the world stage and is delighted to approve your request."

Grant? Whoopee. We'll get new hair bows. I'm so glad I'm out of here.

Terri pauses, looks at all of us, and continues reading. "We look forward to hearing the CD you plan to produce."

CD? We're cutting a CD of our own?

"What do you say, girls?" She's looking straight at me. "Are you up for it?"

Derek's not online when I get home, so I call him. I don't care what it costs. I use the landline, though. Maybe Mom won't notice when it shows up on the bill. And she likes him. She still keeps bringing up Scott—but she likes Derek. Enough to spring for a few international long-distance phone calls. We need to get a cheap plan.

Derek doesn't pick up. It's way late. Practice went over. We sang through all our old favorites trying to decide what to put on the CD. "Take Me Home"—for sure. Our other competition pieces. And all the new stuff Terri chose for me to sing this year.

"You know what would be cool," Leah piped up. "If Beth could get Derek to come and sing that duet with her. We could do the backup."

I turned at least red—probably purple.

Terri winked at me. "I'll check into the licensing if you think he would?"

"I don't know. He's really busy. I'll ask." I'm such a liar. But what could I do?

Derek's voice-mail comes on, and I hang up. Maybe he's asleep. I thought he'd wait up—want to talk. I check my computer screen again. No Derek. I can't do this in an email. No way.

That's when I decide not to tell him until I see him. I'll go Friday. Steal one more night in Amabile's rarified air.

I get there late. He's waiting outside the church. He kisses me too quick and hustles me to the door. "How did it go Tuesday?"

"I'll tell you after."

I can't relax and get into the singing. I'm an intruder. What am I doing here? The wispy-beard director gets an alto and soprano to try the solo I sang last week. It works. They so don't need me.

Derek leans over and whispers, "You were much better."

I shake my head.

He rolls his eyes. "Not even close."

His ex sings the next song with a solo. Her voice is delicate—not breathy like Meadow's but feminine and pretty—fairies sing like that when they dance at midnight. I keep my eyes focused on the music. No way do I dare look at Derek. What if his eyes read regret?

He lost her for me? It doesn't make any sense. He could get her back easy. Maybe, after tonight, he'll want that.

After choir, he makes me hop on the back of his bike. "You aboard is the best way to ensure my safety."

I can't argue.

I press my face into his leather-jacketed back and enjoy hanging on to him. He rides over a bridge and then takes a narrow road down into a park. It's full of old maple trees. When he shuts off his bike, I can hear moving water—close.

"I found us a new bench." He leads me to a green wooden park bench beside the small river that splits London in two. "This is the Thames. Not Lake Geneva—but—"

"I love it."

"Are you hungry?"

"Not for donuts."

He sits down and pulls me beside him. We fall easily into our Lausanne make-out position. It feels so right. I comb his silky dark hair out of his eyes.

"So you're okay? Tuesday wasn't too traumatic?"

I get my mouth on his. I need this first. I need the assurance of his lips pressing harder and harder. I need his arms and his shoulders and his chest. I need to cling to him and kiss. I get hungrier and hungrier.

"Hey—hey. Slow it down." He presses his cheek against mine. "We've got all the time you want tonight."

I press my face into his shoulder.

"You're not cold, are you?" His fingers slide through my hair.

I put a ton of conditioner on it, didn't rinse it all out, and left it wavy. I wanted it soft for him. I can tell he likes it.

"Thanks, Beth. I told you this would work." He shifts me so my head falls back on his arms and bends to kiss me again.

I put my fingers on his lips. "Tuesday. I tried, but—"

It all comes out in a rush. His body goes stiff, and his arms drop away from cradling me. At least he doesn't dump me on the ground.

"I'm sorry. Terri wouldn't have a CD if I left." I wrap my arms around his neck. "Don't hate me. Please."

He's quiet a long time. I don't let go of him—keep my face pressed into his neck. I wait for him to shove me into the dirt, but it doesn't happen.

"Why'd you come tonight?"

"To taste it again and tell you face-to-face."

"You took your time about it."

"I wanted to soften the blow." I get my lips on his neck and chew on his salty sweetness. "If we can't sing together, maybe—"

"Crap, Beth. Knock it off." He pushes me away—stands up so I have to. He heads back to his bike. "Plan C isn't going to be any fun."

I run after him. "Don't get mad. There was nothing I could do."

"You made me look like a fool in front of the entire Amabile organization."

"They don't need me."

He stops, turns on me. "You're right. They let you in because I need you."

"Why, Derek? She's gorgeous. She still loves you; I can tell. Why are you with me?"

A flap of wings and honking sounds come from the direction of the river. He looks toward that instead of at me. "She knows me way too well."

"And I'm special because I don't?" I hate that. I hate it. I hate it.

"You see me in a way she never could." He looks back at me. "I want to be the guy you think I am. When we're together, I almost believe it's true."

I reach for his hand. "I want to be with the guy you are."

"No, you don't." He squeezes my hand and drops it, heads up the path to his bike.

"Why not, Derek," I yell after him. "I've been patient all this time. You have to tell me why not."

He keeps walking away. "That wasn't the deal."

I run after him. "I'm the one who should be angry." I catch up and grab his arm, pull him around to face me. "That's the real me—an angry beast. Ask anyone."

"That's a load of bull you tell yourself so you don't have to try."

"I'm trying—trying so hard, but you have to try, too. I saw your arms, Derek. Back in Lausanne. Those pills you're always swallowing. We both know they aren't vitamins. What are they?"

"You wouldn't understand."

"Does it help you write? The high? Is that where the music comes from?"

"My music? You think I have to get high to write? That's cold."

"Then why do you do it?"

"Drugs?"

"Yeah. Drugs—whatever it is you snort, swallow, inhale, or inject."

"I don't do drugs."

I want to believe Derek standing in front of me. I don't want to hear Blake saying Derek has a drug habit. I don't want to see him swallowing pills. I don't want to touch the tracks on his arms. "I'm not blind."

"Stop with this nonsense. Do I look like some kind of low-life user with a fried brain?"

"Looks?" I know how fake that can be—see it every time I pass a mirror. "You're a genius, Derek. You could make me see anything you want."

He flinches like I hit him in the gut, turns away from me, and gets on his bike. He kicks it to life like he wants to kill the thing. I climb behind him. He revs the engine and takes off. I hold on tighter than I should. He gets to my car way too fast. He stops—doesn't get off to help me or kiss me good-bye.

I slide off the bike.

"I'll call you." He tears fast into the night.

I drive home super-slow and careful, imagining Derek's body mangled under that stupid bike all the way.

chapter 25

REPRISE

He doesn't call. Two weeks. Nothing. If we're over he should at least tell me. I resist calling him. Total invitation to get dumped. He's not online anymore. I think he's blocking me. He's with her again—I know it. They're together talking about me. Laughing. That song I started gets another verse.

> *Don't take it away.*
> *Don't twist me in knots and run.*
> *What else can I say?*
> *Again? Please can I be your one?*
> *The only girl who feeds you—*
> *The girl you said you need, too.*
> *Don't break my heart.*
> *Give me a new start.*

It so doesn't go with that other chorus. Time for a bonfire. My eyes land on Derek's rose lying on my desk. No. I'm not burning that. I'm never burning that. But all the garbage, crap, awful, stupid lyrics I've got scratched on scraps of paper and the backs of notebooks—incineration time.

Scott keeps flirting with me at school. My heart's breaking, and he won't let up the pressure. Not that I tell him my heart's breaking. He would so take advantage of that. Little brat. He's nice to everyone at school but me. He was talking to a nerdy-looking kid who looked familiar one morning.

"See you at practice then." The kid walked off down the hall.

"Who was that?" I watch the kid disappear into the crowd, trying to figure out who he reminds me of.

"You don't recognize him clothed?"

"That kid was the offering?" That awful morning still makes me cringe. "What are you doing with him?"

Scott shoves his hands in his pockets and shrugs. "I helped him get into Quiz Bowl. He's smarter than he looks."

"Thanks for rescuing us last spring." I lean against my locker and study Scott. "Who else have you rescued?"

His ears get red. "I wish you'd let me rescue you again."

"Come on. School's not bad this year with the Horsemen gone." My eyes follow the fluid movements of the muscles in his arms while he reaches for a text on the top shelf of his locker like I'm in a trance.

He turns his head, notices I'm staring. His blue eyes grab mine and won't let go. "You still need to be rescued."

I turn away. "Derek isn't Colby." I chuck my notebook at the back of my locker.

"He's worse." Scott grabs my elbow and spins me around. "He'll hurt you way worse—don't—"

"Shut up." I jerk free of him and slam my locker door. "You don't know anything about it." I stalk away in a huff.

Who am I kidding? Scott does know. He sees the pain I'm in. He sees everything. Like that kid—the offering. All I saw was Colby's tool. Scott saw a person. He made sure his poor, humiliated soul had a place to heal.

That sounds awfully good to me right now. Beautiful even. I remember dancing against him at prom. His face on my chest. Him shoving Colby away from me. Our kiss on the front porch. How wonderful I felt when I finally figured out he wanted that kiss. The look on his face when I told him about Derek.

Derek. I'm committed to him. I love him. I'm not ready to give up on him. He'll heal my heart. I don't need Scott. Derek will be back? No. Be positive. He *will* be back.

Monday after school I turn into my driveway, and Derek pulls up behind me on his bike.

I'm out of the car and all over him before he even gets his helmet off. He's into it, too. "You scared me."

He kisses my ear and whispers, "I'm sorry."

I kiss the side of his face. "Don't ever do that again."

"I had to go away."

"To a land with no telephones or Internet?"

He nods, and I'm so eager to get back to his lips that I believe every word. "I thought I'd screwed it up."

"We should get out of the street."

I lead him into the house.

We're still making out, lying in each other's arms on the family room couch when Mom pulls up. I'm on my feet, running out to talk to her, breathless and giddy. "Derek's over. Can he stay?"

"The night?" She's nervous about it this time.

"Dinner?"

"Of course."

Derek and I mess around, making dinner in the kitchen while Mom watches the news. He's playful and affectionate and makes really good pasta. Neither of us says much. Words are trouble. I'm so happy he's back that I don't care about anything else.

After dinner he wanders over to the piano. The Amabile folder lies on the bench. He sets it aside, glances up at me.

"I wanted it. I really did."

He nods. He sits down and begins to play. His fingers caress the keys and a delicate melody emerges. I've heard this song before. I sink onto the couch, close my eyes, and remember him humming it to me on our bench in Lausanne. He doesn't stop halfway through this time. It's whole and rich and stunning.

"You finished it."

Mom stands in the kitchen with a dirty plate in her hand. "That's a striking song. I don't know it."

Derek gets up from the piano. "It's just something I've been working on."

"It's a lovely piece."

"Thanks." He looks thoughtfully over at me. "It just needs words."

"Derek composes and arranges pieces for his choir."

"Is there anything Derek doesn't do?" Mom looks from him to me and back to him. She puts that last plate in the dishwasher and heads to her den. "Behave yourselves," floats down the hall from over her shoulder.

We flick on the TV, find an old movie, try to watch it, give up, and make out until Mom interrupts us.

"School tomorrow, Beth."

"Okay."

I walk Derek out to his bike. "Why'd you come back?"

"I didn't leave you, Beth." He hugs me. "Honest. I was going to call the next day." His words ache with sincerity.

I believe. I shouldn't, but there's too much love in his voice for doubt to survive. "So," I exhale, "what's next?"

"I don't know when I can get away again. We've got some cool gigs coming up. Maybe you can come to some of them." He caresses my face.

I'm so there—nodding as he speaks, but then I remember. "Crap. We're recording the next two weekends."

"I guess we'll have to make do online." His lips press against my temple. "Thanks for tonight. You don't know how badly I needed to see you."

"Me too."

"I can't believe you didn't tell me to take a hike."

"Me neither."

He kisses me, and I cling to him. When will I see him again? I can't let go of his lips. I get crazy, chewing on his mouth, sucking his lips and tongue, hard and desperate. I press myself into his body.

He groans, grabs my arms, and shakes me. "Do you know what you're doing to me?"

I just get his mouth again.

He pulls me tight. His kisses turn hard, overpowering. His grip on my arms hurts. What happened to my gentle boyfriend?

I should fight him, tell him he's hurting me, but I don't. I'm limp, completely in his control. He scares me, wild like this. He's always been so tender, so careful. I love this, too, though. I don't want him to stop. My beast slips its leash. I get as fierce as he is. Crap. Why is my mom home?

She flashes the porch light.

Derek's head jerks up off my neck. He shoves me away. I stumble, catch myself.

I'll have bruises on my arms in the morning. His neck will be a mess. We're both breathing hard.

He coughs as he gets on his bike. He won't even look at me.

What have I done?

Are we messed up?

I am the Beast.

He kicks his bike to life and drives away. No *good-bye*. No *see you later*.

No *I love you*.

Suddenly the mild October night is bitter cold.

I wrap my jacket close around me and walk slowly up the path to the porch, climb the stairs, and push through the front door.

Mom is waiting for me in the living room. "We need to talk, Beth."

"Not now." I'm a wreck, Mom. Please. I wander up the stairs to my room and fall face down on my bed.

She follows me, sits on the bed's edge, and strokes my hair. "I'm worried about you."

I'm so not having this conversation.

"Derek reminds me so much of your father."

I whip my face to the side and glare at her. "How dare you say that."

"It's true."

She's creeping me out. "Derek is not like him." I shudder against it. "Derek is perfect."

"I thought your father was perfect."

"But you were wrong—I'm not. Go. Away." I pull a pillow over my head.

"No." She lifts the pillow off and hangs on like she needs it for support. "Listen, I can see that your relationship is getting more serious. That you might be thinking about—"

"I don't want to talk about it."

"Neither do I."

"It's not like you're an expert or anything."

"I guess I deserve that. We should have had this talk a long time ago."

"We should have talked about a lot of things." But we didn't—I never wanted to upset her. She's always seemed so fragile to me.

"Linda and I were best friends through junior high and high school. Your father was a couple years older than us. I always had a crush on him. He was so cool—long hair, electric guitar—as irresistible as Derek is in his own way. Lots of girls. He had a reputation for getting what he wanted when he wanted it."

"And you liked that?"

"I knew he was pretty wild, but that made him all the more appealing. I—as you can imagine—was anything but wild. He didn't know I existed. I hung out at Linda's as much as I could just to get a glimpse of him."

I don't know what she's getting at. This is nothing like Derek and me.

"Summer after Linda and I graduated, he was home from college. Bored I guess. Linda and I were in the backyard tanning one day. I went in for a drink of water, and he saw me. I had on a new bikini. 'Look who's all grown up.' I don't think he even remembered my name. 'You still have it bad for me?'"

"He knew about your crush?"

"Linda must have told him. I flushed red, he put out his hand, the next thing I knew we were making out in his bedroom. He had my bikini off before I even knew what was happening."

"I don't want to hear this."

"All I remember about that first time was how much it hurt, how much I bled—"

I so didn't want to hear that. "It's like he raped you?" How can she think he's anything like my Derek?

"No. Took advantage? Yes. But I didn't try to stop him."

"You got pregnant from just that one time?" Was her whole marriage a myth?

She looks down at the pillow. "No."

"You went back?"

"All summer. There's an emotional side that goes along with the physical side. He said he loved me, and I—"

"Couldn't get enough of him?"

"I thought you'd understand now. That's how you feel about Derek, isn't it?"

I nod. I'm starting to see what she's getting at. Derek's not like my father. I'm like her. Now I need the rest of the story. "What happened? After the summer?"

"He went back to college, and I found out I was pregnant. When I called and told him, he gave me the address of an abortion clinic. I couldn't do that. Not to my baby. Our baby. I still loved him."

"What did you do?"

"I broke down and told my parents. They told his, and they forced him to marry me."

"And then I was born, and he hated me." Enter *damn ugly daughter*.

"He didn't love you. He didn't love me. He was totally consumed with himself."

"Derek's not like that."

"Are you sure? I'm not sure I like what's going on with you and him."

She sees way more than I give her credit for. I don't want to go down that path with her. I keep her on the defensive. "How old was I when my father ran out on us?"

She fluffs the pillow, turns and smoothes it gently into place on my bed. "He didn't run out on us." She brushes my hair off my forehead and swallows hard. "We left him."

"What?" I can't have heard her right. "I always thought—"

"You were such a beautiful baby. So sweet. So gentle. A little angel in my arms. I couldn't raise you in that atmosphere. I tried—overlooked a lot. I loved him. I finally realized we only had one option. I moved back home, went to college after all, and—"

"Here we are." The upside-down part of me is in motion. This sudden change makes me kind of dizzy.

She nods her head.

I study her face, finally see who she is. "I love you, Mom." I hug her. "Thanks for making me listen." Tears seep out of my eyes. I always thought she was weak, but she's strong—stronger than I dreamed of.

I need to rewrite an old song I made up about them. Make it true.

> *Now get away.*
> *Magic-carpet ride from this hell.*
> *Fly through the night,*
> *Build a place where together we'll grow.*
> *Just get away.*
> *Your beautiful daughter keep her far,*
> *Far from his sight.*
> *He's not the man we wanted*
> *To love.*
> *Get away.*

chapter 26

STUDY NOTES

The next couple months are crazy. We start recording the CD. It takes forever. Every time Derek invites me to a performance, I've got another recording session. We only manage to get together again once. We keep connected online, but then he'll disappear, sometimes for a few days, sometimes more than a week.

I don't ask anymore. Everything is so fragile right now. I don't want to make him angry. I can't risk losing him. I've decided I don't want to know. I'll close my eyes and savor what he gives me. It's not enough. Maybe someday we can figure out how to get more of each other. As the weeks pass, I grow grateful for every whisper over the phone, every line he writes, every stolen second we get.

I don't know why it has to be stolen and what I'm stealing him from. The time we got together it was here. He won't let me go to his house. I still haven't met his parents.

One night online he surprises me.

Derek: how'd you like to spend a whole weekend with me in
Toronto?
Beth: suddenly it's right?

Derek: I knew you'd take it like that
Beth: this isn't about sex?
Derek: shut up
Beth: only if you tell me how you'll know when it's finally right
Derek: easy . . . my mum says it's wrong unless you're married
Beth: you're a big boy . . . you don't have to do what Mommy says
Derek: you don't know my mum

"And why is that?" I ask the screen. I don't type it, though. Complaining only makes him disappear.

Beth: so you're asking me to elope to Toronto with you? let me
        check my calendar
Derek: maybe next time . . . this time I'm asking you to come sing
        with me again

I get all hot. Singing with him is such a rush—but how can I? I stare at the screen, imagining myself onstage with him again, letting our passion fill our song. I've got so much bottled up in me. It needs to get out somehow. But I wrecked that. Derek didn't give me the full scoop, but I could tell the AYS directors were angry.

Beth: I can't show my face around Amabile again
Derek: it's just the guys . . . they all still think you're the goddess
Beth: me and all those guys?
Derek: you and ME and all those guys . . . Saturday we've got a movie
        premier downtown TO, and Sunday we're doing a live CBC
        Radio broadcast

He is so nuts to think I can do that.

Beth: and you want me to muck it up?
Derek: I arranged "Beth's Song" as a duet with tenor/bass backup...
         I want you to write the words and then come sing it with me
Beth: I can't write lyrics good enough for that song
Derek: don't be stupid
Beth: you write it
Derek: I already did my part ... it's your turn

I can't. I can't. No way. I can't. I'm not hot anymore. Suddenly I'm really cold. Freezing cold. I start typing.

Beth: I've got midterms and a big project due ... our CD-release
         concert is coming up
Derek: this is important
Beth: I can't do it ... all I've ever written is bits and pieces ...
         fragments ... and most of it's hideous and sappy
Derek: apply yourself ... you're wasting your talent

Just because he can write, doesn't mean I can. He talks about music flowing out of him. I have to squeeze out every word. And it's still bad.

Beth: what talent? I'd ruin your song
Derek: no you won't ... you've got plenty of time ... if it stinks, I'll tell
         you and you can try again
Beth: that sounds like great fun
Derek: that's how it works ... I can't remember the date, but it's after
         your Thanksgiving ... the second weekend of December I think

Am I relieved? Disappointed? A mixture of emotions surge in choppy confusion.

Beth: that's when our concert is . . . we're doubling it for our
        Christmas concert
Derek: shoot . . . you did that on purpose

I need to give him something. I flip to the calendar. Sunday's free—totally.

Beth: how about I take the train up to Toronto on Sunday and
        watch your broadcast? that would be cool
Derek: come Sunday and sing with me
Beth: please, just let me hide out in the crowd . . . I'd love to be your
        groupie
Derek: NO . . . I'll email you the music
Beth: I can't

He ignores that last post—I'm sure of it. Within three minutes there's an email in my inbox with an attachment.

I hit reply and type, "There's absolutely no way on earth I can do this."

It's late. I'm whipped, and his hyper-confidence in me makes me angry. It sounds cool—him and me singing a song we wrote on the radio. What I wouldn't give to do that. But that song is too beautiful, means too much. My words would clunk against his music. I don't have beauty inside me like he does. I'm the Beast. Ugly. That's all I can write.

Since that night when I told him I couldn't leave Bliss and we fought in the park, I've been patient and understanding. Crap. I haven't even met his mom. I've let him get away with it. It's all exactly how he wants. He's not going to make me do this.

Next morning I get a text from Derek on my way to my locker to dump my backpack: try 2 lines

I chuck my bag into the locker. "Crap." I key in: 0 lines and mash the send button.

Scott arrives in time for that performance. "I don't like the way he treats you."

"It's none of your business."

"I have to see you like this every day."

"Like what?" I jerk my head around and glare at him. "I'm *fine*."

He frowns and leans against his locker. "Uptight. On edge. Isolated—even from me."

I scowl at him. "I'm really happy with Derek."

"Deliriously. I can see that." Scott folds his arms across his chest.

"When we're together—"

"Doesn't seem to happen much." He leans toward me. "What's with that guy?"

"We're both really busy."

"Too bad. Maybe you should look closer to home."

"You'd like that, wouldn't you?"

Scott's surprised. I haven't given him an opening like that for weeks. He steps closer. "We'd be together whenever we want. At school and after. Weekends." His dark blue eyes get intense. "If you would just let me in."

"I'm busy, though. My choir and the CD. Not to mention all these AP classes I'm taking this year."

"We study well together. Don't you miss that?"

I can't lie. I do.

"How about I come over this afternoon, and we can study for that econ exam we've got Thursday?"

"Maybe that's not such a good idea."

"Come on, Beth. He doesn't own you. You're not his puppet."

Exactly. "This is just to study?"

"Like old times."

"You know, Scottie." My old name for him slips easily out. "That would be nice. I have missed you."

"I'm here. Every day. I'm here."

The bell rings, and we head off to different classes. It's nice to have Scott acting like a friend again. I'm actually looking forward to seeing him in choir today. And he's a lot better at econ than me. I could use his help. My phone buzzes as I sit down. Derek.

1 line?

I painstakingly type, I'm not your puppet out in full and send it back to him.

After school, Scott and I walk out to my car together. "How is your history project going?" I ask to fill the nervous silence.

"So-so. It's kind of a dumb project."

We're supposed to look at how politics or governments were influenced by art or vice versa. "I like it. I'm studying how jazz influenced politics during the Depression."

Scott opens my door for me. "I got stuck with Stalinist-era Soviet art." He slams the door and goes around to the passenger side.

"Stalinist art sounds cool to me." I adjust my mirror while he gets settled. "You could tie it in with communist propaganda."

"Boring. It's not fair. You get to do music. You're an expert."

"Jazz?" I start Jeannette's engine and back her up. "Are you kidding? I sing choir music."

He laughs. "Some of it's jazzy."

"A gospel spiritual isn't jazz." I drive out of the parking lot.

"Want to trade topics?"

"No way."

"I rest my case."

When we pull up to the house, oh, crap, Derek is sitting in the driveway on his bike. Scott whips an accusing look at me.

"I didn't know he'd be here. I don't want to—"

"Rub my face in it?"

Derek's at my door before I can answer, opening it, pulling me up, and kissing me.

Scott is out of his side fast. "Are we still going to study?" He's got his backpack in his hand, looks ready to bail.

I twist around to face Scott. Derek keeps his arms around me. "Of course." I pat Derek's arm. "Scott and I have a big econ exam we need to cram for."

Scott glares at Derek. "You any good at econ?"

"Nope. Must be why I'm always broke." He squeezes me. "If you're busy, I'll take off."

"No."

Scott's face falls. Great. I can spend the next three hours studying with Scott or making out with Derek. And they both know it.

Derek reaches inside his jacket. "I'm just dropping this off." He pulls out some white pages folded in half. "I don't have to stay." He looks from me to Scott. "I don't want to get in your way."

He's taking this so wrong. "That's stupid. We're just studying." I lead the way into the house. "Come on, Scott. We're wasting time."

We spread out our notes and books on the kitchen table and get to work.

Derek wanders into the living room and sits down at the piano. He messes around, improvising jazz—slow, seductive stuff that makes it incredibly difficult to concentrate on econ.

Scott looks up from his notes. "Jazz, huh?"

I get pink and flip to the back of the chapter, hunting for review questions. "Ask me these."

Derek keeps playing. After a while, he comes into the kitchen. "When is your mum home tonight?" He glances at the clock.

"She's got a late meeting."

Derek opens the cupboard under the stove, pulls out a tall pot. "How about pasta then?"

Scott can't like seeing how comfortable Derek is in our kitchen.

"Sure." I turn to Scott. "Do you want to stay? Derek's pasta is pretty good."

Derek puts the pot in the sink and turns on the faucet. "The secret is to cook the pasta al dente and finish it in the sauce so it sucks up the flavor."

"Naw." Scott glares at me. "My mom's expecting me."

"He won't poison you—I promise."

Derek laughs. "Then what will I do with all this hemlock I've got chopped up?"

"You—" I point to Derek. "Shut up and let us study."

Scott and I struggle through another half hour, trying to decipher lecture notes with Derek humming and chopping and frying behind us.

"This is truly a culinary masterpiece." Derek walks around the island with a plate of steaming pasta in each hand. "Sure you don't want some, Scott?"

"I guess I better go."

Derek puts the plates down at the far end of the table. "I guess you better."

Scott slams his book shut and grabs his notes and backpack.

I look up at Derek. "We're not done."

Scott shoves his stuff in his pack. "I'll see you at school." He won't look at me.

I follow him to the door. "Thanks. Maybe we can finish Wednesday. I've got choir tomorrow."

His eyes are full of hurt. "You want to?"

"I can't get that stuff in Chapter Six."

The pain in his eyes eases. "Okay." He drops his voice. "My house?"

"Sure."

Derek is sitting, staring at the steam rising from his pasta. "How long has this been going on?"

"What do you mean?"

"Private tutoring."

I take a big bite of pasta and chew.

"At least now I know why you say you're too busy to work on this with me." He lays the folded-over sheets of paper on the table between us.

I swallow. "School is crazy hard this semester. And econ is my worst, deadliest subject."

"You seemed to enjoy it with Scott."

"Why were you so nasty to him? I thought you liked Scott—at least that I had such a good friend."

"I thought you'd be upfront with me. Going behind my back? That isn't like you."

"I need to preapprove all my study plans with you?"

He snorts. "Studying?"

"That's all we did." I put down my fork and glare at my plate of pasta.

Derek leans closer to me. "And what did you do last night or the one before when I wasn't here?"

"That's a nasty thing to say." I turn my head and meet the storm in his eyes, unleash one of my own. "I'm not the one holding you at arm's length. I'm not the one who can't ever get together. I'm not the one who won't take his girlfriend over to his house to meet his parents. I'm not the one who disappears off the face of the earth for days at a time with zero explanation. I'm not the one who comes up with wild, impossible plans. I'm not the one—"

"Sorry. I thought you were." He puts down his fork, picks up the papers. "I'll quit bugging you." He stands up and looks around for his jacket.

"What do you think you're doing?"

"Getting out of your way. Call Scott and tell him I'm dumped, and you can finish whatever you two really planned to do." His face goes from angry to sincere little boy devastation. Quite an act.

"No way." I glare at him. "You're not getting rid of me that easy. Sit down and eat."

He obeys.

We both shovel pasta and chew.

He swallows first. "It's obvious. I'm making you miserable."

"That's not true."

He reaches across the table and touches my cheek. "That's not a happy face, Beth."

I catch his hand, hold it on my face. "If you would just—"

"It'll probably get worse before it gets better." He gets out of his chair and crouches next to mine.

I look down at his deep, tortured eyes, the concern spread across his brow. "*Will* it get better?"

"Maybe. No guarantees." He stands up. "Go be happy with Scott, and I'll disappear."

I get to my feet. "Don't you dare." I put both hands on his chest. "I couldn't live if you left me."

"No. Don't say that." He grabs a hold of my hands. His are cold. "Don't put that on me."

"Too late." I lean toward his trembling lips. "You're stuck." He lets me kiss him. "I'd rather be miserable loving you, than happy with anyone else."

He kind of devours me at that point. Good thing Mom keeps the kitchen floor so clean because we don't make it to the couch. We sink down, roll around, get lost in lips like we did back in Lausanne during that concert.

I sit up and squirm out of my hoodie so I've just got a tank left on. I skipped the bra today. He stares—then pulls me back down beside him. I meet his lips, wrap my legs around him. He kisses me back, then chews on my bare shoulder, smoothes his hands across my back. His lips slide to my neck, down my throat. He presses his face on my chest. I'm dying for his skin. I need to get my lips on his body. I unzip his sweatshirt, go for his T-shirt.

He grabs my wrists. "Don't do that."

I fight to get my hands free. He distracts me, kissing my lips again. I stop fighting him. He relaxes his grip but doesn't let go. We're locked together. I roll onto my back, bring him along so he's on top. I stretch my arms, with his still attached, up over my head, and go crazy kissing him. He lets go of my wrists, runs his hands down my arms—

I grab the back of his T-shirt, fast, yank hard.

He wrenches free, pushes away from me. "Damn it, Beth." He pulls his shirt back down, but I see the Band-Aid on his stomach—in the same place it was in Lausanne. "I said don't."

I lay on the floor stunned. Ice-cold misery flows through me, twisting the fiery passion that throbs me into stark pain.

Damn it, Beth.

Damn it, Beth.

Damn it, Beth.

Then Derek is back on me, but he's not the same person now. His kisses are too deep, out of control. He presses his body against mine, too hard, jamming me into the unyielding tile floor. I go nuts, try to fight him off. He fights back—overpowers me.

I yell, "You're hurting me, Derek!"

He groans and rolls on his side. "Damn it, Beth. I don't want to hurt you." He grabs his hair and kind of chokes. "I don't want to hurt you, but—"

I scramble to my feet and gather up my sweatshirt. I hurry to the far side of the room, turn, holding my sweatshirt up like a shield. My other arm is out, hand raised to ward him off. I'm trembling, terrified. *Damn it, Beth. Damn it, Beth.* That's all I can hear. He's saying something else, but it doesn't get through.

Isn't this exactly what I want? What I've dreamed of? What I've begged him for? Why am I flipping out? I want the heat to surge again, but it's frozen into a dagger, cutting me inside. "Go away, Derek."

"Damn it, Beth. We can't leave it like this." He starts to cough.

I run up the stairs to my room, lock the door, press against it. I brace for him to follow and pound on it, knowing I'll let him in, remembering I love him, reassuring myself I want this. He'll be gentle. He'll be sweet. He won't hurt me.

He'll tell me everything after this. We'll share everything after this.

I wait and wait.

No steps on the stairs.

No gentle knock.

No voice whispering that he loves me, he wants me, he needs me.

Only the creak of the kitchen door and the brutal sound of his motorcycle tearing open the silence of the night.

chapter 27

TREATMENT?

I hate my mother for telling me all that crap about my father.

I hate him for calling me *damn ugly*.

I hate Derek.

I hate music.

I hate singing.

I hate pasta.

I hate Lausanne and Lake Geneva and stone benches.

I hate Scott.

I especially hate AP econ.

I fall asleep before I finish the list—before I come to the only person I really hate. This morning I stare at her in the mirror and see the truth.

It messes you up. Derek's famous advice about sex. We didn't even manage to do it, and we're utterly messed up. I'm massively messed up.

And Derek? What about Derek? Crap, he's messed up, too. Why would he curse me out over his T-shirt? Does he really never want to do it with me? Am I that gross after all? I think back through it all, over and over and over.

Was it that Band-Aid on his stomach exactly where it was in Lausanne that made him angry? It's so not a mosquito bite. Could it be a scar?

Why the Band-Aid then? Is it a needle mark he doesn't want me to see? What kind of scary drugs do you inject into your stomach? Over and over, exactly in the same place?

The whole thing is so, so disturbing. I don't even know how to feel anymore. What I wouldn't give to peek under that little flesh-colored vinyl strip.

When I see Scott at school, I break my date to study with him.

"He won't let you?"

"I'm not being fair to you. I'm with Derek. Nothing is going to change that."

Scott closes his locker with a clang, steps so close I can smell his citrus cologne, and whispers, "We'll see."

The rest of the day, he's funny, cute, friendly Scott again. He brings his econ notes to lunch and goes over the stuff in Chapter Six with me. In choir he can't get his tenor part. He scoots his chair up against mine and leans over so we're almost cheek to cheek—so he can hear me sing his part better.

"Why don't you hate me?"

He shrugs his shoulders. "Masochist."

I laugh. "Thank you, Prince Charming."

"Any time, Beauty."

Here he is saving me again. I should love him. I really should. I wouldn't have made it through the day if not for him.

As I drive down to choir, all I can think about is that Band-Aid on Derek's stomach. Guys don't use Band-Aids. If it was a cut or a mosquito bite, why would he care if I saw it? Why is it still there?

It all seems . . . medical.

The Band-Aid.

The cough.

The weight loss.

The pale, pale skin.

The mysterious disappearances.

Even his advice about doctors. Those pills he's always popping. Dumb Blake and his idiot *drug habit*.

It all adds up. Not to an addiction, but to an affliction.

I couldn't live if you left me. And what did he say? *Don't put that on me.*

Is he planning on leaving me because he's . . .

No, that can't be right. Oh, gosh. He could be sick. Really sick. Not just allergies or a cold that goes away.

For an ugly second, I worry if I could catch it. What is it? Could he have HIV? That's why he won't—no, no. Not that. Diabetes. They stick themselves all the time. It's probably just that. Are diabetics pale? Do they cough? Maybe it's leukemia. He can go to a hospital and get treatments. He's going to be fine. People recover from leukemia. Bone marrow. He just needs new bone marrow.

It will get worse before it gets better.

That fits.

He can't be that sick, though. Most of the time, he's fine. He just coughs. It's bronchitis or something. Maybe mono. But mono's catching. He'd tell me if he had mono.

What disease makes you cough?

Just dumb stuff like colds, flu, pneumonia. I had that once. I coughed forever. Old smokers cough. But that doesn't work for Derek.

Why won't he just tell me?

I can't bring it up—confront him. Not for a while. Not after last night. We need to get back to where we were before I threw him out. Oh, crap. I threw him out.

Late in the night after choir, I check for Derek online, but he's not signed on. I write him a text about wanting his body. I'm still kind of crazed. Delete it. Simply send, I miss you, and go to sleep.

In the morning, I check my cell. Nothing gushy and sweet in reply. No voice-mail messages. No posts. No email. I'm scared. After everything that happened Monday night, I need to know that he's all right with me—that we're all right—before he slips off into that awful nothingness. I promise not to ask about the phantom Band-Aid on his stomach. Crap. It could have been there all along. He's always got a sweatshirt on. Or a thick leather jacket. We've been dating for a few months now, and I've never been close enough to him to see his bare chest. Isn't there something wrong with that? I feel dread in the pit of my stomach. His anger. His violence, even. There's just so much about Derek I don't know.

But I won't ask. I promise to be the perfect, pure thing he asked me to be back in Switzerland.

What else can I do? I love him.

Days go by.

Weeks.

How can he expect me to bear this? I'm helpless, delusional, don't know where he is, what's happened to him, what's happened to us. Are we messed up forever? This silence shakes me up. It's so much longer and louder than before. I can't break into it.

Stuff starts showing up on his profile. He hasn't posted since before that night with me, but his friends start adding messages. There's one from his AYS ex: You're going to make it. I love you. That one makes me scream.

Blake posts, Hang in there, bud. It's going to work this time.

There's a bunch of Come back soon! and We miss you! kind of stuff.

At least I know he's alive somewhere. I don't post. No way. Too public. Too humiliating that I don't know what's happening. That he doesn't want me to know. Won't let me know. I stuff his inbox with private messages that get more and more pathetic as each day passes.

It's sounding more medical—scary medical. I'm so stupid. If I would have joined the AYS like Derek wanted, I'd be chummy enough with those girls to have a link independent of Derek to find out what's going on—no matter what he's told them I can't hear.

I think about phoning Blake. Try it once. He doesn't answer. Derek's orders? I don't know.

How can he do this to me? Just cut me off. I'm his girlfriend, aren't I? Maybe not.

His ex posted "I love you" on his wall for all the world to see.

Maybe he's back with her. Maybe he thinks I'm with Scott. Maybe he's paying me back.

No. He believed me that night. I'm sure. I have to keep believing. He'll appear in my driveway on his bike like he always has before. Be patient, keep loving him—keep resisting Scott.

Scott's not making it easy. He's there at school, every day, warm and friendly and real. His muscular shoulder is right next to me all the time, bumping into me. He's always joking around. No way can I let him suspect what's going on with Derek. If he offered to comfort me, I'd let him and then what would I tell Derek?

I delude myself, pretend everything is cool and that I know where he is and what's up. I send Derek a dozen texts every day, email him what's up with me. No questions. No complaints. He'll be back. Any day. Any second. I almost convince myself.

I download the sheet music he sent me for "Beth's Song," study it, hum the melody with a pen poised ready for inspiration, but I can't fool myself that much. I throw down the pen and stare at the wall.

I search my room—gather up all my pathetic efforts at song writing that I meant to burn. Maybe I can pull something from one of these. I read through my scrawls.

I'm bones, blood, and flesh

Not clay to be pounded....
I bleed when you wound me....
Can this be me?
Taking the stage for gold dreams....
Touch the sky?
Who am I kidding?... The dream turns to dust
As I bow to do your bidding....
Can she be beautiful?
Will all the people love me?...
Beautiful prince who says
He'll keep me warm—

I come to the verse I wrote after the prom about Scott: *The scent of you on my fingers / Makes me crazy while it lingers.*

Scott loves me. Scott wants all of me. He doesn't expect me to do this stuff I just can't do. It's way too hard to go on with this masquerade. I grab "Beth's Song" and tear the pages in half again and again and again.

It's too late, anyway. Derek's broadcast is this weekend.

I go on the Amabile guys' Web site and print off the details. I told him I'd be up on the train. If he's anywhere, he'll be there. I don't know if I have the guts to confront him, maybe lose him, but I have to see him again soon or I'll lose my mind. I Google it and manage to buy myself a one-way ticket online. I'll get a taxi to take me where they're singing and make Derek take me home.

What will he do when he sees me there in the audience invading his turf? That's how it feels. I know it's stupid. Why am I going? Why don't I just leave him alone? Call Scott. No. Derek wanted me there. Correction, he *wants* me there.

———

Saturday evening our early Christmas concert to celebrate our debut CD's release is packed. Halfway through our first number, Scott slips into the back and stands by the usher. He smiles at me and gives me a thumbs-up. I smile back at him and feel like I'm totally betraying Derek.

We get through the first half and swish off the risers, a mass of shimmery crimson in our gowns that still feel new and special. We file out of the room. I hope the people in the audience don't want their money back. I'm singing fine, but I can't find the magic that transforms me and the power to bring them along. Our CD is for sale in the foyer. Maybe I've just killed its success.

We crowd into the big room in the back of the building with faded Bible pictures taped to the wall that we use for a dressing room. It's better than the basement, but not by much.

I pick up a water bottle and go over to a window, stare into the dusk while I gulp it down. I set the bottle on the sill and put my forehead against the cool glass.

"Hey, Beth—look what I found." Sarah waves me over to an old TV in the corner. "It's them. Oh, gosh, there's Blake."

I turn and stare at her.

"Did Derek tell you they were going to be on TV?"

I feel like I'm moving underwater, but it's thick, like honey, won't let me through. Somehow I'm across the room peering through the blurry TV at Derek in his tux standing in the middle of his choir, singing at the movie premiere in Toronto. He's incredibly pale. Almost blue. Maybe it's the lighting. He looks ultrathin, too.

Crap. He looks so sick. How could I have been so blind all this time? Blinded. That's what it was. Totally blinded. I saw what he wanted me to see.

Sarah turns to me. "Derek looks awful. What's wrong with him?"

"I don't know."

She looks at me funny. Other girls crowd around now, pushing to see. While we're watching, Derek sways and pitches forward. He'd be flat on his face if the two guys next to him didn't have quick reflexes.

I make a weird startled sound.

The camera cuts away to the director. Mr. Tall Wispy Beard keeps going like the guy I love didn't just turn white as death and keel over. When the camera goes back to them, the boys are singing as if nothing happened, except Derek and his two rescuers aren't in the picture.

The whole choir stares at me. I'm frozen. I've got to move. I've got to get up there. Now. How far is it? Will Jeannette get me all the way to Toronto? Of course. She's solid, but how will I find him?

I don't care. I don't care. I don't care.

I thaw enough to hold out my hands. "I need cash."

Girls in long shimmering red run to purses, shove fives and tens in my hand. Meadow's got a stack of twenties.

I grab my purse and jacket and head to the back door. "Tell Terri I'm sorry. You guys can do it without me."

"Your gown!" Leah calls. I'm not supposed to go outside in it, but to hell with that. I'll try not to drag it through the snow and mud in the parking lot.

I push through the door and plow smack into Scott.

He catches me by both elbows. "How did you know I was out here?"

"Let me go, Scott." I try to wrench away. "I have to leave."

"Are you okay?"

I can't answer him.

He still doesn't let go. "Listen, Beth. I'm just going to say this one more time. I'm here. Look around."

"Let me go!" I flail my arms and break his hold. "I don't have time for you, Scott." I turn and rush away, cringe at how cruel those words echo in Scott's stunned silence behind me.

He shouldn't have gotten in my way.

He shouldn't have gotten in my way.

He shouldn't have gotten in my way.

If I say it enough, I'll believe it. Maybe even he will, too. As much as my heart is racing for Derek, I don't want to hurt Scott. I care for him—more than I should. And I owe him. He'll never know it, but he rescued me again and again during this impossible blank time.

As I speed up I-94, the numb shock that got me out of the concert and onto this freeway pushing Jeannette to her max speed warps into absolute terror. What ravaged Derek like that? What's taking him away from me? He said it would get better. I believed and believed and believed. Crap. He just fainted on TV, and they all kept on singing.

I'm going to find him and force him to tell me everything. No more nice, purring Beth making believe everything's fine, waiting and waiting and waiting. The Beast is loose, and she's not going back in her cage.

My cell rings as I'm passing that dumb giant tire marking the outskirts of Detroit.

"What in the world—"

"I don't even know, Mom. It's Derek. I'll probably stay up there."

"Where?"

"I'll call back when I know."

I get all the way to the border before I realize I don't have a clue where I'm going. There's a line of cars way backed up, so I start dialing Blake's cell. Over and over and over. He finally picks up.

I yell, "Where did they take him?"

"Beth?"

"I'm on my way. What hospital?"

"They're going back to London." Blake's voice is maddeningly calm.

I pound on the steering wheel with my free hand. "All the way to London? Are they crazy?"

"The bleeding stopped. He's okay."

"Bleeding?" Oh, my gosh. "Are you in the ambulance with him?"

"What ambulance?"

A car honks behind me. "Stop confusing me." I pull Jeannette forward.

"His parents took him back down to the lockup in London."

"Crap—he's in jail?" Is it drugs after all?

"Geesh. You're stunned." Blake laughs. The creep laughs. "You know that's what he calls the hospital."

"The lockup?"

"We sprung him for this weekend. He refused to miss it."

I'm pressing the phone so hard into my ear it hurts. "He was in the hospital!" I yell into the phone.

"How can you not know that?" Blake yells back at me. "He practically lives there."

I pull forward again as a sleek black sedan rolls through the border crossing.

Blake is still ranting at me. "What kind of a crap girlfriend are you?" His vicious tone rips me apart. "You should have been there with him every second you can. He needs the motivation to hang in there. Look at today."

"It's not my fault." I bang the steering wheel with my hand. "You can't blame me. He doesn't tell me anything."

"Oh, sheesh." Blake doesn't say anything for a long moment. "You don't know."

The cell slips in my sweaty hand. I grapple with it, get it back jammed to my ear. "Tell me what he has, Blake." My voice cracks. "I'm going crazy." I'm trembling, trying to control myself from breaking down with the shock that's starting to register.

"Forget I said anything." The jerk hangs up on me.

I throw my phone into the passenger seat and pull forward. Three more cars to go. Two more. One more. My turn. I pull up to the Canadian border booth thing and roll down my window.

A friendly looking guy in his twenties puts his hand on my roof and leans over to speak through the window. "Passport, please."

"Passport?" The Canadians up at our crossing at Port rarely want ID.

"You locals need to learn."

I fumble in my purse and grab my wallet. "Please." I shove my license at him. "My boyfriend's in the hospital."

"You're in love with a Canadian?" Oh my gosh—is he flirting?

I just nod.

He gives me back my license. "I hope he's okay. Godspeed."

I get a lump in my throat as I drive off. I sniff and rub my eyes. *Pull it together, girl. You've got to drive.* I glance down at my gas gauge. Shoot. All I've got are American dollars. I pull off at one of the gas stations in Windsor past the border crossing. They're happy to take my dollars— rip me off on the exchange. I buy a big bottle of water and some gum. I should eat, but the smell of stale chips, cookies, and jerky blended with diesel churns my tense guts into knots.

As I head up the 401 in the deep cold of a black night, I try to stay calm, but the border guy undid me. Tears attack. Burn my eyes and face. It starts to snow. Dumb snowbelt. Stupid Great Lakes. Stupid winter. I so don't need this tonight. I follow the signs to London, push Jeannette up to seventy-five, as the snow falls thick and fast, deadening the sound of our passage, but it doesn't muffle the way I'm crying. Snot runs down the back of my throat and then over my lips. I catch it before it drips off my chin and stains my blood-red gown.

I have to stop this. I'll scare Derek looking like this. I don't want him to know—

But I do.

He needs to know.

He should see the destruction. I've felt like a ball of hot tears and snot inside all this time. Why not let it out? Let him see. No more pretenses. No more faking it. He has to let me in.

If he loves me at all, he needs to see this. This mess I've become.

I curse and cry and yell stupid things at him. He's sick, and I'm flipping out livid at him. I hit a drift that throws a sheen of snow into my headlight's beam. Jeannette gets pulled hard to the side of the road, but I crank the wheel, get my old girl straightened out and back up to speed.

Jeannette and I fight through drift after drift, me sobbing, her engine throbbing, the two solid hours it takes to get to London from the border. My voice is wrecked by the time I flick on my signal and take the Wonderland Road exit.

I plan to stop at a gas station and raid the yellow pages for hospitals, but I see it before I even spot a pay phone. Red brick sprawling giant off to the right. I slow down and turn in, follow the maze into a visitors' parking lot, and shut off the car. I pull my pink choir T-shirt out of my bag and wipe my face with it. I catch a glimpse in the rearview mirror. All the makeup's rubbed off. I reach for at least a cover stick. Stare at it. A bitter laugh erupts from my throat. I toss the magic wand aside.

I bang through the glass doors, into the florescent-lit lobby, and march over to a chubby middle-aged guy with a red face under an INFORMATION sign. "Derek Collins, please."

"Derek, huh?" He types in the name. "Only family allowed up." He notices my dress, and his eyebrows shoot up. "It's late for a hospital visit."

"I'm his sister."

"Another one? My old buddy, Derek, has got to tell me how he does it." He hands me a map with a room starred on it. Then he notices my face, my ski jacket thrown over a shimmering gown, and compassion fills his eyes. "I'm sorry. You head right upstairs and cheer him up."

Am I the only girl on earth who's never been here?

"Tell that boy he owes me three chocolate bars for this."

I run away from his friendly voice. Get on an elevator. Stare at the map. Crap. This can't be right. I ask a young red-haired guy who pushes a cart of pills onto the elevator at the next floor for help. I show him the room number, helplessly.

"That's Derek's room."

"Why does everyone here know him so well?"

"We have our favorites. And that kid—the way he comes back and sings to everyone, brings his friends. We're all pulling for him."

My eyes are blurring up again. The guy reads my gross red-blotched, puffed-fat face and how I have to bite my lips to keep them still. "Here. I'll take you."

He puts his freckled arm out for me to grab onto and leads me down a long corridor, up another, through a bunch of doors into another elevator. He hustles me past the nurses' station.

I want to hug him by the time we're standing in front of the door that matches the room number written on my map. He opens the door and pushes me inside and pulls the door closed behind me.

Derek's there, lying in a hospital bed, with a mask strapped on his face. He has to fight to get each breath in. His face looks blue against the stark-white hospital sheets. His damp hair stands out dark against his pale skin. His eyes are closed. The eyelids are purple, and he's got dark shadows under his eyes. His long black lashes look wet. There's a bag of clear liquid hanging on an IV pole. My eyes follow the narrow tube out the bottom of it to where it turns into a syringe sticking into his chest. There's another pole holding up a bag of yellowish murky stuff. It has a tube, too. A bit fatter. That tube disappears under the sheets. Oh, gross. I think it's going into his stomach—where that Band-Aid was. I peer at his face. Tiny clear tubes run into each nostril.

I must have made a noise—a sharp intake of my breath. Maybe I sniffed.

His eyes open, and they focus on me. "No, Beth." He closes his eyes again.

"*No?*" I say it too loud, too harsh.

"Not you."

"Who else?" I'm losing control.

He pulls down the mask he was breathing into so he can talk better. "You're not supposed to see this." His voice is thick and raspy. "Go away."

"Look at me." I move to the foot of his bed. "Open your eyes, *damn* you." It's my turn to curse. My turn to scream.

He won't open his eyes.

I go around to the side of his bed and pry an eyelid open. His skin is hot and slick, but I persist.

He sees me well enough. He turns his face away.

My fingers slip into his dark, damp hair. I lean down and speak in his ear. "This is what you're doing to me."

"Go away."

"It's not that easy."

He turns to face me, brushes my face with his fingers. He holds me there with the love deep in his feverish eyes until I can't bear it anymore.

I turn away this time, stumble over to a chair by the door, and break down.

"Oh, Beth." He struggles to speak. "Please, Beth. Don't cry like that."

I jump to my feet, fear fueling that anger I uncovered in the car.

"What am I supposed to do?" I screech in his face. "Tell me, Derek. Whatever it is—I have to know."

"I didn't want this to happen."

"That's so stupid." I scream. "I love you. How can you be so cruel?" I whip my head back and forth and keep yelling. "I hate you for doing this. I hate you." I lunge at him with my fists balled up, screaming, "Stop lying. Damn it, Derek. Stop!"

The door to his room flies open. A short, sturdy woman with Derek's eyes darts into the room and gets between me and Derek's bed. "Control yourself, young lady." She grabs my wrists. "I don't know who you think you are or what you think you're doing here, but you need to get your evening gown theatrics out of my son's room."

I stare at her. "But I'm Beth."

She lets go of my arms. "We don't know any Beth." She herds me toward the door.

"Derek!" He can't lie there and let her do this to me.

"Stop, Mum."

"She doesn't even know who I am." My knees buckle, and I sink to the floor, crimson gown and all.

His mother whirls around to face Derek. "Do you know this girl?"

"We met in Lausanne."

"No. You said Blake met a girl in Lausanne."

"Not like the one I met." He sucks in air and whispers. "She's the best thing that ever happened to me."

Hearing that makes my tears start again. His mother stares at me and then back at him. "You didn't tell her? Oh, Derek. How could you do that?"

She comes back to me, helps me up, and hugs me. "I'm sorry, honey." She keeps an arm around me, and I lean against this woman I don't know. Maybe she'll tell me—if Derek won't.

From his bed, Derek struggles up onto an elbow. "I was going to tell her once I got back on the active list, but it's taking way too long. Go away, Beth. Forget you were here. I don't want you in this world."

Active list? What is that? I'm sure he thinks I'll leave him here like this—that I'll ever leave him again. "How can—"

"Hush, dear, he doesn't mean it." His mom turns back to him. "It may never happen. You have to tell her—now." I like this woman. A lot. She emanates sense and strength.

She leads me back over to Derek's bed, leans over him, smoothes his hair off his forehead, and kisses the spot.

She squeezes my arm, bites her lower lip, and leaves us alone.

chapter 28

TRUTH

I'm not angry anymore. The terror returns.

"Can you go back to the chair and sit for a minute." The only thing I hear in his voice is utter weariness. "I need to finish this." He puts the mask back on, lays his head on his pillow, and breathes, with kind of a gasp and a rattle, into his mask.

I move the chair close beside his bed and take his hand. He worms it away so he can hand me the tissues from his bedside table. I use up half the box, wiping my runny face. Then I lay my cheek down on his upturned palm.

In a few moments he starts to speak. "Did you ever wonder why my skin tastes so salty?"

"No." I kiss his hand and lick my lips. "I just like it." I didn't get past Scott's mouth. Derek's the only guy I ever tasted.

"I was a really sick baby. Always a cold or pneumonia. I screamed all the time and wouldn't eat. Then I'd eat and eat and eat until I started screaming again."

"Poor Derek."

"My poor mum. My dad worked nights—even back then. She couldn't keep me quiet so he could sleep. And then I'd scream all night, too."

"What was wrong?"

"Nobody knew. Her doctor said she wasn't producing enough milk. Stuck me on formula."

My eyes go to the bag on the second IV pole. That's what the stuff in it looks like, baby formula.

Derek pushes the sheet down past his waist and pulls up his hospital gown. The tube is attached to a plastic disk embedded in his stomach. "Now you know why I always wore bulky sweatshirts, backed off when you got too close, went ballistic when you tried to take my shirt off." He notices my eyes following the tube to the bag of stuff on the pole. "It's a feeding tube. People with my condition need a lot more calories to thrive than normal people."

"But you eat. I've seen you."

"Not enough. I was a skeleton baby when the doctor finally stuck me in the hospital. One of the doctors suspected and gave me a sweat test." He nodded. "I have CF. That's why my skin tastes so salty."

I lift up my head. My face pulls into a knot. "But you're not in a wheelchair. I can't believe *your* brain is messed up."

"No. You're thinking CP—cerebral palsy. Cystic fibrosis, CF, makes all the mucous in your body extra-thick and sticky. That's why I cough."

"That could be allergies—or asthma."

"No, Beth. It's CF. It blocks up my pancreas and messes with my liver, too. I have to take a handful of enzymes if I want to digest anything. I was a snot-nosed brat who wouldn't eat, so Mum stuck me on the tube." He glances at the IV pole and bag. "I've been doing night feeds at home to keep my weight and growth normal since I was a kid."

"Then why do you have to be in the hospital now?"

He closes his eyes for a minute to nerve himself, opens them again. "I've got a jungle of exotic bacteria growing in my lungs."

"Why don't they give you antibiotics?"

"Like that?" He glances at the IV. "And that's what I just breathed in, too. I live on antibiotics." His face turns bitter. "Too much antibiotics."

"Your drug habit?"

He manages to lift his eyebrows. "That's just the beginning."

I sit up straight, wipe at my face, feeling stupid for not catching on that he was sick—not being here for him sooner. Blake was right. What kind of crap girlfriend am I? But it's going to be fine now. He's safe in the hospital, getting treatment. Antibiotics will fix him. I squeeze his hand. "Why didn't you tell me? You wouldn't believe what I've been going through."

"My whole life I've been the boy who was going to die." He struggles to pull air into his lungs.

Die? He's not going to die.

His scratchy voice continues, "All my friends know I'm going to die. My ex back in Amabile was the heroine because she loved the boy who was going to die. Every girl since junior high who liked me knew I was going to die." He coughs and lies back on his pillows.

I plaster a brave smile on my face. "But you're in the hospital. They are taking care of you. You're not going to die."

He squeezes my hand. There's no strength behind it. "I needed a place where I wasn't sick. Where I could just be the boy who loves you."

"I still would have loved you."

"Not the same way. I needed a whole heart once in my life. Is that so wrong?"

"You've got my heart." I get up so I can lean over him. "All of it." I smooth back his hair like his mom did. "And you're going to get better. I can help you now."

"My CF is kind of severe. I got listed for a double lung transplant two years ago."

I draw back, afraid. "They want to cut you open and take out your lungs?"

He nods. "Last spring, after we got pegged for the Choral Olympics, I took a real dive. Lots of hemoptysis—coughing up blood."

I try not to flinch. I don't think he noticed.

"The bacteria took control. I got a massive infection. They almost lost me twice."

My lips start trembling. I struggle to keep them still. Bite them. Hard.

"You better sit down."

I sink back in the chair, confused. Except for a bit of a cough, he was fine in Switzerland. And every time I've seen him since. He was always tired. Coughed a bit. Other than that, he seemed fine. But how much can you tell from a phone call or an online chat?

"My mom got me into a drug trial for a brand new cocktail of treatments—including a heavy dose of a new space-age antibiotic. I survived—that usually doesn't happen without a lung transplant. It's kind of a miracle I made it to Lausanne. My choir—wanting that trip—hearing your voice and deciding I had to find you—got me out of the hospital and onto that plane. Poor Blake." He sort of shakes his head, hardly moves it. "Our room was like a clinic."

I nod, starting to get there. "That's why you flipped about him taking Sarah there."

He touches the tubes that run into his nose. "I had to have oxygen on the plane—and all night and the mornings except when we performed." He weakly lifts a hand and points to a black mound of Kevlar on top of the dresser. "I took my vest and inhalation mask. Three times a day, I inhaled antibiotics and this stuff that thins your mucous, and then I was in the vest for twenty minutes."

"What does it do?"

"Moves the gunk in the smaller passages of my lungs into the bigger ones so I can huff it out."

"Huff?"

"Like a cough without a cough." He closes his eyes. "Before I got the vest, the guys used to put a piano bench on a flight of stairs and pound me. Blake's almost as good at it as my mum."

He's losing me. "You sang, though. Your voice was totally pure."

"I did extra treatments before performances. I spent the night in the hospital twice for IV antibiotics. Modern medicine is great."

He wasn't weak like this. I'm still confused. "How did you do that and keep up with the schedule?"

"I skipped out of most of the practices. I did performances and you."

"But after, you were so active."

"That might have been a mistake. I mean exercise is a good thing. My adrenaline cravings kept me strong and alive for years. I'd been so weak and sick, and suddenly I was alive again, relatively healthy again—and pumped full of you. You're better than any drug, Beth."

I shake my head.

"I went overboard after you left trying to keep up with Blake. Mountaintops aren't a smart place to be if you have trouble breathing. I had to take my portable O2 tank with me when we went snowboarding. I got a few good runs in, sucked oxygen in between them. It was my last shot to live."

He went overboard that last night with me, too. "We stayed out way too late. And then you had to go rescue Sarah."

"That wasn't so bad. I took a taxi. I took a lot of taxis in Lausanne. The only time I walked was with you. You just thought I was getting a cold."

"You totally faked me out."

"After I dropped Sarah off, I didn't go back to the hotel room—went straight up to the hospital. The Swiss doctors were great."

I remember him coughing as our bus rolled away the next morning.

"I crash-landed when I got home—right back to the hospital."

"No cottage?"

"I lied, Beth." His voice drops to almost nothing. "I lied a lot." He closes his eyes, exhausted from all this talking. "I don't expect you to forgive me." There are tears behind his words. "Say hi to Scott." He can't stop the pain that takes over his face.

"I'm supposed to leave now?" I should be livid. Angry. Hurt. Scared. I look at his pale, sunken face, tinged blue and bruised, his lips more purple than pink, watch as he takes a labored breath and tries to control his emotions. He looks so young—especially with his hair slicked back like that. There's nothing left of the confident singer, the intimidating composer, the sensitive boyfriend who wants to keep me a nice girl. He's just a small boy, and all I want to do is take care of him. He's not beautiful anymore; neither am I. But what I'm feeling inside is. I love him more than I ever did.

I lean over him again. "You're going to be fine now. I'm here."

His eyes flicker open. "I came to see you as soon as they let me out. Whenever I could escape"—his eyes take in the equipment around him—"this."

"How did you expect to keep me in the dark if I joined the AYS?"

"I think there was a part of me that wanted you to find out. They let me out for practice when I'm up for it. I planned on getting better, not . . ."

"I'm sorry. I would have been here, Derek. Every day."

"I know." He motions me close so I can hear him whisper. "The median life expectancy for CF patients is thirty-seven."

I swallow. "That gives us loads of time. Remember? You told me they're doing stuff with genetics."

"Thirty-seven is the median age. That means half of us die a lot sooner."

"Not you, though."

He puts his hand up to my face. "I can only father a baby in a test tube."

"You can't—"

"No. That works. The sperm can't get through my clogged tubes."

"So we won't have to worry much about me getting pregnant. You're the perfect guy for a mutant like me."

"Last spring after they saved me, I tested antibiotic resistant. I guess they used too much of that new stuff. That meant I had to go inactive on the transplant list until they can fix me."

"So you'll get better without them cutting you up?" I like the sound of that.

"Impossible."

"What?" I'm not believing him. "You did last spring—"

"That helped me . . . for a while. Mum's trying to get me reinstated on the active list. I don't think I'm going to make it."

I lay my face on his pillow. "Yes—you are." Derek dying? No way. It's not real. I won't let him. I kiss his salty face. "You are going to stay right here and do everything the doctors tell you to do."

"Story of my life." He shakes his head.

"You are never riding that motorcycle again. I'm going to sit beside you and make sure it happens."

He opens one eye. "In that dress?"

I glance down. "Do I look like a fool?"

"You're gorgeous. You don't have to stay. I already have a mum."

I stand up. "But you've been so stupid. Look at all the time we wasted."

"I thought you had school and your choir?"

"If we only have until you're thirty-seven—"

"Beth, stop—" He reaches out, and my cold hand meets his fevered one.

I bend over him and press my lips on his salty, dry mouth. "Your mom can't do that." I kiss him again. "You don't want to see the scene I'll pitch if somebody tries to make me leave."

"You'll stay for my sponge baths?"

"If they'll let me help."

"I'll get the nurses to train you—right away."

"You talk dirty when you're helpless."

"It's all I can do." He grins, but the pain and bitterness are back in his voice. He pushes a white button pinned to his bed where he can easily reach.

A nurse appears.

"Hey, Meg. This is Beth. You think you can find her some scrubs? She says she's moving into my lair."

The nurse, Meg, smiles at me. "I'll be right back."

I change in Derek's bathroom. The pants are way short and surgical green doesn't help my bright-red face much. I stare at my hideous reflection and promise myself Derek will never see me cry again. I wash my face and fix it best I can. Nothing close to beautiful.

I call our home phone. Good, Mom doesn't answer. I manage to say, "Derek's in the hospital in London. I met his mom. She's letting me stay over. He'll be fine," all in a fairly normal voice. I turn off my cell— hospital rules.

I hang my gown in his closet next to his tux.

Meg looks up from where she's working on Derek's IV. "I'd like to see you two at the ball."

"We sing," Derek says.

"Together?"

I swallow the lump in my throat and nod. I hope we can do that again. Wherever and whenever he wants.

Meg leaves us alone.

"My mum came back while you were changing. She was relieved you didn't strangle me."

I sit down in the chair. It's still where I left it close by his bed.

"I told her you wouldn't leave."

"What did she say?"

"Thank you. She's going home to sleep in her own bed."

My eyes dart around the room, expecting to find his mom hiding somewhere. "How can she leave you here alone like that? What if—?"

"You're here."

"*Me?*" She doesn't even know me.

Derek coughs. I can tell it hurts. He gasps for a minute.

I stand there helpless.

He whispers, "If I turn blue in the middle of the night, buzz for Meg."

"You're already blue, babe."

"Bluer."

"That's not funny." I want to hit his arm, but I don't dare. "I'm not staying if you're going to do that."

"But Mum's counting on you." He's not joking. "She needs a break. I knew you were bluffing."

I go over to the door and look up and down the hall. It's empty. I turn around. "They're leaving us together—all night? Is that allowed?"

"I'm kind of helpless here. I'm sure they figure you're safe."

"What about you?" I shut the door, lean against it with my hands pinned behind my back. "You're too weak to run away from me again."

"*You* ran away from *me*."

My eyes drop to the floor.

"I don't blame you, Beth. Who'd want this?"

I cross the room to his bed. "I won't this time." I plant my lips on his salty neck.

He whispers in my ear, "Probably a bit more excitement than I can survive."

I pull back—am I hurting him?

He manages a weak smile. "But that would be a good way to go. Do you want to take out my catheter or should I?"

I'm not sure if I'm laughing or crying. "You're gross."

"I tried to protect you as long as I could."

I slide back in the chair and try to get comfortable, cross my arms, and prepare to stare at him all night.

"What are you doing?"

"Settling in to watch for blueness."

He slides over in his bed. "I'll share."

"What if I get tangled up in your catheter?"

"Stay on your side."

I climb onto the bed and lie down next to him, roll on my side so I can study his face.

He pushes a button and the lights go out.

I kiss his forehead. "Good night."

"I can't sleep. Do you think—"

"I'm not touching that catheter."

"Could you sing to me?" He caresses my face.

I close my eyes. And sing.

> *I take me down to the river,*
> *The sweet, sweet river Jordan,*
> *Stare across the muddy water,*
> *And long for the other side.*

His fingers trace my cheekbones and eyebrows, they play over my lips while I sing, *Take me home, sweet, sweet Jesus. / And wrap me in your bosom*— His hand draws away. I pause, open my eyes, he nods, and I sing, *Lord, I long for the other side.*

Does he long for release like that slave girl? Is that why he loves this song? Is that why he loves my voice? *Take me home, take me home, take me home.*

No. Not allowed. He's not going anywhere. I change my tune, hum our duet. Sing to him,

> *It's gotta be, it's gotta be about you, you, you, you....*
> *I raise a kaleidoscope up to my eye,*
> *Twist it once and watch the bright colors fly, and the picture is so*
>   *clear—*
> *It's gotta be you.*

He sleeps. I don't. I lie there, wishing I'd never run away from him, wishing he'd come up those stairs to my room, wishing I'd left his T-shirt alone. My heart fills with the enormity of how much I care for him. I smooth his hair back and cherish him like a child while I sing with the slave girl again. *But my babe, Lord, my sweet child / Wraps his sweet, sweet fingers so tight around my heart....* I look up at the ceiling, close my eyes, and whisper, *He ain't ready for Jordan.*

Is anyone ever ready? Could I ever be ready to let him go?

No way. Never. He's staying here with me.

Pulls me back, pulls me back, pulls me back.

chapter 29

REALITY

I wake up. The room is still dark. Derek lies on his side with his head propped on one hand. He's tracing the features of my face lightly, barely touching me. He's close enough to kiss, so I do. He's not as hot now.

"Hey."

"Hey." I kiss him again.

"You taste kind of nasty in the morning."

I pull away from him and cover my mouth. "Recovered enough to be a brat. I liked you better helpless."

I kiss the top of his head. He raises his face and catches my mouth. He doesn't taste that great, either.

"How about we brush our teeth?"

I hurry into the bathroom. I've got a toothbrush and stuff in my bag because of the concert. I brush my teeth fast. My hair is a wild mess, but I don't have time for it. I find Derek's toothbrush in a shaving kit by the sink, load it up with toothpaste, fill a glass with water, and run a washcloth under warm water, wring it, and head back to Derek.

I catch him disconnecting the tube that goes into his stomach. I stand there dripping while he finishes. "You do that yourself?"

"Half my life." He pulls the sheet over the plastic port in his stomach.

"I used to have to thread a tube up my nose and down the back of my throat. This is easy."

I go to stick the toothbrush in his mouth.

He snatches it from me. "I'm not paralyzed." He presses a button, and the head of the bed raises until he's sitting up enough. He takes a maddeningly long time brushing his teeth. "Where am I supposed to spit?"

I whip a plastic cup off his bedside table and hand it to him. He gives me the toothbrush. I run to the bathroom to rinse it, so I don't have to watch him spit. Not really a turn on. Neither is a hole in your stomach. Or a syringe taped to your chest.

I get back as he's taking a last swig of fresh water. I pick up the wash-cloth—good, it's still kind of warm—and wipe his face. Slowly. Major turn on. Makes up for everything else.

"Now that feels good."

I move it down to his neck, run it over one shoulder. "About that sponge bath—"

He tugs me toward him and our lips connect. I manage to get myself onto the bed without breaking the kiss. The head of the bed lowers—smoothly—while his tongue slips softly into my mouth.

I'm lying kind of sideways—half on, half off him. I try to be careful. He's still so weak, and I don't want to bump the syringe that drips into the permanent port into his vein hiding just under the skin. "You're awfully good at making out in a hospital bed."

"Home-court advantage." His mouth captures mine again. His hand moves under the loose scrubs top I've got on and caresses my back. I didn't sleep in my bra. I savor his touch on my skin, kiss him harder—roll onto my back without falling off the bed and lie there waiting for him.

He shifts onto his side and caresses my stomach. I close my eyes—every part of me concentrating on his tender, pulsing fingertips.

"Would it kill you this morning?"

"You and your one track mind." His face clouds up. "Don't go there, Beth." He draws his hand away.

I groan.

He lets the mask drop. I see his longing and frustration. "It hurts too much." His face contorts. "Everything we won't have."

I roll on my side, take his face in my hands, and kiss him softly, as gently as I can, and whisper, "When it's right."

He turns his face away. "It won't be, Beth. All I am is disease."

He lets me kiss him again. I whisper, "Once upon a time there was a hideous beast who met a handsome prince. The prince saw the Beast's agony and bestowed on it his magic kiss."

"I'm the Beast, Beth."

"Shhh." I place my fingers over his mouth. "The magic kiss changed the Beast forever. She became human. She learned to love and loved the prince with all her heart."

"And he loved her."

I hold his eyes as I say, "And they *will* live happily ever after."

He doesn't argue, lets me kiss him again. And again. And again.

There's a sound at the door, and I jump up, flushed and breathless.

His mom, followed by a solid man about Derek's height with silver and dark-brown hair, enters the room. My face burns and my antiperspirant fails.

"Hey, Dad." Derek relaxes back on his pillows as if they didn't just walk in on us making out in Derek's hospital bed. "Meet Beth."

His dad nods at me and winks. Why do these people like me so much? He actually walks over to me and kisses me on the cheek. "Welcome to the team." He squeezes my elbow and smiles Derek's melting smile.

His dad turns to Derek and raises an eyebrow. "Rough night?"

Derek reaches for my hand. "Slept like a baby."

His mom takes up station on the other side of the bed. She examines his empty bag of formula on his feeding IV pole. "Did you take your meds yet?"

"No, Mum. You even beat Meg here."

"She's late." She goes off to find the nurse.

His dad sits down in my chair.

Derek puts the head of his bed up again. "How was work?"

His dad shrugs. "The usual."

I retreat into the bathroom. When I come back out, his mom is back with Meg and lots of pills. Derek dutifully swallows everything.

His mom notices me standing back by the closet. "I'm going to take Beth home while you get your therapy out of the way. Dad's staying."

I don't want to leave. "Can't I?"

Derek gets comfortable with his hands behind his head, challenging me to throw that fit I threatened.

"You get some rest, young lady." His dad can't help yawning. He picks up the vest and shakes it out.

"I don't need to rest. Aren't you tired?"

He shakes his head.

"Come on, Beth." His mom puts her arm around my waist. "You've done enough for now."

"I want—"

"We've got so much to talk about."

I glance over her head back at Derek. He puts his hand over his eyes and shakes his head.

I stick my tongue out at him. "If that's the case—sure."

"When will you be back?" There's an anxious note in his voice that makes my heart flip.

I glance at his mom.

"A couple hours."

He points at his mom. "Don't scare her off."

His mom makes me phone mine on the drive to his house. My mom doesn't yell at me, but she says I have to come home tonight and go to school tomorrow.

"But—this is an emergency. I need to stay with him."

Derek's mom puts her hand out for the phone. I obey.

"We'll make sure she gets there. No, no. It shouldn't be late. She's been wonderful. All right. Good-bye." She hands me back my cell.

I slip it into my bag. I don't dare argue. She's in control and wants me to know it. "I wasn't wonderful last night—more like a disaster. Why are you making this so easy for me?"

"He says he loves you. Do you love my son?"

I nod.

"Then why wouldn't I do everything I can to keep you around? I need an ally."

"Against him?"

"For him. When he was almost five, a doctor told me he would only last two, maybe three more years. I've been fighting since then to prove that man wrong."

"Derek—resists?"

We get stopped at a red light. "He fought therapy and meds when he was little. Fed his formula to the dog—stuff like that. But that's all second nature now. He resists in other ways—dangerous ways. For a while it was girls. Then he got together with a nice girl in his choir. But he still needed to rebel. His entire life is drugs—so he didn't go down that road." The light turns green. She steps on the gas.

"How could you let him get that motorcycle?"

"He's nineteen." She shudders. "His dad was for it. What could I do?"

"He was crazy in Switzerland."

"Ever seen him on a skateboard?"

Stupid adrenaline. "You should have—"

"Tied him up?"

"Padded cell."

She puts on her left turn signal. "I caught myself looking forward to his hospital stays so I could watch him round the clock." She makes the turn and shoots me a grim smile.

"The lockup?"

She nods. "But lately he's taking living seriously." She glances away from the road. "Thank you."

"Me?" I roll my eyes and fling my head back against the neck rest. "I got everything so wrong."

"I don't think so."

"I need to help."

"You already did." She reaches over and pats my knee. "Last night I was a thousand miles past exhausted—but how could I leave him? And then there you were. Derek's angel."

"I didn't act like an angel."

She laughs. "I had to take his word for it." She focuses on the road, drives, silent for a moment. "Derek should not have played with your happiness like this. Not many girls would have stayed. It will get painful."

"It can't be worse than not knowing."

"It can, Beth." Her eyes catch mine. "It will."

I draw into myself—refuse to hear her. He's going to be fine.

We arrive at a small two-story house in a little town west of London. Derek's bike is pulled up by the side door. We both shoot it nasty looks on our way into the house. She takes me in through the laundry room stacked with dirty clothes—like I'm a part of the family—and into an open kitchen and family room. There's a waist-high, long black table, narrow and set on a downward slant behind the couch.

She notices me staring at it. "The vest needs help some days. I used to pound on the poor kid forty-five minutes four times a day to get him to cough up that gunk in his lungs. You can imagine how much he liked that."

Cases of formula sit on the kitchen counter. She opens the dishwasher, and it's full of all kinds of medical stuff. She finds a couple mugs in there. "You hop into the shower, and I'll make us some cocoa." She directs me to Derek's room. "Don't mind the mess."

I wade through his dirty clothes, stop at the foot of his unmade bed, stare at his body's imprint. There's an IV pole next to the bed with clothes thrown over it. His computer is almost buried in papers and stacks of sheet music. On the way to the bathroom, I stub my toe on a keyboard floating in the mess. The bathroom is clean enough. His mom must have got it ready for me. I doubt Derek left those fresh towels laid out on the counter last time he was in here.

I take off my borrowed scrubs and get into his shower. The hot water feels so good. I've got tears and sweat and snot dried all over me. My hair is caked with hairspray from my performance updo. I find more pins while I wash my hair with his shampoo. I lather up with his soap, scrub until I'm tingling fresh, and rinse it all down the drain. The smell of him lingers on my skin even after I towel down.

My jeans are in my bag, so I put them on. I forego undies. Not usually my style, but the ones I peeled off are nasty. The bra is fine for another day, but my pink T-shirt is stained and crusty. Gross. What was I thinking? I borrow a white one from a folded pile on top of Derek's dresser. His mom doesn't mention it when I go back out.

My hair dries into a frizz while I sit in their kitchen and sip cocoa with marshmallows.

His mom leans across her steaming mug. "Tell me how you met— and everything. If I ask Derek, he'll just grunt."

I blow on my cocoa and try to figure out where to start.

"Please?" Her eyebrows lift. "It isn't true what they say about mothers. We don't hate our sons' girlfriends. The sleazy ones—maybe. But we're mostly delighted and a little startled when a wonderful girl loves our son. And relieved the son is smart enough to love her back. I'm grateful, Beth."

"I'm not wonderful."

"I'm sure you are. Derek has very good taste."

I slurp up a melting marshmallow—much louder than intended, and we both laugh.

"It started with Meadow, I guess." I tell her about Meadow's stage fright and how I filled in. My absurd makeover. Derek up on that mountaintop already knowing my voice. Him coming after me and finding me on that bench. She nods her head when I explain my genetic problems—understanding my pain like no one I've ever talked to before.

"You're lucky in a way. We didn't know until after Derek was diagnosed. I wanted a houseful of kids, but the risks . . ."

"I know." Our eyes meet. "Kind of awful. Derek was . . . incredibly comforting." I flush and my hands get sweaty. The hot cup of cocoa I'm holding is no help. I set it down and lean back in my chair.

His mom grins and shakes her head. "The opportunistic little devil."

"No." How can I explain how much that meant? "I'd never had a hot guy like him do anything more than hurl abuse at me. Then doctors were saying they were right. I really am beastly."

She shakes her head and stirs her cocoa.

"And then there was this beautiful boy holding me while I cried. When he kissed me, my world changed forever. I'll never be the same. Cystic fibrosis? What difference could that make to *me*?"

She gets teary while I tell her how magical the rest of our time in Lausanne was, how scared I was when it was over, how relieved when he showed up on that motorcycle—until he took me for a ride. I look at the trappings of his condition all around us. "Now I know why he kept me away."

"And why he didn't tell me about you."

"Where do we go from here?"

"I'll manage the medical establishment. You manage him."

"He won't like me bossing him around."

"That's not what I mean. He wants to live—for you. He wants life. With you. Keep him hoping. Keep him fighting. Until they can save him."

My heart gets tight, but I look up at her and nod. "All right. Should be easy."

She reaches across the table and places her hand on top of mine. "It may be the hardest thing you ever do. Are you sure?"

"I'm not afraid."

Her mask of calm drops for a moment, and she whispers, "I am."

chapter 30

EXISTENCE

Getting my butt out of bed Monday morning is painful. I hit the snooze button three times. Mom has to drag me out from under the covers. I throw on an old sweatshirt and slide into my Levi's. I capture my hair and jam it through a black scrunchie. I treat my face so the sore spots on my chin and forehead don't erupt on me, but I don't bother with makeup.

I grab a banana for breakfast. Mom pours me juice.

"Please—can't I go back to the hospital?"

"After school. But take your homework."

"It's December. Christmas break starts in two weeks."

"And you have finals in all your semester classes."

"Who cares?"

"Every college you'll be applying to in a couple of months."

Applications? Colleges? What planet is she on? "Get real. I can't bother with that until Derek's okay." I filled her in when I got home last night. She took it pretty hard.

She looks down and stirs her coffee. "What if he's not okay?"

I slam the juice glass on the counter. "Why are you being so mean?"

"Reality sucks, but you need to face it, honey."

"He's not going to die."

"He tricked you. He tricked both of us."

"Shut up. Don't talk about him like that. He needs me, and that's all that matters."

"I don't want you to throw away your happiness." She closes her eyes and her tone drops. "Like I did."

"You said you loved my father."

She nods and sighs. "You have to do this. I understand."

"Good." I run back upstairs to my room, pull my suitcase from the summer out from under my bed, dump the junk that's still in the bottom, and start throwing underwear and T-shirts into it.

"Whoa." Mom barges in. "Hold on." She grabs my arm. "Slow down." She takes a stack of jeans out of my hands and gathers me close. "Let's think this through for a minute."

I drop my head onto her shoulder. "I have to get back up there. What if—"

"Is he that bad?" She lets me loose.

I sink down on my bed. "How can I waste time on school when he—" I take a deep breath and steel myself to say it. "When he could be dead tomorrow?"

"It's that close?"

I fight hard to keep my emotions steady. "No one knows. It could be. This new medication they've got him on seems to be helping." His mom filled me in when we went back to the hospital Sunday. "How long it will help and how much is a mystery. They have to keep him alive long enough for him to get the transplant. Only problem is they have to get him so he's not antibiotic resistant anymore first."

"How's that going?"

"It's not." I sniff and start to blink. "If they take him off his antibiotics, the infections will win."

Mom sits beside me. "I'm sorry." She's fighting back tears, too. "So, so sorry." She puts her arm around me and squeezes. "Okay. Let's take it one day at a time. Go to school today. Get your assignments, and you can take off tomorrow."

"Really?"

"Sure. I'll see you tomorrow night. Try to make it before midnight." I had a hard time leaving Derek last night. "I love you, Beth." She leans her head against mine. "I'm here. Whatever I can do. I'm here."

I kiss her cheek, hug her, jam a change of clothes and my zit stuff into my bag, and tear out of there.

I get to school late, but Scott's still at his locker. I was so awful to him Saturday night. I need to apologize—explain. "Hey, Scott. I'm so—"

He whirls around with his arms full of books. "To hell with you, Beth." He walks past me, to the far end of the hall.

The locker beside mine is empty.

I hear books thud and a locker door slam down the hall. I feel like he hurled those books right in my face.

He's not in choir.

At lunch I see him with a tiny junior girl who's new this year. On my way out after school, he's making out with her by the front doors.

Crap. He's taking my stupid, stupid advice. I should be happy for him. I've got Derek to worry about. No room for a friend who wants more than I can give. I relied on him and that's not really fair. Better to have Scott occupied. Right now he's more occupied than I want to know, but he deserves something. He can't really like her. She's tiny and pretty and perfect for him, but he can't love her. He loves me. She's probably had a crush on him since school started. And now, oh my gosh, he's got his hands on her butt.

I hurry by them, chuck my bag on Jeanette's passenger seat, and drive fast for London. No line at the border between Port and Sarnia. I've got my passport today, but the guy glances at my license plate and waves me through. It's snowing again, but the road is fine. I make it to the hospital in under an hour. It's easier than driving to choir. Shoot—choir. We have a practice tomorrow. I'll have to call Terri. Maybe I'll just update my status on my page. Everyone will get the message that way—

Oh my gosh. My page.

Derek friending me—curious about the rest of me.

What a brat. He was right, though. The Amabile guys beat us. He got his way with me, too. He always gets his way.

He'll get those lungs. It's Derek.

I burst into his room. He's asleep with his inhaler thing strapped to his face. His mom, poor woman, is nodding off, too, balanced on that uncomfortable chair. I gently shake her shoulder. Her eyes flutter open.

"He's still good?" I whisper.

She blinks and nods. "Get him to finish that. Then his vest."

"I can stay. Sleep in tomorrow."

She gathers her purse and knitting, leaves a stack of books about cystic fibrosis for me. "Make sure he doesn't skimp his treatments in the morning." She hugs me and stumbles out.

I steal the table that swings over Derek's bed for meals, push it over by the window, lower it, and spread out my books. I grab the chair—catch him spying at me through one eye.

"Are you awake?"

"No."

I drop the chair and very gently, mindful of his IV and how weak he is, attack him.

He kisses me back and breathes, "You're going to make my monitors go off," into my ear.

I press my ear to his chest. His heart races back. "Too much excitement?"

He presses the magic buttons and the bed sits us up. "Bring the table back over here."

"Not until you finish with your vest."

I bring it over to him, help him get it strapped on. It vibrates him for twenty minutes, and then he huffs gunk into a basin.

Meg sticks her head in the door. "Need any help?" She sees the green tinge to my face and comes in. "I'll take over. Get some air. Don't push yourself too fast."

I walk up and down the hall, berating myself until Meg comes out. "He wants you again. He said something about a sponge bath."

That makes me smile. I go back in the room, push the table back to his bed, and dutifully study with his head resting on my shoulder. He falls asleep like that—drools on my neck. I don't dare move, keep studying until late.

He wakes up when I try to lower the bed. He takes the controls and makes the head go down and the foot go up. "I think my ankles are swelling."

"Like a pregnant lady?"

"I'm not a pregnant lady."

"I noticed."

"Turn around. I'll never get back to sleep with you looking at me like *that*."

I kiss him. "Are you sure?"

"My mom's cot is under the bed. If you don't stop torturing me, I'll make you sleep in it."

"You didn't offer me the cot Saturday. I thought she slept in the chair."

"I can't keep my eyes open. Meg upped my morphine." He gets these awful headaches.

"I'm supposed to watch you. This isn't about sex. I thought you knew that."

He manages a drowsy laugh and lies back, closes his eyes, and he's out.

I lie on my side, wanting him, and wonder how I can feel like this when he's so sick.

The next two weeks, I only go to school for tests. Mom manages everything with my teachers. I get way more studying done in Derek's hospital room than I ever did wasting time in class. Derek's headaches get worse. He's on so much morphine now—sleeps and sleeps and sleeps. So I watch him and study. And ace everything except econ.

I try to talk to Scott after that test, but he cuts me cold.

The week before Christmas is peaceful. Mom lets me go up for the whole time. Derek's mom takes advantage of me being there to get her shopping done and mail stuff. I help her wrap Derek's presents. I get him black leather riding gloves to match his jacket.

I sleep in his mom's cot. I can't lie beside him night after night and not go crazy. I love him more every day and with that love come other feelings I'm not sure I can control. Not next to him all the long, silent night.

The info-desk guy brings up a steady flow of notes, gifts, and cards from people he can't let up. Amabile—seems like the whole amazing family stops by at one time or another.

Before their Christmas concert, his choir—all those guys in their tuxes—stand in the snow outside his window and sing to the twilight. I open the window a crack to let in the sound. At first they just sing, "Oh," in rich harmony as old as monks and cathedrals. Then they slowly unwind the gentle hymn. *Lo, how a Rose e're blooming from tender stem hath sprung!* Their harmonies build and dissipate, break into a celebration at the solemn birth and salvation. Then close with a single voice in the night.

O Savior, King of glory, who dost our weakness know;

Bring us at length we pray,
To the bright courts of Heaven, and to the endless day!

It's the only time I ever saw tears on Derek's eyelashes.

Meg gets me to go caroling around the hospital with a few other nurses. "Last year Derek brought his choir friends and guitar and sang for all the kids."

I think of him back in his room, lying on his bed with his mom sitting in her chair, knitting a scarf out of bumpy purple yarn.

We sing for old people and sick people and sicker people. I don't want to leave the kids. One climbs on my lap and sings along, patting the beat on my cheeks with tiny chapped hands.

My mom comes for Christmas. We're having it in Derek's hospital room. She brings turkey and stuffing, gravy and potatoes. A big pumpkin pie. He makes Meg dial back on the morphine a little so he's more alert for an hour or so. In pain but alert. I kiss him good-bye that afternoon and follow Mom home. It's Christmas. She needs me, too.

Mom lights the fire. It's gas, but it's still cozy with all the snow. We eat hot buttered microwave popcorn and watch *It's a Wonderful Life*. Mom lives for Jimmy Stewart.

We both cry at the end.

It feels so good.

As we watch the credits and blow our noses, Mom puts her arm around me and draws me under her wing. "How is he—really?"

"Alive."

"And the transplant?"

"He's still on the inactive list."

"No change in his resistance?"

I shake my head.

chapter 31

HOPE?

The week after Christmas is a disaster. The nasty bacteria in Derek's lungs fight back. For some reason no one can explain, the antibiotic they had him on can't contain it anymore. His lungs fill up and his temperature spikes. He chokes and coughs continuously. I've been there for his therapy so much now that I'm used to him coughing up crap. It's nothing like this. Blood. A lot. Cups of it.

They almost lose him twice.

I'm not there, either time. His mom is back at his side, full time. I sleep on the couch in the visitor's lounge down the hall. It scares me to even think of going all the way home.

He's shrinking—no matter how much they pump into him, his weight drops. A little of him slips away from us every day.

They finally get him on something experimental from a European clinical trial. His mom had to move heaven and earth to get a hold of it. At first there's no change.

School starts, but I don't go back.

And then his fever drops. "Beth?" It's a feeble whisper.

I rush to his bed and take his bony hand. "Hey."

"I'm doing this for you."

I kiss him gently and then move aside for his mom.

I go into the bathroom until I can pull myself together. I splash cold water on my face and go sit by his bed.

I hold his hand all night long.

Next morning, Mom picks me up. Derek's mom called her. I sleep all the way home, fall into my bed, and sleep the rest of the day. I haul my butt over to the school after it's out to pick up textbooks and talk to my teachers.

"When will you be back?" my counselor wants to know.

"After he—" I pause, clench my teeth. "After his transplant."

It will happen. It has to happen. Derek's mom will make it happen. I'm keeping him alive—as painful as it is. I'm keeping him alive.

Mom won't let me go back to the hospital. His mom phoned in a good report. I collapse on my bed, wake up with a cold, and they won't let me near him.

Two long weeks.

And they won't let me near him.

I'm not even that sick after the first couple days. I go to school, call his mom at the hospital a hundred times a day. He seems to be doing better. His mom lets him talk to me on the cell. All we say is "Hey," and then he starts to cough again.

I make up the work I missed and work ahead.

I notice Scott is with a different girl. He is way too good for this one. Sleaze is putting it mildly.

He catches me on my way out of English. We have it together this semester. "Beth."

I stop and turn to him, can't help raising an eyebrow.

"I hear he's in the hospital."

I nod.

"I'm sorry."

I duck my head and bolt.

———

When I finally get to go back, Derek's mom is totally exhausted, leaves me on watch. He looks so much better than the last time I saw him. He tugs me down onto the bed with him as soon as we've got the room to ourselves.

It feels so right to have his lips slipping over my face and down my neck, and then back on my lips, responding to my open, hungry mouth with his sweet, soft tongue. He's weak—can't keep it up very long—but he gets me wondering. How hard can it be to take out a catheter?

"You're making me crazy." I chew on his earlobe.

"Sorry. Couldn't help it."

"How much better are you?"

"I don't think it would kill me."

I start to get excited, kiss him long and slow, pressing my body hard against his.

"The trouble is," he finally says, "this medication that's saving my life—makes my extremities go numb." He runs his hands over my shoulder. "I can't feel this."

I capture his hand and kiss his palm.

"That either. No sense violating you if I'm not even going to feel it."

"But I'll feel it." I start to undress but he stops me.

"Save it for Scott, Beth." There's a resignation in his voice that frightens me. "I owe him that much for letting me have you all this time."

"What are you talking about?" I cuddle up to his chest. He doesn't know about my rupture with Scott.

"When I'm gone—" There's anger, pain, and sorrow in those three words that neither of us can bear to admit.

"Stop that. You'll be fine."

"Beth, listen—"

"No. This is going to work. They'll put you back on the active list."

The whole transplant thing makes me angry. They let smokers on it.

People who crapped up their lungs on purpose and not my Derek. It's supposed to be too risky because they have to give him lots of immunosuppressants after the operation. A lot of patients get infections post-op. If you are resistant to all antibiotics, you die. But what's the alternative? They could try. Why would his new lungs be resistant? I don't get it at all.

"Listen." I draw spirals on his chest. "I've got two lungs with five healthy, pink lobes." At last being an absolute Amazon is a good thing. You have to be mega-tall to be considered as a living donor. "You can have one."

He ignores me. Derek saw me reading those books his mom left. I've gone through them all three times. If I give Derek a lobe, then we'd just need an uncle or friendly giant to give him another one. They usually only do living lobar transplants on small women and children who have small ribcages for the smaller lungs, but wouldn't little lungs be better for Derek than no lungs? "I'm going to get tested. If you don't want it, I'll give it to somebody else."

"No one is cutting you up."

That gets to me. I can't talk anymore or I'll break that promise about losing it in front of him. I don't want him to know there's a lump in my throat too big to swallow. His arms wrap around me, and I relax on his chest. He falls asleep holding *me*, comforting *me*. I think he does know.

I don't want to move. He'll wake up. I can't sleep. What if I relax my grip, and he slips quietly away? I lie there, hour after hour, listening to him fight through each breath. Meg and another nurse come and go all night like I don't exist. This is strange. What aren't they telling me? They up his oxygen flow, put a new bag on his IV, plug his feeding tube in the slot in his stomach, punch up his morphine pump.

All this stuff that keeps him alive—it used to scare me.

Now I love that IV. I love the tube. I should be nervous they want to cut him open and take out his lungs, but the only thing in my heart is *hurry, hurry, hurry*. Make him active again. Ship him to Toronto. Let's do this thing. Take part of me if it helps.

At four in the morning, he stops breathing.

I jam the call switch and start to shake him. "Derek. Come on. Please."

The nurses rush in with a medical team right behind. Meg shoves me out of the way.

I stumble into the bathroom, sweating cold, and wretch over the toilet.

Meg appears behind me, hands me a damp washcloth. "How long was he out before you buzzed us?"

"Seconds. Is he—"

"Asking for you. You saved his life."

"This time."

She goes off to call his parents. His mom left strict instructions for updates.

I sit by his bed, holding his hand, while therapists work to clear his lungs—gently. They roll him onto his side and pound his back with cupped hands like his mom used to do every day, four times, morning, noon, afternoon, and night. Whatever clogged his throat is gone now, but he starts to cough up thick green phlegm and blood—chokes on the mess, gasps, manages to somehow breathe again. They give him an inhaled antibiotic treatment and more Ventolin, the thinning stuff.

Things calm down by the time he's finished the treatment. Meg checks his monitors one more time. "Call me," she orders and leaves the door open.

I take Derek's hand again and look at him. It's trembling. I look at his gray face and closed eyes. I realize these past two weeks have been filled with false reports. He faked it pretty good this afternoon. Kind of like how he faked me out ever since I met him. What did those nights that he stole away from the hospital to see me cost him? And this afternoon, what did those few minutes of exertion cost? Have I killed him?

His fingers move against my hand, and he opens his eyes. "You brought me back."

I shake my head. "It was them."

"No. It was you." His eyes drift closed again.

I lean over him. "Derek. Derek. Come back."

"I've been waiting . . . for you. Next time—" He opens his eyes and stares at me.

I shake my head, can't stop denying what he's saying. "Rest now. You'll be fine."

His eyes drop closed. "You need to let me go."

I kiss his forehead and whisper, "I can't." I'm not ready. I'm so not ready.

"The place I'm going—I've been there a couple times now. There's peace—love—a joyfulness I can't explain. Let me stay. Next time . . . I'm ready to stay there."

Take me home, take me home, take me home.

He wants to go, but I can't leave him. "Take me with you then."

He frowns. "Not allowed."

"Have you told your mom?"

"Will you?"

I bow my head over his hand. Pain throbs in my chest. I can't do this. I can't let him go. I only know how to hang on. I wish I knew something about praying—had the strength of that slave girl in my solo singing down by the river Jordan.

Oh, the glory of that bright day
When I cross the river Jordan.

She knew something I don't. "Give me that," I whisper. "Please."

The weight on my heart doesn't lift, but a calm, soothing sensation flows from Derek's hand into mine. Comfort emanates through me. "How are you doing that?"

"I'm not."

"Maybe it's deliverance."

"Sing it for me, Beth."

"My solo?"

"It's in the drawer." He closes his eyes. "Sing me to sleep."

I pull open the nightstand drawer. There's a sheaf of wordless music on the top. "Beth's Song." "I don't have any words."

He doesn't answer.

I wish I could find phrases to match his music that could tell him how much I love him, but all I can do is hum the melody, add "oohs" and "aahs." His parents arrive while I'm singing. I start to leave—Derek's mom doesn't need me to tell her anything. She knows. She stops me, though. Keeps me there with them, singing to Derek.

I sing his song over and over again—aching for some kind of meaning to match this delicate melody so full of life and love. I'm afraid to stop singing. Afraid to let go of him.

A hint of dawn reaches the room. His eyes flutter open, his mouth eases into a smile. He looks like an angel already.

No one moves when his breathing stops.

"Good-bye, my Derek-boy." His mom bends over and kisses his forehead.

I touch my lips to his one last time.

His father pats his head, awkward and manly. "You fought a good one, son."

Derek's machines sound off. Meg comes running. His mom caresses his hair off his forehead. "Let him rest."

Meg backs out of the room, tears streaming down her face.

I wish I could cry like that. It's not fair. She's just his nurse. Give *me* those tears to soften the desolation I feel as he goes. His mom is crying. So is his dad. What's wrong with me? Why am I so cold? Where did the music go?

I look down at Derek. His hand in mine is no longer warm. Oh, dear God, it isn't him anymore.

I let go of the hand and lay it gently under the sheets. I shiver, have to clench my teeth to keep them from chattering. I am so cold, so, so, so cold.

Doctors and nurses grow around us like dandelions in the lawn. Meg guides us gently out of the room.

I stop and look back. "What are they doing to him?"

"Nothing."

My mom is in the waiting room. I don't know how she got here. She holds me and cries. I pat her back and try to remember how it felt to hold his hand.

chapter 32
WORSE

It's dark. Even with my eyes staring wide open.

A bar of light falls across my face. I jam my eyes closed.

"Beth, honey, why don't you try school today? I'll drive you. *It'll make you feel better.*"

A stack of books on my desk. Notes from my teachers. They all look forward to my return—*as soon as I'm better.*

Sarah, Leah, and Meadow appear at the foot of my bed. How dare Mom let them in. There's no music left inside me. "We miss you, Beth. Come sing with us. *It'll make you feel better.*"

Better? I don't want to *feel better.* Even the damn minister at the confused blur that was Derek's funeral so many days ago said Derek was better off now. No more suffering. Even Derek said it. Leaving me was *better.*

I am worse. Buried in worse. Cling to dusk and the four walls of my shadowy bedroom. I play his voice over and over and over. Hold him in my dreams, but he dissolves, and I'm left in the dark turning to stone.

No tears come to wash him away. I'm filled with cold, dead empty that started the night he died and grows and grows and grows.

———

A whisper comes to me when I wake in the night and stare out the window at the gloom of February snowstorms. *Follow him, Beth. You'll feel so much better.*

I bury that voice. Hear the evil in it. Derek would be so angry if I did that. I'm supposed to live. I want to live. But how can I without him? If he could see me now—crap—what if he can? He'll hate me.

Mom again. Pale light. "I'm not sure she'll talk to you."

I roll over—shade my eyes against the brightness. She hands me the phone. It finds my ear. His mom again? No. A guy's voice. Who is this guy?

" . . . Would you be in it?"

"Is this Blake?"

"That's right."

"Can you say that again?"

"Amabile is holding a memorial CF benefit concert for Derek. You're not the only one, Beth. We all miss him."

"You want me to come?" Leave my safe darkness? The shadows? This solid pain that keeps reality at bay.

"We want you to sing."

"For Derek?"

"Will you do it?"

"Yes. Yes. Yes. Thank you, Blake. Yes."

With trembling hands, I pull down the heavy quilt blocking my window. Gray winter day flows through the cracks and crevices of my den. The first thing I see—lying half-buried under undone assignments from school—is Derek's pale pink rose, dry, delicate—but real. As real as my love. As real as my loss.

I rescue it, cradle it in my palms, and lift it to my lips. That faint scent, sweet but dead, finds its way through my senses. I glance around at the mess, searching for a safe place. It doesn't exist in this chaos. I step on a roll of tape. Use it to secure the rose to the piece of wall I see if I lie curled on my side in bed. I try it, lie there, staring at Derek's rose.

Something brings me to my feet, stumbling through the mess again and searching through the bag I haven't touched since Mom brought me home from the hospital, darkened my window, and tucked me in bed.

I find white papers, carefully folded over. I press them to my heart and run back to my bed. My nightstand drawer yields a pencil. I pick up my choir binder off the floor. I sit cross-legged on my tangled blankets and lay the binder on my knee, unfold the music, smooth it out with a caress.

"Beth's Song."

I pencil in "for Derek" under the printed words.

My eyes close as his melody winds through my soul. Words come slowly at first and then in a torrent. I weigh them, choosing, discarding, searching again, fitting the puzzle pieces together, clothing my bare words in the richness of his music.

My room fills with light as the thick gray clouds outside shift enough for the sun to break through.

chapter 33

FOR DEREK

The concert starts with the Amabile boys singing "Sing Me to Heaven." People talk about Derek. Somebody gives a lecture on supporting assumed-consent legislation and keeping an organ-donor card in your wallet. The AYS sing. And chamber. Their young boys' concert choir steals everyone's heart with the soaring height of their pure voices. Even the youngest Amabiles take a turn. I listen from the sidelines, standing in my crimson choir gown so I won't crush it.

My name is announced, and my feet carry me onstage. I've practiced. I can do this tonight for him. The piano plays a tinkling introduction. A violin comes in. I gaze into the sea of people who loved him long before my solo magically brought him into my life.

My eyes close and I begin to sing.

> *Don't steal away your love.*
> *Don't steal away your touch.*
> *Without your smile I'll never find*
> *The star you shine.*

I take a deep breath and shake my head, open my eyes to the blur in front of me.

Don't leave me empty here.
Don't leave me without hope.
Don't say it's for the best, love,
When I'm lying here alone.
Please stay, 'cause I can't make it on my own.

I draw a deep breath as I move into the chorus. I'm not on that stage. There's nobody out there. It's just Derek and me.

Who will be the boy who heals my heart?
Who will be the boy who feeds my art?
Where will I find a friend?
Who will be the boy who rescues me?
Who will be the boy who makes me sing?
You made me live, made me who I am.
If you're leaving, take me with you,
Here's my hand.

My voice falters. I take a deep breath and sense a touch in my palm. His hand, his strength, his peace flow into me again like the night he died.

You spoke of peace and rest,
A joy that filled your breast,
And then you closed your precious eyes.
God set you free.

As I sing, Derek fills me up and promises he'll never leave me.

So I will carry on,
Forever sing your song.
If I have to live without you now,

I'll love the best I can,
But whisper when you're near me, and I'm home.

I move into the chorus repeat, and the audience comes into focus. They're with me, tears streak their faces, and I realize they are searching, too. Searching for beauty. Searching for love. Searching for life. I found all that when Derek took my hand, smiled, and said, "You sing me to sleep." I know what *beautiful* is now, because of him. I know what love is because of him. I know I can be strong. Please, God, help me to be strong.

The key shifts through the bridge, and somehow my voice rises full of strength that isn't mine.

Together, love, we'll find somebody who—
Will help us keep on breathing without you—

The note stretches out. I hold onto it as long as I can. The sea of strangers blurs and one face emerges.

Scott's here, his face full of pain, witnessing how much I loved Derek. My eyes find his and my chorus changes.

Will you be the boy who heals my heart?
Will you be the boy who feeds my art?
Please, will you be my friend?
Will you be the boy who rescues me?
Will you be the boy who makes me sing?
Will you make me true to who I am?
If you're leaving, take me with you,
Here's my hand.
If you're leaving, take me with you,
Here's my hand.

I finish the song. The applause is reverent. Everyone is still crying. I move through the crowd to Scott. The people stopping me and hugging me were Derek's real world. The people he let in. The ones who really knew him. His old girlfriend from the AYS. Meg and his doctors. Blake. The Amabile directors. All the guys. This giant wonderful family he grew up with.

I'm a fantasy. A myth. A digital recording—deleted with ease. I'm something else. Somewhere else. I don't belong here.

But I am here. I would have cared for him and loved him for the rest of my life. I held his hand while he went beyond. The pain I feel is every bit as real as that pretty petite girl I unwittingly stole him from. I loved him. I still love him. I'm clogged with the ache of it. I can't bear to look back.

When I look forward, there's Scott, and he catches my arm, supporting me like I'll faint.

I lean on him. "How'd you get here?"

"Your mom."

I see her now—standing in the back. "Will you ride home with me? I'm not sure I can drive."

He nods. "You bet." He takes the keys and guides me out of there.

All the way home, I sit slumped in my seat with my head down.

Scott doesn't speak. I'm grateful for the space.

We get to the house. I still sit there like a zombie. He comes around and opens my door. A gust of clear, crisp air sends a shiver to my core. Scott takes my hand and helps me to my feet.

We've been here before. His warm arms go around me—feels like home.

I drop my head onto his shoulder.

The tears come. Slow and hot. Each one agony to produce.

Scott caresses my back and says, "I'm sorry, Bethie. I'm so, so sorry."

It doesn't make any sense. What does he have to be sorry for? All he ever did was love me. It makes sense in my heart, though. His soothing hand and comforting voice—his shoulder mutes my sobs, opens my heart, and wrings it out.

I can't control the cascade his tenderness forces from me.

Mom arrives. "Beth, don't—"

Scott stops her. He knows I need this. He knows I'll need his shoulder again and again and again. After all I've done to him, he's willing to give it to me.

Mom leaves us out there.

I raise my face. The front of Scott's jacket is soaking. "I did this to him, too. In Lausanne. And he held me—just like this."

"I don't mind being second, Bethie. As long as I'm last."

"You're not second, Scottie." I kiss him then. The touch of his lips makes me cry even more.

He kisses me back—tender, so soft, like I'm fragile as Derek's dead pink rose taped to the wall next to my bed.

I trace his lips with my fingertips, marveling that he's here, a whole solid person, with his arms around me. This boy I grew up with, who knew me before any of this. Who loved me as I was—and as I am. He should hate me, but I can tell by the grief in his eyes that he still loves me—will always love me.

And I can love him now.

I learned how from Derek.

I clutch at Scott. He draws me closer, holds me tighter and tighter, his familiar scent surrounding me, calming me. I *am* home.

"Don't let go." I press my lips on his to seal my plea. "Please, Scottie, don't ever let go."

author's note

Sing Me to Sleep has given me the chance to remember Matt Quaife and share his spirit. Derek isn't Matt. To try to re-create Matt in fiction would have been presumptuous and impossible. Matt's life and death are sacred and private. But Matt inspired this story, and it is in honor of his memory that I share it with you.

Matt grew up singing in London, Ontario, home of Canada's world-renowned Amabile family of choirs (www.amabile.com). I remember him burping the alphabet in one festival when he was a member of the Boys' Concert Choir. Later, he became a fixture of Amabile's famous Young Men's Choir.

Matt didn't talk often about his cystic fibrosis. He was too full of life for that. He didn't complain about therapy, medicine, and regular trips to the hospital. Matt passed away November 25, 2007. He was just eighteen.

Thirty thousand people around the world live with cystic fibrosis. To learn more about their struggle and the remarkable research that has a cure in its sights, go to www.cff.org or www.cysticfibrosis.ca.

Thank you . . .

Joyce, dear friend, for smiling on my efforts, sharing your son's journey, and helping me get the medical stuff right.

Amabile Choirs of London, Ontario, Canada, for all those years of music and letting me use your name and fame for the sake of my story.

Rachel, for mining your memories and giving them to me.

Allie and Jared—your love was a catalyst. You *will* live happily ever after.

Heather, for sharing your heartbreak one afternoon in the Cougar Eat and setting me up with your cousin.

Mike and Tina and your beautiful family, for James.

Joelle, Connie, Rachel, Jenni, and Kristin for brilliant and timely first-draft critiques when I was freaking out. You saved me months of revisions.

Lexa, for insisting Beth needed a boy back home, asking for lyrics, and all the other excellent work you and everyone at Razorbill do on my behalf.

Allen, for your love and support. I couldn't pursue this dream without you.

And my boys for your patience. The time-traveling space pirates will make it into print some day.

photo appendix

IN MEMORY *of* MATT

Matt, left, in his Amabile tuxedo.

Amabile combined choirs.

Amabile boys. Matt is in the front, far left.

Amabile boys, goofing off.

Matt in his hockey jersey. At their Christmas concert,
Amabile had this framed and presented it to Matt's parents.